WILD HEARTS

The if  line

WILD HEARTS

An IF ONLY *novel*

Jessica Burkhart

BLOOMSBURY
NEW YORK   LONDON   NEW DELHI   SYDNEY

First published in the United States of America in May 2015
by Bloomsbury Children's Books
www.bloomsbury.com

Bloomsbury is a registered trademark of Bloomsbury Publishing Plc

For information about permission to reproduce selections from this book, write to
Permissions, Bloomsbury Children's Books, 1385 Broadway, New York, New York 10018
Bloomsbury books may be purchased for business or promotional use. For information on bulk
purchases please contact Macmillan Corporate and Premium Sales Department at
specialmarkets@macmillan.com

Library of Congress Cataloging-in-Publication Data
Burkhart, Jessica.
Wild hearts : an If only novel / by Jessica Burkhart.
pages   cm
Summary: When residents of a small Wyoming town protest her developer father's plan to build
a hotel on land used by mustangs for grazing, sixteen-year-old Brie, who enjoys the excitement
of moving to a new place each year, finds herself falling for a young protester who rescues and
rehabilitates mustangs.
ISBN 978-1-61963-259-2 (paperback) • ISBN 978-1-61963-258-5 (hardcover)
ISBN 978-1-61963-260-8 (e-book)
[1. Moving, Household—Fiction. 2. Land use—Fiction. 3. Real estate development—Fiction.
4. Mustang—Fiction. 5. Horses—Fiction. 6. Love—Fiction. 7. Wyoming—Fiction.] I. Title.
PZ7.B92287Wi 2015   [Fic]—dc23   2014031989

Book design by Amanda Bartlett
Typeset by Newgen Knowledge Works (P) Ltd., Chennai, India
Printed and bound in the U.S.A. by Thomson-Shore Inc., Dexter, Michigan
2 4 6 8 10 9 7 5 3 1 (paperback)
2 4 6 8 10 9 7 5 3 1 (hardcover)

All papers used by Bloomsbury Publishing, Inc., are natural, recyclable products
made from wood grown in well-managed forests. The manufacturing processes
conform to the environmental regulations of the country of origin.

I couldn't have finished this book without the support and cheerleading of Bri Ahearn. Bri, thank you for welcoming me into your home and your city!

CHAPTER ONE

Cowboy proverb: The bigger the buckle, the better the cowboy.

Mom shrieked as Dad slammed on the brakes. Behind us, tires squealed, and several people blew their horns. I twisted to look out the back window and counted four pickup trucks.

"My God, Michael, you don't have to speed everywhere!" Mom said, smacking her hand on the gray dashboard.

Rolling my eyes, I leaned around her to see what was in front of us. I loved my parents, but we had spent excessive amounts of time together over the past several days. Being trapped in the car 24/7 with parents wasn't anyone's idea of fun. Welcome to another one of the Carter-Brooks family's permanent vacations, otherwise known as a move. The current destination: Wyoming.

I pulled out my earbuds and paused the music I'd been listening to. "What is it?" I asked, looking through the windshield. Eight bison lumbered across the pebbled road. I stared. Real live bison that weren't in a zoo. The massive brown animals didn't glance up once or hurry away from cars. One by one, they walked in front of our SUV and into waist-high grass in the field on the other side of the road.

Truck engines rumbled and two cars joined the lineup. Tourists eagerly piled out of the cars, their cameras in hand or hanging by a strap around their necks. Almost all the tourists wore some form of WELCOME TO WYOMING hoodie or sweatshirt. Their trunks were probably stuffed with knickknacks—mugs, key chains, shot glasses—for friends and family back home. Locals stayed in their trucks and I could almost feel the drivers' impatience. I imagined that they were bored with the bison after living here for however long.

I shifted in my seat, trying to decide what to do. I wanted to get a closer look at the bison, but I didn't want the locals—my new neighbors—to lump me in with the tourists. "Dad, can I get out?" I tapped the back of his seat.

"For a minute," Dad said. "Stay close to the car, Brie." He eyed me in the rearview mirror. "Never know what those animals will do."

Unlike Mom and me, Dad had a strong distaste mixed with annoyance for animals and anything wildlife related. He was much more of an office-chilled-to-sixty-five-degrees type of guy. Dad had three trademarks: tasseled leather loafers, sunglasses, and his phone. If he had to spend six months on a deserted island, I knew those would be the three items he'd choose to bring.

"I'm going to take a photo," Mom said.

She rooted around for her camera, and Dad dug through the SUV's cup holders.

"You see my phone?" he asked Mom.

"Daaad," I said. "You're not going to get reception here. We're in the middle of *nowhere*."

Dad, ignoring me, found his BlackBerry, held it up in the air, and moved it around until his arm was outside.

"I pay enough for this damn service," he grumbled.

Time to get out of the car.

As soon as Dad *did* get reception, he'd be on the phone with the provider, chewing them out for the minutes of service he'd lost. Mom and I had been around for a zillion of these conversations. We'd pointed out that despite how much Dad seemed to hate the service, he kept renewing the contract. Every. Year.

I left my Canon T3i, Mom's old camera from last year, in the backseat. I wasn't in the mood to take pictures—I just wanted *out*. I glanced through the window before opening the car door, letting in a rush of cold March air. There was even some snow on the roadside—the one-lane roadside. "Road" was maybe giving the *path* we'd been driving on for hours too much credit. This road was practically nonexistent and in desperate need of a pave.

I looked far beyond the bison and saw a scattering of tops of houses and buildings. Somewhere down there, at the base of Blackheart Mountain, was our new home.

Mom, beside me, held her camera. Her sandy-brown hair was twisted into a messy bird's nest.

The huge animals moved with surprising grace across the road. Their shaggy coats had prickly burrs and there were dreadlocks around their hooves. A few wagged their stubby tails at buzzing flies.

Now at least ten cars had halted behind us and people were crowding forward snapping pictures. I chuckled to think of the poor friends and family members who would no doubt be subjected to a slide show upon the travelers' return.

"Look at that little guy," Mom said, pointing to a cute bison calf. "He's perfect for a wildlife magazine." Mom frowned at me. "You should have brought your camera, honey."

I shrugged. Mom's photos always made mine look like cheesy glamour shots. Eccentric and creative, Mom could take a photo of anything and make it frame worthy. She had been teaching me about photography for years. After growing up with Annie Leibovitz as our family friend, photography was something that I liked to dabble in. I wasn't ever going to be good enough to make it professionally like Mom, but I was okay with it being just a hobby.

I zipped up my jacket to ward off the late March chill that seemed to tumble down the mountain. A fresh breeze, smelling of flowers and, ugh, farm animals, blew gently in my face. Mom aimed her camera at a bison as it plodded across the road and headed for the grass. She took her time, zoomed in on its head, and waited for the right moment. Just as the bison turned to face the cars, Mom snapped its picture. *Click.*

"Good timing," I said quietly.

Mom crouched down on the road and swiped at a stray lock of hair that flopped in her eyes. I wouldn't be surprised if she ended up on her stomach and crawling toward an unsuspecting bison. I admired her dedication. Once, she had waded through a horsefly-infested swamp to capture pictures of a northern bog violet for *Flowers Monthly.*

Then she stood and put her camera in my hand.

"Mom," I protested. "I don't feel like taking a picture right now. Let's just get to our house."

"One," Mom said, holding up her pointer finger. "Then we'll go." She didn't wait for me to argue—she walked around the front of the SUV and got back into the passenger seat.

Mom would know if I rushed it just to get done. Then we would be here even longer. Sighing, I gazed around for the perfect shot. The tourists had begun to go back to their cars. Like Mom, I crouched low and rested my elbows on my knees. I adjusted the lens, turning it until it was just right, and waited for the bison I'd focused on to—

An engine revved *hard* behind me. Still on the ground, I turned and a rusty black Ford revved at me again. Against the sun, I couldn't see the driver, but I shot him my index finger in the universal wait-a-sec gesture before turning back to the animals.

"We have an entire corral of these in town for tourists to photograph!" a guy's voice shouted from behind me.

That did it. The bison scattered, moving awkwardly through the brush and disappearing over a small hill.

I got up, slapped dust off my jeans, and walked over to the driver who had just ruined my photo. "What is your *problem*, jerk? Do you really have somewhere so important to be that you couldn't wait five more seconds for me to take a picture?"

Eyes the color of dark chocolate met mine. A guy who couldn't be much older than me sat behind the wheel.

"And FYI," I continued, my voice a little less angry than I wanted it to be. "I'm not some tourist trying to cause a traffic jam. I'm moving here."

His eyes widened a bit and he tipped his chin in a nod.

God, his chin was really chiseled. I took in his long-sleeve plaid shirt, jeans, and leather belt with a large silver buckle. I squinted to read the inscription.

"It says 'Triple M.'" The guy's voice was deep and playful at the same time.

"What?" I asked. I yanked my eyes from his waist to his face.

"My buckle," he said, grinning. His tanned skin set off his beautiful white teeth. "Sorry to disappoint you, but it doesn't say 'jerk.'"

A blush crept up my neck. "Oh, well, maybe you'll get another one for Christmas." *Really?* I yelled at myself. *That was the best you could do?*

"I'll have to try and be good for the rest of the year. I better find some way to apologize to you so Santa doesn't give me coal in my stocking." He smiled easily.

I fought to keep my angry, nonchalant posture—a hip jutted out with my hand casually resting on it, head held high, and narrowed eyes. But *he* was making it insanely difficult. Just looking at him made me want to forget this whole thing and promise him that Santa wasn't going to give him coal this year.

"I'm Logan," the guy said, shifting in his seat. He stuck a hand out of the window.

I clasped his rough, hardened hand in mine. His tan skin made my own look almost translucent.

"I'm—

"Brie, let's go!"

I released his hand and rolled my eyes. "I don't even have to introduce myself now. My dad did that for me."

Logan smiled again.

"See you around, Brie," Logan said. "Welcome to town. I work at WyGas, so I'm sure I'll see you around. It's the only station in town."

"Oh, cool. See you."

I turned away from his truck and sauntered—really, walked; I had no idea how to *saunter*—back to our Explorer. Once I got inside, Logan's truck rumbled past us, barely scraping by on the narrow road. A giant red piece of paper in the back window caught my eye, but the tires kicked up too much dust to read it.

Dad grinned at me in the rearview mirror. "Remember that we're going to be living here for a while. Try not to chew out every person in town on our first day."

"Ha-ha," I said. "Ironic, coming from you."

Dad shrugged, feigning innocence. We both knew where I got my temper.

My dad, the Michael Brooks of Michael Brooks, Inc., developed land. His projects ranged from condos to strip malls. The jobs usually lasted a year or less, and his work required him to be constantly on the job site. Mom and I moved wherever Dad's work took him.

I'd been measuring my life in 365-day increments ever since I could remember.

In the backseat, I pushed my books and iPod out of the way. The drive from Houston to Wyoming hadn't been an easy trek. After nearly twenty hours in the car and days of driving, I couldn't wait to see our new home. Lost Springs was about to become another one of Dad's projects.

Sixteen years ago, when Dad had first started his company, Mom, Kate, and I had lived in Seattle. Dad had flown back and forth between his job sites and home to visit us every month. Soon Mom had grown tired of raising a baby and an eight-year-old daughter on her own; and with her career in photography flourishing, she needed Dad back.

My parents decided we would move with Dad to each new development site. It sounds crazy, but it works for us. I grew to *like* moving. Although it had become a little lonely since Kate had moved to LA. My big sister had always been obsessed with Hollywood news and gossip. Now, at twenty-four and after graduating from UCLA, Kate had managed to land her dream job as an entertainment reporter at *Star Access*—the top-rated nationally syndicated entertainment news show. She was already eyeing the anchor chair.

It helped that we still talked on the phone several times a week. She had made me promise to tell her everything about Dad's new job, building an extended-stay hotel for tourists at the edge of town. Dad had said the closest hotel was over an hour away.

Dad started the SUV forward, and gravel crunched under the tires as the vehicles behind us started moving. In all our years traveling for Dad's job, we had never been to Wyoming. Still, the excitement of getting to see someplace new never faded. I glanced up at Blackheart Mountain. It looked like something you'd find on the cover of a calendar featuring the country's best mountains. The mountain reached thousands of feet into the air—the black rock was snowcapped, and jagged peaks jutted out at all angles. Thick fir trees covered the mountain's base, and a lone buzzard circled high above the trees.

Virginia had been hilly when we'd lived in Roanoke, but that had nothing on the Breeze River mountain range. This looked like a movie set.

The tiny U-Haul we pulled behind us swayed as Dad drove slowly along the road that spiraled down into the valley near Blackheart Mountain. Guardrails were bent or missing on most of the road; it would be a long way down if our car skidded off. Gulping, I redirected my gaze forward.

"Can you get any reception, Nicola?" Dad asked Mom as he squinted at his cell phone screen. "I called the company yesterday and they swore we'd get reception out here."

"We're in a valley, Michael," Mom said, shaking her head. "You really expected to get service here, did you? We'll be in town in minutes."

"I expected service because I was promised service everywhere. Now I'll have to call again and speak to a supervisor."

The road started to level off as we pulled up to a lopsided, rough wooden sign. "Welcome to Lost Springs," I read aloud. The words were burned into the wood, and the sign was nailed to four wooden posts that weren't exactly even.

"Please be alert of the wildlife and don't call emergency services to report bear sightings." I shook my head. "Sorry, but I'm disregarding that last part if a bear comes near me."

Mom and Dad nodded, laughing.

We were finally here. This time, I vowed to make the house and town feel like home even if I only lived in Lost Springs a short time.

The Explorer started up the narrow street. According to Google Maps, there was only one road, Main Street, which went straight through the town's center. We passed a boxy building, its white paint yellowed with age. Unvarnished wooden planters filled with deep-purple and light-blue flowers lined the building's front. Brown trim framed the large, spotty glass windows. A black Lab wearing a red collar sat on the building's stoop and wagged its tail so energetically it thumped his body up and down. Painted above the door was a red sign with white block letters. LOST SPRINGS RUGSTORE. With the *D* missing, it looked completely archaic. Like something out of a black-and-white film.

Across from the drugstore, an archaic-looking gas station, complete with attendants dressed in hunter-green jumpsuits, was servicing two pickup trucks circa the late 1960s, while the truck owners chatted with the attendants.

"Can we get a soda?" I asked, the words surprising me as they tumbled out of my mouth. Dad probably wouldn't stop. His number one priority was always setting up computers at home. He always connected the Internet before he moved in anything else so that he could start working right away.

"Yeah," Dad said, whipping the SUV into the desolate parking lot. "Go get us a few drinks, and I'm going to find a pay phone."

I blinked, surprised. I almost regretted my request. I reached into my purse for my compact mirror and cosmetics bag. I looked into the mirror at my green eyes. They were lightly lined with black kohl liner. This morning, I'd used my Naked 2 palette and had done a brown smoky eye that was perfect for daytime. I touched up my lashes with CoverGirl mascara. My cheeks didn't need blush—they were lightly tanned. I swiped on Lip Buxom in a peachy shade and snapped my mirror shut. I ran my fingers through my shoulder-length light brown wavy hair, catching a few tangles.

"I'll wait here," Mom said, rubbing her hand across her makeup-free forehead. She did that when she was exhausted.

At least we didn't have much to unload from the U-Haul. The rental house was already fully furnished—it was too much work and cost to move furniture of our own.

Dad parked, and I tossed my flip-flops onto the parking lot and stepped into them. There were actual wooden hitching posts on the edge of the parking lot. Did people still use horses for transportation around here? I walked away from the Explorer and headed inside the gas station. The smell of honeysuckle filtered through the air. The reddish brick building looked dim inside, and the front door was held open by a chipped concrete block. This was the first gas station I'd seen with a wooden porch and rocking chairs out front. A WYGAS sign hung crookedly above the door, but the porch and store were swept clean. I'd half expected the station to be full of straw and horsehair or something.

Passing the empty counter, I avoided the wooden case of candy, chips, and various junk foods. Gobstoppers sounded good, but I'd probably already consumed half my weight in candy on this trip. I peered around for Logan, but I was the only one in the store.

Instead of a normal display refrigerator, I found a line of blue and red plastic coolers against the back wall with papers on them that said "diet," "regular," and "water." At the far corner of the store, a large refrigerator took up most of the wall space. Inside the refrigerator were Styrofoam cups with plastic lids. In squiggly handwriting, the cups were labeled. "Crickets, worms, live bait," I read aloud. "Whoa." Not your typical gas station snacks.

Closing the bait fridge, I grabbed three Diet Dr Peppers from the red cooler. I headed up to the checkout and placed the sodas on top. There was still no one behind the counter, and I twisted around and looked for an attendant. A flyer was taped to the counter. *If no attendant on duty, please place correct change in jar. Thank you for using our honor system.* No way. A jar like this wouldn't last five minutes in my old town. I dug in my jeans pocket and pulled out enough money for the sodas. As I counted the bills, *he* suddenly appeared behind the counter.

"Hey," he said, his eyes meeting mine. He'd taken off his cowboy hat to reveal cropped flaxen blond hair.

"I got a good photo, thanks," I snipped back at him.

Logan hung his head a little. "I was a jerk. Sorry."

I shrugged. I pointed to the jar. "The honor system, huh? That's pretty rare."

"Well," he said, taking my sodas and putting them into a brown paper bag. "We know where everyone lives around here, and when the sheriff can track you down in five minutes, no one has much interest in stealing."

"That'll be nice for a change." I tried not to look over his shoulder at Dad, who was pacing back and forth as much as the pay phone cord would allow. He was gesturing wildly with his hand. I jerked my attention back to Logan.

He pushed the bag toward me. "So you're really moving *here*?"

"Yeah, moving in today."

"Most people just pass through," he said, putting the hat back on his head.

So was I, in a way. Logan dropped a couple of quarters in the jar. "For later," he said. He smiled and revealed a dimple in his left cheek. "I usually grab a snack."

I took the bag and headed for the door. "Thanks."

"I owe you one, so maybe I could show you around sometime, if you want."

"Maybe." I shrugged. "See ya." I headed out of the store and walked down the porch's creaky wooden steps.

I wondered about Logan's smile. Did he have the I-think-I-like-you face? Or did he give every girl the same grin he'd given me? Whatever.

I held the bag up so Dad could see I was ready to go and went to the car. Mom walked back from where she was examining a stone well in the nearby grassy lot. When I opened the bag to grab a soda, my hand touched something crinkly. I reached inside and pulled out a Snickers bar. This wasn't mine. Why would Logan give me a candy bar? He didn't even know me, and he slipped me candy. That was *not* the honor system. I could take the candy back inside, but then I'd have to see him again. *Oh.* That's what the quarters were for. I unwrapped the candy and bit into it. Welcome to Lost Springs, indeed.

CHAPTER TWO

Don't worry about bitin' off more'n you can chew;
your mouth is probably a whole lot bigger'n you think.

The rest of the ride through town was a blur. All I could think about was Logan. The hair, the eyes that peeked from underneath his cowboy hat, and the smile that came easily to his face. Was it *like at first sight* or something? I'd never thought so much about a guy I'd known for five minutes.

Less than ten minutes later, Dad slowed the SUV and turned off the main road onto a gravel path. "I thought you girls would like an authentic Western house," he said. "May as well enjoy the entire package while we're here." That was guilt talking. Probably because of our Belize house. We'd be happy if this house had electricity, hot water, and a clean yard. Our rental in Belize had been hours away from Belmopan, the capital city. The tiny two-bedroom house was old and crumbling, but it was the only place available near Dad's job site. During the summer we were there, the dense jungle suffered from soaking rains and constant thunderstorms. Sometimes, we had been stuck inside for days filling pans with water from the dripping ceiling. Our power went off for up to a week at a time, and we had to boil water from a local well and haul buckets for showers. Despite the challenges, I loved living there. The people were friendly and as interested in learning about our culture as we were in learning about theirs. Mom and I had spent lots of afternoons exploring the beaches and jungles with local families.

"Honey!" Mom exclaimed to Dad, folding the map on her lap. "This is huge! How big is it?"

I peered over her shoulder at the house in front of us. Sure, Dad had shown us photos on the Realtor's website, but this was the first time we got to see it *live*. Bonus: we were arriving a day early since we'd skirted around big cities and hit little to no traffic in many areas.

Dad slowed the car so I could see the yard. He drove across a wooden bridge over a clear, rushing creek lined with small boulders. "Four bedrooms, four baths," he said. "That's a gazebo attached to the left side, and a hot tub."

The SUV eased up the driveway, and Dad parked in a small gravel lot beside the house. The log cabin was a light reddish wood with a dark green roof. It had two wraparound porches, one on the lower level and one on the upper, each with a sliding glass door for access. The house's roof had a sharp peak in the middle, and there was a triangular window in the center of the peak. A stone chimney jutted out from the back. There were no flowers or trees planted near the house, but a forest filled in the space behind the cabin.

"I love it!" I shouted.

Dad turned off the car and handed me the house keys. "Go on and look around," he said, rubbing his neck as he got out of the SUV. His blue-and-white polo shirt was wrinkled from the drive. "We'll be right there."

I trotted across the gravel and headed up the wooden steps. The gazebo gave a startling 180-degree view of the mountains and trees. I looked out over the wooden railing. Beyond the driveway and across the creek, treetops and Blackheart Mountain loomed in the distance. A cloudy haze of gray encircled the mountain's top and I wondered if anything survived up there. Puffy white clouds felt close enough to touch, and the stress of the trip started to fade.

I glanced down at Dad, who was slinging some of our duffel bags over his shoulder while he talked on the phone. Mom, looking toward the forest, had her special Kate Spade notebook tucked under one arm as she framed potential shots with her fingers. She had her photos, Dad had his building, Kate had her Hollywood news and gossip, and I had . . . I needed to find my own project.

Turning my gaze away from my parents, I slid the key into the sliding glass door and stepped into the brightly lit living room. The polished and shiny wooden floors matched the log walls. Wooden support posts in the living room were decorated with carvings of birds so detailed, they must have taken weeks to whittle. Most were owls, but a few eagles were scattered on the posts.

I stood in front of the mahogany leather couches and stared at the beautiful stone fireplace. The mantel was a log sawed in half and mounted to the stone. Above the mantel, a huge silver flat-screen begged to be turned on. I left the living room and stepped into the adjoining kitchen. The cabinets, counter, and bar were wood. I flipped up the handle on the faucet, squinting—afraid what color the water might be—but clear liquid streamed out. Whew. Our Belize kitchen had brown water sputtering into the sink most of the time.

"Brie?" Mom called.

"Coming!" I said.

"What do you think?" she asked, carrying a pink duffel bag on each shoulder. Dad came in behind her, staggering under the weight of the four suitcases he carried.

"It's definitely awesome, and just enough rustic," I said. I nodded toward throw blankets with outlines of horses on them that were draped across the couches. "I really, really like it."

I took the duffel bags from her and headed off to search the rest of the house. It felt like an "after" episode of a home make-over show.

A dining room adjoined the living room. There was a pool table that Dad would love, if he ever actually put down the phone and picked up a cue. Since that was unlikely, I would beg Mom to play with me. She was quite the pool shark. Sarah Lawrence art history majors aren't so innocent after all.

I wandered down the hallway and passed the master bedroom and a smaller room across from it. A short staircase led to a second floor. I walked upstairs and found a bedroom with double glass doors and gauzy white curtains opening up to a balcony. This was *so* my room.

The bed had a tall wooden headboard and a bare queen-size mattress. A dresser sat directly across from the bed and a large plain mirror hung over it. One window was directly to the left of the dresser and the same gauzy curtains covered it. I reached for the handle on the sliding glass door and pulled it back—the balcony was bigger than it looked from inside my room. I could envision sitting out here with a giant glass of pink lemonade and a book. The balcony overlooked the driveway and showed a gorgeous view of Blackheart Mountain. Even though I'd seen the mountain earlier, I loved how dark and almost moody it looked against the lush grass and happy flowers. I was already in love with this place.

I stepped over my bags and headed downstairs. Mom was in the master bathroom running her fingers over the ledge of the Jacuzzi tub. This house was more like a resort than a rental. Outside, Dad paced around the driveway with his cell phone pressed to his ear. He threw a hand into the air.

"This house isn't terrible," I said.

"It just makes the cut," she agreed.

"Is it okay if I bike into town for a bit?" I asked. "I just want to look around."

With our constant moving, it wasn't easy finding the time to get my license. I loved running and biking, though, so driving wasn't really high on my list anyway.

"You won't get lost, will you?" she asked. She wiped down the counter with a cloth and sprayed Windex on the mirrors. Each time we moved into a new place, she cleaned no matter how sanitary things appeared. It was part of her routine to ease us into a new house. I liked that she used the same cleanser—so it made the house smell like home. I always lit candles, too—ones scented like roses and strawberries. Having familiar scents calmed me.

I started for the door. "There's not much town to get lost in."
Mom nodded. "Take your phone just in case."

She went back to cleaning the counter, and I left. When I opened the back door, Dad's voice carried across the yard. "Are you kidding me?" he said into the phone. "Why weren't these people handled before I got into town?" His free hand was balled into a fist. Then he saw me.

Dad uncurled his fingers and waved at me. Or rather, he waved in my general direction. All his attention was on the phone call. I grabbed my yellow bike and headed down the gravelly driveway. Exploring a town solo was one of my favorite things about coming to a new place. I intended to soak up every second of Lost Springs.

CHAPTER THREE

Timing has a lot to do with the outcome of a rain dance.

The crumbling road to town was almost deserted. There weren't any houses even remotely close to our cabin, and when a solitary pickup truck passed me as I biked into town, the driver lifted three fingers from the steering wheel and tipped his hat to me. Three fingers? Not one or two? Did three mean something? If you flashed three fingers in a lot of the places I had lived, it would have been taken as a gang sign.

In town, I passed a small post office—a wooden building with a tin roof that stretched into an overhang above the steps and small porch. A wooden sign, flapping gently in the breeze, said WATSON'S GROCERY STORE. The gravel parking lot was nearly empty, and attached to the grocery store was a smaller building. SPRING SUPPLY: SEED & FEED. Their parking lot was packed. Pickups with dogs in the truck beds were jammed into the crowded space. People trickled out of the store with burlap bags of what I assumed was feed for cattle and horses, bales of hay, and other unidentifiable farm supplies.

I headed for the grocery store. Our usual ritual was to come to the new grocery store and shop together as a family, but maybe I could pick up a few things now and save Mom and Dad the trip.

The grocery store was more like a market. Dozens of fruits and vegetables filled large bins, and smoky-smelling ham was suspended from the ceiling by twine in a corner of the store. Mom would probably buy out the fruit section when she saw all that Watson's offered. I grabbed milk, bread, and a container of pre-sliced turkey and headed for the checkout. The *one*-lane checkout.

"Hi," I said to the cashier, who looked about my age. She had chin-length black hair and, like, a hundred metal buttons with smiley faces, clovers, and other tiny pictures pinned to her uniform. "Ask me" was written on her name tag.

"Stocking up on travel food?" she asked as she rang up my items.

"Kind of," I said, handing her cash. It was going to take a little getting used to how everyone knew everyone here. This was the smallest town we had ever lived in.

"Hope you've got a cooler for the milk. It's going to get really warm tomorrow," she said. "You're one of the few tourists to shop here. Usually, everyone buys water and stuff from the vendor in the town center."

"Actually, I'm living in Lost Springs for a while," I said. "My dad has a job here." I smiled at her. "I'm Brie Carter."

In our family—even though my parents are married—Mom, Kate, and I are Carters. Mom, on a super-feminist kick when

Kate and I were born, had convinced my dad to let us keep her maiden name as our last name.

"I'm Amy Banks," she said, smiling back. "Your dad is the new ranch hand at McCoys', huh? I heard he was supposed to be moving here soon. I didn't know he had a family."

I took the bag, holding back a smirk, and shook my head. No one had ever mistaken Michael Brooks for a ranch hand before. Mom would laugh her butt off.

"My dad's here for different business," I said. "It's him, my mom, and me. I've never heard of the McCoys."

"Oh, suck," Amy said, handing me my change. "Not suck that you're moving here!" she added quickly. "I was just disappointed for a friend. His dad is the one waiting for the extra help. It would have taken a lot of responsibility off Logan's shoulders."

Logan? Maybe it was a super-common name around here. "I think I met a guy named Logan," I said casually. "He worked at the WyGas."

"That was him," she said. "Logan's always working. He's due here for his shift any minute."

"Awesome," I muttered. "So he works *everywhere*." I said that part louder.

"He has to," Amy said, leaning closer even though the market was empty. "He works two jobs outside his dad's ranch. The Triple M is pretty big around here. Well, *was*, I guess."

"Did something happen?" I asked.

"The economy," Amy said. "They need lots more hands, but they're only able to hire one person right now."

"Oh." Now I felt like a brat. My parents didn't spoil me, but I'd never had to go out and get a job. Sure, I worked for my dad, but Mom always said, "School is your job."

But Logan, who couldn't have been more than a college freshman, was out in the real world with three jobs. I spent my days exploring, doing schoolwork, helping my dad, taking pictures—or, at least, fiddling with my camera—and reading.

"You picked a crazy time to move here," Amy said.

"Why?" I asked. I put the brown-bagged groceries at my feet.

Amy leaned back against the counter. "I'm guessing you just got here today?"

I nodded.

"Lost Springs is—spoiler alert!—a tiny town," Amy said.

"No!" I said, laughing a little.

"No one *ever* moves here," Amy continued. "If someone comes here, they're like a rare species. The locals, especially the old people, go insane trying to meet the new people, bring them baked goods, and ask a ton of questions. You know, normal behavior like that."

We both laughed.

"Uh-oh," I said. "I better behave now that the whole town is going to be watching me."

Amy held up her pointer finger. "Actually, you're in luck. Your family, too. The McCoys' new ranch hand should be here any day now. But . . ." Amy paused, frowning. She folded her arms. "There is a guy moving here that *everyone* is in a frenzy about. He's the biggest jerk on the planet. He's supposed to get here tomorrow."

All the bubbly niceness had evaporated from Amy. She pressed her lips together in a line, shaking her head.

"How do you know he's a jerk if you haven't met him yet?" I asked. "And the *entire* town doesn't like him?"

My stomach flip-flopped a little. Amy wasn't talking about . . . no, she couldn't be.

"We don't just not like him," Amy said. "We *hate* him. At last month's town meeting, we all learned that some big shot was coming here to destroy our town."

"Destroy?"

I had a sinking feeling I knew exactly who Amy was ranting about. My hands clenched and I stood up straighter. I was in flight or fight mode.

"Destroy. He's a land developer or something like that. The mayor had Googled the guy's name before the meeting and we all got flyers with info from this jerk's website."

"What's his name?" I asked, my tone flat.

"Michael Brooks," Amy said, practically spitting it out. "I'm *so* glad that you're not with him! I'm sure you're really busy unpacking and everything, but if you want to know more about him, you should look him up online."

Anger burned in my chest. Not one of these people had ever met my dad. Amy made it sound as if Michael Brooks were a part of the Mexican cartel storming the city with weapons and drugs. I took in a slow breath through my nose.

"I could look him up," I said. I caught Amy's eye and held it. "Or, better yet, I could ask him. Since he *is* my father."

Silence.

Amy opened and closed her mouth. Twice.

"I'm going home," I said. "And the person who is coming to 'destroy' Lost Springs is there." I bent down and picked up my grocery bag.

"I'm sorry," Amy said. "I was a little harsh."

"A little?"

"Well, your dad *is* coming into town to do something that none of us wants. He's going to clear acres of land. That impacts the wildlife and the quality of life here."

"Thousands of trees are chopped down every year," I said. "As for wildlife, give the animals some credit. Birds and squirrels and whatever else will find new homes. We've coexisted with them for a *long* time, haven't we?"

"Yes, but this is different. Lost Springs is home to—"

I cut Amy off with a wave of my hand. "Whatever. When the hotel is built and it starts bringing money into town, you'll be thanking my dad."

"I don't think so," Amy said. "No one wants this. Not one person in town."

I clenched my jaw. "So what? All twelve residents of this dinky town hate my family? I think we'll survive."

I walked away from the counter almost feeling fumes of hot anger radiating off my body.

I heard Amy call my name just as the door swung shut. I kicked a rock on the pavement. If that was how it was going to be around here, at least I had a little warning.

In the parking lot, a *very* familiar black Ford was parked next to my bike. The empty truck's windows were down. I could get right inside if I wanted to. Maybe the whole town ran on the honor system.

I walked behind the truck and saw a bumper sticker on the back with three uppercase *M*s in a row. No question about whose truck this was. In the back window, the red paper was a flyer that looked like it could have been for a candidate running for office. Except it was a picture of my dad with a giant NO sign over it.

I got on my bike, balancing the bag carefully on the handle-bars. We hadn't even been here for twenty-four hours and I already wanted to move.

CHAPTER FOUR

*Horses are only afraid of two things—things that move
and things that don't.*

"MONSTER!"

I sat up straight in bed, my hands gripping my coffee-colored sheets. *It was just a nightmare*, I told myself. *Everything is totally fine.*

Faint light filtered through my blinds. I grabbed my phone off the stack of boxes next to my bed and checked the time. Barely six in the morning.

"MURDERER!"

"Omigod," I said aloud to no one in my room. I scrambled out of bed and my bare feet slapped against the wooden steps as I went from the second floor to the first. I ran to my parents' bedroom and knocked on their closed door, feeling like I was four or five again and needed my mom and dad after a bad dream.

"Mom, Dad," I whispered. I cracked open their door. "Dad," I said louder. "Mom! Wake up." Part of me felt like I needed to be quiet or whoever was outside would hear me.

"Brie? Honey, what's wrong?" Mom asked. She sat up in bed and reached out an arm to me.

I navigated through the maze of boxes and let Mom wrap her arm around my waist.

My dad hadn't moved. He could sleep through anything.

"I heard voices and thought I was dreaming, but somebody's outside," I said. My heart thumped hard in my chest. "Someone was screaming—"

"GET OUT OF LOST SPRINGS!"

"Michael!" Mom yanked on the covers and pushed Dad's shoulder. "Michael, wake up. NOW."

Dad blinked and sat up. "What?" he asked. "What's wrong?"

"Dad, people are outside screaming," I said. "We have to call the police."

"WE DON'T WANT YOU HERE, BROOKS!" a man's voice yelled with that weird sound to it that voices get from megaphones.

"Oh, great," Dad said. "The real-estate agent told me that we'd probably have protestors. I don't know why they had to start so early in the morning."

Mom gave him the Death Stare. "Why didn't you say anything and why did you just make a mockery of it? By the sound of it, there's more than one person outside protesting my husband's business at *our* home. I wouldn't refer to it with such a laid-back attitude." Mom's voice kept getting louder with every word. "You told me *nothing*!"

Mom got out of bed and gathered her hair into a messy topknot. I stood beside her, both of us staring at Dad.

Dad dropped his head for a second. "Sorry," he said. "It was something that I always handed off to Brody. I didn't think anyone would ever really show up."

"I can't even talk about this right now," Mom said. She reached behind me and yanked her purple cotton robe off a pile of boxes. "I'm going to call the police."

"Nicola, we're not calling the cops," Dad said. He straightened his red T-shirt and black cotton pants while slipping his feet into black Nike sandals. "I'll go outside and handle it."

"No," Mom said. I took a slow step backward, not wanting to be caught between them.

Dad and Mom locked eyes.

"Michael," Mom said. "You don't know any of those people. They're angry with you. What if someone wants to hurt you?"

Dad shook his head and started for the bedroom door. "I'll be fine. They're a bunch of noise."

He walked out of the bedroom and Mom turned to me. We looked at each other as Dad's flip-flops slapped against the wooden floor. Without a word, Mom and I both hurried out of the bedroom.

Dad was already at the front door, pulling it open. Crisp early morning air hit my bare legs and I shivered—both from fear and cold.

I stopped just behind Dad and peeked around him.

Signs.

Signs were *everywhere*. People stood all over our driveway and some spilled onto the yard. Red, blue, black, green. The colors almost blended together as the signs waved back and forth. The words made me freeze.

A white poster had a red circle with an image of a black horse. Above the image, the text screamed at me, PLEASE DON'T EAT ME!

Another sign: SAY NO TO HORSE SLAUGHTER!

SAVE THE MUSTANGS!

Something stirred in my belly as I stared at the signs. Dad's job was endangering mustangs? The horses wouldn't *really* die, would they? Dad wouldn't let that happen no matter what he was building. I paused. *At least I* think *Dad would protect the horses*, I thought.

There had to be at least thirty-something people. Thirty-something *angry* people. Lost Springs wasn't a big town. Most of the population was probably standing in front of me.

"Go back to the city, Brooks!" a woman yelled.

"Leave our land alone!" someone else added.

My eyes stopped on a white poster with red letters. THIS IS THEIR HOME, the sign read, and silhouetted horses ran underneath. The sign moved high above the holder's head, and he pushed back his cowboy hat.

Logan.

It felt as though every cell in my body froze. I couldn't believe *he* was here. I backed up into the shadows.

"Get off my property!" Dad yelled. He walked down the porch stairs and headed right for the crowd.

"Michael!" Mom shouted.

But he kept walking as if he hadn't heard her.

I looked at the crowd and there was a man who was almost identical to Logan, only older. The man raised his hand in the air, quieting the group.

Dad stopped just short of Logan and the man in a black cowboy hat.

"We are not here to scare or upset your family," the man said. "However, we *are* here to make you see how many of us are against your plans for Lost Springs. This is our home."

The crowd clapped and whistled.

"We'll continue to protect our horses, no matter the cost," the man said.

"And I'm going to continue to do my job, *no matter the cost*," Dad said in a mocking tone. "Do you want this town to get poor?" He shook his head. "Let me rephrase that."

"Brooks, it's not about money," the man said. "It's—"

Dad laughed, silencing the stranger. "It *is* about money. Look at this town. It's not exactly thriving in this economy."

"Go call the police," Mom said to me.

Mutely, I nodded. I found one of the phones charging on the kitchen counter. I pressed 911 and waited for the operator.

"Lost Springs nine-one-one," a cheery female voice said. "What is your emergency?"

"Um," I said. "There is kind of a protest in front of my house right now."

There was a pause. "What kind of protest? Does anyone have weapons?" the woman asked.

"I don't know about weapons. There are people with a bunch of signs who are protesting my dad's land development here."

"Oh," the operator said, her voice not so cheery anymore. "I'll send an officer to your location. Someone will be there in a few minutes."

"Wait," I said. I heard her rapidly pushing buttons. "I didn't give you my address. I'm calling from a cell phone."

"I don't need your address," she said. "You must be Michael Brooks's kid, right?"

I nodded, even though she couldn't see me. "Yes."

"I know where you live," the woman replied.

I hung up, staring at the phone for a minute. I shook my head and hurried through the living room to find Mom. She hadn't moved from her place in the doorway. I slowed down and crept up behind her.

"I called the police," I said.

"Good," she said, keeping her gaze on Dad. He hadn't moved—he and the protest leader were staring each other down.

"Brooks, you know damn well who I am," the guy said.

Dad laughed. "Do you have any idea how many people I talk to in a day? Do you really think I'd even *take* your calls?"

"Someone in your office did," the man said. "I'm Jack McCoy. I left messages with your people, but you never returned my calls. Think of how much trouble you would have saved if you had only spoken to me."

"I don't have time to return phone calls to idiots like you," Dad said. "I'm here to do my job. I've dealt with radicals like you before, trust me."

Jack crossed his arms. "You have *no* idea who we are. These mustangs—"

"Are not my problem," Dad interrupted. His face was going through various shades of red. Now it was nearing tomato red. "Listen now, because I'm only going to say this once," Dad continued. "I would be stupid not to have my people run every possible check or test to make sure I won't have any problems. The hotel that I'm going to build doesn't violate a damn thing. And those horses can certainly find other places to run around."

"All right, Brooks," Jack McCoy said, shaking his head. "I don't think you understand—"

He was cut off as a cop car with a severely rattling dented fender pulled into the driveway and creaked to a halt.

"What seems to be the problem, gentlemen?" the officer asked as he got out of the car. He sounded bored, almost as if he already knew what the problem was. He pushed back his brown hat and the sun hit his weathered face.

"There's no problem, Officer St—" McCoy started.

Dad cut him off. "There certainly *is* a problem," he said.

The rest of the protestors were silent.

"Honey, go inside," Mom said.

"Why?" I asked. "I want to make sure that Dad's okay."

"*I'll* be sure." Mom tipped her head in the direction of the living room. "Go."

I wanted to argue with her, but I watched her chew on her lower lip—something she did when she was nervous or stressed. I didn't want to make it worse.

Nodding, I headed inside. Mom shut the door behind me and the house was quiet. I started toward the window facing the back-yard, but changed my mind. I half jogged upstairs and grabbed my phone. I sat facing my sliding glass door. From my spot on the bed, I could see Dad, McCoy, the sheriff, and the protestors.

"Kate," I said the second she answered. "I'm so glad you picked up."

"What's wrong?" my sister asked. I could hear the panic in her voice. "Brie, where are Mom and Dad?"

"Sorry, I didn't mean to scare you," I said. "I totally forgot about the time difference."

Kate took a deep breath. "What's going on?"

"Something kind of scary," I said.

By the time I'd told Kate everything, the officer had driven off, and Dad had made a beeline for the front door.

"I think it's over," I said. "I'll text you later."

Jack seemed to signal to the rest of the group to head down our driveway to the road. I squinted and could just make out Jack and Logan walking side by side.

CHAPTER FIVE

Never approach a bull from the front, a horse from the rear, or a fool from any direction.

The next morning I woke to silence. I stretched, and the sore muscles in my arms screamed in protest. I'd been up until midnight unpacking. I'd gone to bed and woken up around two because all I could hear was Dad and Jack McCoy arguing in my head. Then I saw *his* face. Logan standing at the front of the crowd, looking on at his dad talking to mine.

When I'd finally been seconds away from drifting off to sleep, a bone-chilling howl had made me freeze and hold my breath. It wasn't as if I hadn't heard coyotes before, but it freaked me out. The coyotes hadn't stopped howling until three thirty, and I was wide awake. After I got up and went around the house and checked to make sure every window and door was locked, I lay in bed listening for sounds—imagining the protestors quietly creeping onto our lawn, ready to sneak-attack us in the morning. I finally fell asleep around four.

I rolled over and buried my face in my pillow. I felt like a coward. I'd stood behind Mom during the entire argument. I'd hidden in the shadows of our house like a scared little kid. I almost wanted to apologize to Dad for not appearing at his side. I frowned, mentally scolding myself. I'd never cared what people thought of me. I was always the new girl, and that made me stand out. So why hadn't I jumped to Dad's defense?

Because Mom would have freaked if you'd gone out there, I told myself. But even I didn't believe my lie.

I slid out of bed and opened my blinds. I'd had the window cracked open all night for air and the bedroom was chilly. I slid on jeggings and ankle socks and pulled on a black graphic tee with a rhinestone skull on the front.

Quickly, I did my morning routine: brush hair and pull it into a high ponytail, wash face and apply BB cream with sunscreen, brush teeth. I slicked on a coat of Sugar Fresh Rosé lip gloss and, pocketing it, headed downstairs.

Mom and Dad were already up and in the kitchen.

"Did you guys hear the coyotes last night?" I asked, pulling out a high-backed chair from the island. Before sitting, I went to the window and scanned our lawn. No protestors.

"Coyotes?" Dad said. "Really?" His brown-gray eyes looked at me.

"I can't believe you didn't hear them. They howled half the night. Then I was too freaked to sleep."

"I didn't hear them, either," Mom said. "Probably because we fell asleep with the TV on."

Mom poured me a glass of OJ and slid it across the counter

to me. She went to the coffeepot and topped off the coffee in her favorite yellow mug.

"Can I have a cup, please?" I asked, sipping my OJ.

Mom shook her head. "Not until you finish your juice. Your father"—Mom shot Dad a look—"is on his sixth cup of coffee."

Dad grinned, looking up from his iPad. "My love," he said. "It's not my sixth cup."

I grabbed a raspberry-filled breakfast bar from a wicker basket on the counter.

"You haven't had less than six," Mom said, folding her arms.

"I never said *less*," Dad said. He had a gleam in his eye, like he was excited to be getting away with something. "I had two cups before you woke up."

"Michael," Mom said, shaking her head. "It's not even seven o'clock. At least drink some juice or have a piece of fruit."

Dad kissed Mom's cheek. He tore a banana from the ripe bunch near the breakfast-bar basket.

"If we don't get our morning coffee, it stunts our growth," I said, putting an arm around Dad's waist and grinning at Mom.

Dad laughed and kissed the top of my head. Mom was barely able to conceal a smirk.

"You are your father's daughter," she said. "Now, hon, Dad and I need to talk to you about something before you leave."

"Okaaay," I said slowly.

"We didn't talk much yesterday about what happened," Mom said. "You know there's a very good chance you might run into protestors at the development site this morning. Or maybe even this afternoon."

"I'm not afraid of them," I said, shrugging. "Dad's not doing anything wrong."

"You were really quiet after everyone left," Mom said. She did her Mom-Scan of my face, looking for any signs that there was more to the story.

"Brie, you *can* stay home today," Dad said.

"I'm *really* okay," I said. "Stop."

I looked away when Dad leaned in to kiss Mom.

"Like we talked about last night," Mom said to Dad, "I'm going to be on a video call with another photographer, and then I've got to order a few new pieces of camera equipment."

"Okay, hon," Dad said to Mom. "You almost ready?" Dad asked me.

When I wasn't working on my homeschool curriculum, I worked for Dad in his office. I'd been Dad's secretary and website designer since I was twelve. He had started me out with small tasks like filing paperwork. Then, after a month, he taught me how to answer the phone with a "How may I help you?" and not a "What's up?" By that point, I realized that Dad didn't have—and really needed—some sort of online presence for his company. So, I got a book from the library about how to design a website. A few months later, Dad's company website went live and business really started to pick up. I was glad to have learned all that I had from him and wouldn't take back the hours I put in for anything. Still, I was almost jealous of everyone else in my family. They all had their own "thing." I wondered if I would ever find mine.

Under Mom's eye, I swallowed the rest of my juice and took the last bite of my breakfast bar. I made puppy dog eyes at her, and she went, shaking her head, to the coffeepot and poured the remainder of it into a stainless steel travel mug. The mug was the one and only thing I insisted had to be safely packed and not left behind during any of our moves.

There wasn't anything special about it, but *it* was special to me. The mug was covered in My Little Pony stickers and "BRIE" was spelled out with alphabet letters on a slant. I'd been almost six when Kate—fourteen—had presented me with the stickers. One day, I put them all over her coffee mug, and instead of being mad, Kate rinsed out the coffee and washed the mug. She filled it with apple juice and gave it to me. The stickers were faded—some gone from one too many times in the dishwasher. The steel had dulled and had a million scratches everywhere. I even had to take off the top and sip from the mug because the seal had worn away years ago. I'd ended up with coffee down my shirt or on my jeans too many times before I'd given up fighting with the lid.

"Coffee for the road," she said.

I nodded, gratefully taking the mug. "Thanks, Mom."

I turned to Dad. "Is there going to be enough coffee for us and the guys at the site? Do you have extra in your trailer in case we run out?"

"Oh, my gosh," Mom said, faking a horrified look with her mouth open and a hand on her heart. "How ever would you go on if you couldn't have afternoon coffee?"

"I wouldn't," I said through my smile. "I'd be asleep, drooling on Dad's couch."

The words took me back to the last time I'd been in the trailer. It was almost like a second home to me.

At thirteen, after spending an entire summer working in Dad's cold and boring trailer, I'd *begged* him to remodel it to at least make it more of a comfy work space. For years, Dad had a stuffy, formal office setup inside. Uncomfortable wooden chairs had come well before the couch. Harsh fluorescent lights beamed down on us, giving our skin a greenish look.

I didn't need to walk the new job site to envision the setup. No matter what, Dad always had a silver trailer at the far back left of the lot—a weird superstition—and the rest of the crew shared RVs on the lot. I'd known Dad's work guys since I could walk. His crew of ten had been with Dad from the beginning.

"Is everyone here?" I asked. "Did you tell them about yesterday?"

He nodded, not needing any more explanation to know what I meant. He reached for the sugar bowl. "Brody and the rest of the guys got in last night. They're already at the site doing a preliminary check before we start."

"The guys are there right now?" Mom asked, leaning against the countertop.

Dad nodded. "No one else is there, hon. The village idiots were smart enough not to bang on the trailer doors of a bunch of guys who would make it hard for them to knock on another door for a *long* time. Don't be nervous."

"Well, I am anxious," Mom said.

"Hey," Dad said. He walked over to Mom and hugged her. He took her hand and led her into the foyer.

"Michael, I don't want . . . my daughter is . . ." Mom's voice was too low for me to hear every word.

When Mom and Dad finally came back into the room, she didn't look happy.

"What's wrong?" I asked.

Dad opened his mouth, then hesitated. "Your mom and I are concerned about what we might be walking into at the lot."

Mom frowned and put her hands on her hips. "I'm a little more than 'concerned.'"

"Can you just tell me what's going on?" I asked. "Are there more protestors at the site?"

Dad shook his head. "As of five minutes ago, no. Brie, I should have told you and your mom about the controversy around this job before now. I completely understand if going to work there would make you uncomfortable."

"I'm not afraid of them," I said. But my heart rate increased a little. What if Jack McCoy was there and he and Dad started fighting again? I tried to push away the question forming in my brain, but I couldn't stop it. What if *Logan* was there?

"Hon, you don't have to go," Dad said, looking into my eyes. "Are you sure?"

"Totally," I said. "After all, I am your secretary and webmistress." I paused, and grinned. "Plus, I need money."

Mom and Dad laughed.

"Okay, okay," Mom said, throwing up her hands. "But you *both* better come home and let the police handle the situation if it's out of control."

"Promise," I said, hugging Mom with one arm. "I'll be back for lunch," I called. Dad had already strapped my bike to the rack. The job site wasn't far from home and I didn't want to work all of Dad's long hours.

After Dad said another good-bye to Mom, we grabbed our stuff and headed for the Explorer.

"You're in *trrroooouble*," I sang teasingly.

Dad sighed and shook his head. "I am most definitely in trouble. Your mom was not happy that I didn't tell her about the protestors before we got here."

I clicked my seat belt and put my coffee in the cup holder.

"Why didn't you tell us?" I asked. Dad turned on the engine, backed the SUV around a concrete birdbath and eased it over the little bridge, and started down a bumpy, barely paved road toward the site. Bright sunlight streamed through the windows. I reached down to my Fossil messenger bag—a gift from Kate— and found my pair of Dollar General sunglasses. "We always talk about *everything*."

Outside my window, a giant herd of black cattle grazed calmly. A tangled barbed-wire fence choked with weeds ran along the road. Chunks of the fence were missing, and I wondered why the cattle didn't escape through the fence holes. I kept expecting to see someone either jump out at us with a sign or start following us to the site. But the road was eerily quiet.

"Honestly, hon, the real-estate agent did speak to me about the possibility of all this. But I didn't expect anything to really happen—especially not at our *home*. I just hope you or Mom don't need to deal with that when one of you is home alone." Dad sighed again. "I'm sorry that you had to wake up to that. I never want you to feel vulnerable in your own space."

He eased up on the gas pedal as the single-lane road changed from concrete to a black-tarred road. We hadn't passed one car yet.

"I don't," I said. "They aren't showing up to *hurt* us."

"I know, but I don't want you around them again. Brie, you have to promise that you *will* go home if that idiot McCoy and his merry men show up at the site," Dad said. He put the turned-off Bluetooth device in his right ear and pressed it. The light turned from orange to green.

"Okay," I said. "But, Dad, I would worry."

He looked over at me, then back at the road. The Explorer eased up just a notch.

"Worry about what?"

"You. What if McCoy and those people get *really* mad? They probably all have guns or bear tranquilizers or something."

The corner of Dad's mouth curled up and he laughed.

"Um, what's funny?" I asked. "I was talking about people possibly hurting you!"

"Sorry, sorry," Dad said, his black polo shirt still shaking a little. He reached over and took one of my hands.

"Honey, if someone wants to shoot me with a bear tranquil-izer, well, I'm out of luck."

"Dad!" I yanked my hand free and crossed my arms. But I couldn't stop the smile from forming.

"They'll tranq me, let me stumble around like I've had too much to drink . . ."

Dad and I looked at each other, and we both burst into laughter.

Dad reached over and took my hand again. "I'm happy that you're up for working for your old man again this summer," he said. "Soon you'll be in college and you'll be doing something way more interesting than this."

A pang hit my chest. I felt like I'd worked on and off for Dad forever.

"I'll be home on summer breaks," I said. "And please, as if you could find an intern who would put up with you."

Dad laughed and nodded. "Touché." He took a left and veered off the main road onto another dusty path. Three yellow bulldozers, a crane, and a trailer popped into view.

"There's Brody!" I said, straightening in my seat. His burly shoulders and backward red baseball hat were unmistakable. He stood near one of the bulldozers and talked into a radio. Mom had told me how he'd dressed up as Santa for me for three years in a row when I was little.

Dad parked the SUV, and we both got out. "Careful," he said, touching my arm. "I didn't get a chance yet to read what kinds of snakes are out here."

"Okay," I said. I tried not to think of *Anaconda*. "I'm going to say hi to Brody. Then I'll meet you in the trailer."

I turned, and Dad already had blueprints in one hand and his finger on his earpiece, turning it on.

I stepped through the knee-high grass and made my way over to Brody.

"Long time no see," I said. I reached out my arms and wrapped them around him.

"I thought you had forgotten all about me," Brody said, squeezing me, then letting me go. "Doing okay?" he asked, his freckled forehead crinkling.

"Can't complain so far," I said. "Aside from our friendly neighborhood protestors."

"I like it here, too. But yeah, I could do without those

sign-waving idiots. Honestly, though, even *with* those sign-waving idiots, the conditions here are much better than the sweltering condo lot we did last time. I heard they came to your house. I'm sorry, B."

"They were so angry and just . . . ahh!" I said, tossing up my hands. Logan's face popped into view as I visualized the protestors again. I was starting to annoy *myself* with the Logan visuals.

I looked around at the plain sprinkled with tall, thick trees. Most of the lot was already empty and the land was barren, but it was also uneven and would need serious leveling before any work started.

"Brie!" Dad yelled from the trailer across the space. "Can you come here?"

"Yeah!" I had to go or he'd keep calling for me. Patience wasn't in the Brooks blood.

"Bye," I said.

Brody nodded and climbed into the cab of a bulldozer. He had told me once that he liked to sit in there and work out plans before he actually started bulldozing. But we both knew it was more about getting peace and quiet from Dad. We joked that Dad knew it, too.

Leaving Brody, I ambled across the field. I took my time stepping around the pink and orange spring flowers intertwined in the grass. A smooth stone gleamed in the sun, and I leaned down to pick it up.

Collecting little representations of where we lived was something Mom and I had started doing years ago. Some of my favorite things were white sand from my favorite beach in Belize, a conch shell from Miami, Florida, and a lighthouse replica from Maine.

As I started to stand, the ground rumbled beneath my feet. It started to shake slightly and then harder. My feet didn't want to move, and I heard blood rushing in my ears.

I looked back for Brody. He was still in the bulldozer's cab, and large black headphones were around his ears. The trailer was halfway across the lot. Adrenaline pushed me forward and I kept my eyes locked on the trailer.

Wyoming didn't get earthquakes, did it? Maybe there were geysers around here.

The ground rumbled harder and a low *hum* came from the woods. I broke into a run, sprinting toward the silver trailer.

"Dad?" I yelled. "Dad!"

My flip-flop caught on something, and I fell on my knees. I pushed myself up, and a large blur appeared at the wood's edge. *Bear. It has to be a bear!* Despite my heart hammering in my chest, I couldn't tear my eyes away from the trees.

Horses burst out of the line of trees and galloped toward me. I'd ridden horses before, and had taken lessons over the years, but these didn't look like stable horses. Instead of shining, brushed coats and neatly trimmed manes, these horses were fuzzy. Some had mud caked on their bodies. The horses—mustangs—matched the photos of wild horses that I'd looked up on my phone last night.

The fluidity of the herd of at least fifteen was mesmerizing. Mostly sorrels and paints rushed at me. Everything inside me screamed to run. But I knew I couldn't outrun them. I'd be trampled by the thousand-pound animals that barreled in my direction.

Dad's office door flew open, banging against the trailer's side. Dad looked toward the sound and then he saw me.

"Brie! Run, for Christ's sake!" he yelled. His voice was barely audible over the thunder of hooves. He gripped the railing on the trailer steps and he froze.

I hugged myself. Horses were smart. I knew enough about them to know they wouldn't run into a solid object on purpose. I had to be still. I shivered and my teeth chattered as if the temperature had dropped below zero.

The first horse, a dusty sorrel, galloped by and the sea of horses enveloped me. I couldn't see anything but blurs—backs, manes, and tails flashed in the sun. The horses almost brushed me as they ran. A few coarse tails stung my face. For the briefest of seconds, I wondered if they were headed for the field on the other side of the lot. I couldn't breathe. The horses didn't look afraid or angry. They were simply running.

More horses swerved around me and the rumble of hooves disappeared almost as fast as it began. I gasped, as if I hadn't taken a breath during the rush of horses. My heart beat almost as fast as they had galloped by. Fear melted into awe as I turned my head in the direction of the horses' destination. I had never known what true freedom really looked like until seconds ago.

I waved to Dad. His shoulders sagged in visible relief, and he ran across the field.

"I'm fine!" I called as he reached me and grabbed me in a tight hug. I could almost hear Dad's heart—it was beating so loud and fast. He kept me in the hug, squeezing me before letting me go. His heart pounded fast against my chest, and his jagged breath whooshed against the back of my neck.

"You could have been killed," he said. "Why didn't you run?"

The bulldozer cab door opened. "You all right?" Brody called. His headphones were around his neck as he started down the cab steps. Three of the guys who had been marking trees with spray paint were looking in my direction. I waved a hand at them.

"Totally good," I called.

Dad's eyes were wide. Beads of sweat formed along his hairline. Usually, he was preoccupied with work and he looked through me and on to something else, something more important than me. Our exchange on the way here was a rare thing. Something I missed. Now Dad was actually looking at *me*. He wasn't staring over my head or panicking because he could be missing a phone call. Dad's face slowly changed from pasty white to its normal color.

"The horses would have run me over if I'd moved," I said, finally answering his question. "I couldn't outrun them."

"Thank God you weren't hurt," Dad said as he slung his arm across my shoulder and led me toward the trailer. "I wanted"—he cleared his throat—"to run at them, but I was afraid they'd spook."

My heart rate started returning to normal, and I almost skipped ahead of Dad. "There was nothing you could have done, Dad. They were beautiful, weren't they?" Exhilaration kicked in as my fear dissipated. I stepped inside the cool, roomy office. I flopped on the gray love seat, and Dad sat in front of his giant Mac screen.

Dad snorted and rolled his black desk chair under the computer table. "Those scraggly menaces aren't getting near the property again. I called the secretary of the BLM, but—"

"Dad!" I said, stopping his tirade. "What are you talking about? What's BLM?"

"Bureau of Land Management. They oversee every aspect of the mustangs, including where the horses live. They assured me that the horses were far from this lot. The last thing I'm going to deal with is horses on a construction site."

I stood, walked over to Dad's desk, and picked up a stack of papers in what I knew was his "to be filed" tray. I started sticking papers into the giant metal filing box.

"What are you going to do?" I asked him.

He picked up the corded phone and started dialing. "I'll put pressure on them to get the horses moved immediately," he said, his lips pressed together.

Shrugging, I went back to filing.

In Belize, he'd had to call the local animal control about a nest of parrots. Displacing animals went with the territory—I knew that. I glanced at Dad, then back to the files. That rush of raw power in the middle of the herd had made me feel *something*. I wanted to do something—anything—to feel like that again.

CHAPTER SIX

If you come to a fork in the road, take it.

The sun had just peeked over Blackheart Mountain when I climbed out of bed and quietly crept downstairs. Last night, Mom and Dad had decided that Dad would take the morning off to accompany Mom into town. She needed to find a location for her latest photo shoot. One of Mom's editors had called last night, and she wanted Mom to photograph local creeks and rivers to accompany an article in *Traveling Woman*. Dad wanted to go in case Mom ran into any locals who had something to say to Dad.

Things had been quiet since the first protest, though, and I hoped it would stay that way. I opted to get up early and explore on my own. I pulled on well-worn jeans and a graphic tee that had an owl on the front. In case it was cold, I took my jean jacket off the back of my desk chair.

I pulled a scrap of paper from one of the kitchen drawers and scrawled: *Went exploring. Got my cell. Be back later. ~B.* I left the note on the counter. I put on sunglasses and laced up my hiking boots. Grabbing my camera, I eased open the back door and shut it behind me as I stepped onto our wooden deck. The morning was a little chilly. I was glad I'd brought my jacket.

I stood on the porch—feeling dangerously on sensory over-load. What had to be miles of woods and mountains surrounded me. The air smelled like fresh honeysuckles. I drew in a deep breath and took the few steps down to the driveway. The only sounds were my boots crunching on the gravel. I could actually hear myself think.

I crossed our bridge and walked along the road. It wasn't long before I heard the whine of an engine in the distance. It grew louder and louder as the vehicle neared me.

A red four-wheeler whizzed toward me and its driver lifted three fingers. Again, that local version of a wave. The ATV halted in my path and I sidestepped it to go around. The driver pulled off his hat and, suddenly, I was looking into Logan McCoy's face. *What the . . .*

"Hey," he said.

His tone was friendly. Not what I expected, since he had just been on the front lines of a protest at my house the day before yesterday.

"Leave me alone," I said, walking away from the ATV.

The ATV engine silenced. Logan jogged up from behind me, using the four-wheeler's handlebars to push it along.

"What are you doing out here this early?" Logan asked.

"Why do *you* care?" I replied, glaring at him.

"Okay," Logan said, taking a deep breath. "Do you want to talk about the protest?"

His question completely threw me. It wasn't like I didn't expect to talk about it—I did. I guess I thought it would be more one-sided—him yelling at me about my father the horse and land killer and me having to defend our way of life.

"I saw you," I said. "I was behind my dad. You didn't see me, but I watched you. You were shouting along with everyone else. That was a total ambush on my family. I know where you stand and you can probably do the math. Our ideals—our entire ways of living—they don't mesh well. I'm definitely not going to be friends with someone who could show up on my lawn tomorrow with a sign."

Logan put on his cowboy hat. He looked up at me. "It's not personal—"

"Not personal? Are you kidding me?" I laughed. "You're being ridiculous. It has everything to do with my family and me. You and your posse protested my father's business. That business is something my dad built. He loves it and so does the rest of my family. So don't ever think again that it's not personal."

I turned on my heels, ready to bolt.

"Just one more thing and if you say no, I'll leave you alone," Logan said. "Would you at least listen to our side of things? I promise I'm not going to attack your dad or sound like some infomercial."

I didn't think. I just turned around. "Okay," I said, my voice less edgy. "I can at least listen."

"Do you have some spare time?" Logan asked. "I'd like to show you a couple of really cool things in Lost Springs."

"I don't know, I thought we were just going to—"

"It's much better if I show you. I won't keep you. Promise." Logan smiled.

"As long as we're not gone for more than an hour," I said, finally. "What were you doing around here, anyway?"

He grinned. Logan kind of looked like a modern cowboy with an ATV instead of a horse.

"I live on the other side of town, but I four-wheel out here because it has the best trails."

"I understand that," I said. "I'm super into hiking. I did a little mountain climbing, too, when we lived in Virginia. When it was off season, I started indoor rock climbing at a gym."

Logan toyed with the key chain and looked back at me. "Maybe I can take a few extra minutes to point out the best hiking spots. Plus, we've got trails for riding, for exploring the creeks and waterfalls, and for climbing the mountain base."

I can't believe you are having a conversation with the guy that's part of a mob to bring down your dad! I yelled at myself.

Blinking fast, I snapped out of my thoughts and looked at Logan. His brown eyes stared into mine. He held my gaze. Finally, I lowered my eyes to the ground. I felt the heat already building in my cheeks. It had felt like he had been searching my eyes for something else. Or something more. I didn't know.

"What?" I asked. "Why are you staring at me?"

"I was just thinking that I should warn you . . . when you do try these trails, it's not going to be like rock climbing at your old local gym or jogging on the school track. You're a city girl, right?"

"City girl? You don't even know me," I said, my voice rising. "I'm hardly a city girl. I've lived everywhere."

This guy had been nothing but a judgmental jerk from the second we'd met. No way was I wasting my time with him. I mean, he'd been nice at WyGas, but that was erased the moment he had protested against Dad.

"Really?" He smiled and adjusted his hat.

"Really," I confirmed as I started to walk away from him. He could go ATV-ing all by himself.

"Hey," he called after me. "I still owe you."

"Don't worry about it. I'll write Santa and tell him that Logan McCoy was good this year," I said as I continued to walk and adjusted the camera hanging around my neck. "I'll be fine hiking alone, thanks."

"Alone?" he asked, following me. The engine rumbled as he got back on his ATV and rode it alongside me.

"Yeah, a girl going off alone into the woods," I said. Now he was pissing me off. "Does that violate cowboy rule one oh one? Do you think I should be at home baking or sewing?"

Logan gunned the four-wheeler and skidded to a stop in front of me. "You thought *I* was judging you? Not every guy who wears a cowboy hat is somebody with three kids and a wife at home."

His smile was gone. I knew exactly what I was doing. My subconscious never let me form bonds with anyone because of all the moving. Even though I would *never* be friends with Logan, I was going out of my way to tick him off.

The sun was in my face and I looked down at his leather boots. "I'm sorry," I said, sighing. "That was bitchy. It's just . . ." I paused. "Like I said, I saw you at the protest at my house. Is it like my family came to town and brought a giant wrecking ball with it?"

"No, it's more like your dad is tearing up a great piece of land that local mustangs use for grazing and accessing the local streams and rivers."

"But it's just a *tiny* piece of land," I said. I waved my arm, palm up. "You have all that room. Won't the horses be fine if they're relocated?"

Logan stared at me. "How much do *you* like relocating?"

I clenched my teeth to stop my jaw from dropping. "I like moving!" I said. "Actually, I love it because the next move will be somewhere without you."

I waited while Logan spun the ATV away from me and sent a dust cloud my way. I *did* like moving. Not the packing or unpacking parts, but living in a new place was always exciting. The tangle of horses that had run around me flashed through my mind.

"I'm glad you like moving so much," Logan said. "But the horses don't. Take a quick detour with me, and then I'll bring you back here."

I shook my head. "I'm good, thanks. Anyway, the mustangs *are* animals. They'll probably forget that they've moved a day later."

"C'mon, Brie," he said. "Can we start over? We'll stop talking about horses. Let me give you a ride," Logan said. "You can cover twice as much ground on a four-wheeler. Let me show you just a few hiking trails." His tone was light.

"That's okay," I said. "I'll find my way around."

"There *are* bobcats and bears," he said. That made me turn and look at him. He wiggled both eyebrows. "And mountain lions."

"Oh." It came out in a whisper. "I'm not, um, afraid."

My body flashed hot and cold at the thought of running into one of those animals. Unlike the horses, I didn't think a bear would just pass on by.

"Okay," Logan said. "Long as you're cool out here. Make sure you have pepper spray."

Logan turned the ATV away from me. I swallowed hard.

"Wait," I said. "I'm *not* afraid, but you do owe me. So I'll do you a favor and let you play tour guide."

Logan kept a straight face, but I could tell he was fighting the urge to laugh. The corners of his mouth twitched.

I slid onto the back of the four-wheeler and tried to keep at least a few inches of space between us. My palms sweated and I stared at his back, knowing I'd be touching him in seconds. I felt awkward leaning forward and encircling his waist. His chest muscles tightened against my interlocked fingers.

He fed gas to the engine and we moved forward. He gave it a little more gas as we zipped down the road.

"You okay?" he asked. "Tell me if I'm going too fast."

"I'm good," I said. I almost couldn't believe that I had my arms around Logan—the guy who had honked his truck horn at me less than seventy-two hours ago.

I realized I didn't know anything about him, aside from what he'd told me and what little I'd heard from Amy. My image of cowboys was probably skewed with footage from old black-and-white Westerns that Grandpa and I had watched together.

"What do you do, exactly?" I asked. "I heard that you have a ranch or something."

Logan took a smooth left and headed off the road and into a grassy field. He stopped and got off the four-wheeler.

"My dad and I run it together. I herd the cattle, gentle foals—you know, getting them ready for riders—take care of the livestock, and do whatever needs to be done." He lifted the wire loop that was placed over a fence post and opened the rusty gate. "Can you drive through?" he asked.

"Sure." I slid forward and squeezed the gas. I'd driven plenty of ATVs around Dad's lots. The four-wheeler eased through the gate and I put on the brakes and waited for Logan to close it. *Foals.* Logan had a hands-on connection with horses. Enough of a connection that he'd protested my dad's arrival.

"Are we allowed to ride in here?" I asked. Mom and Dad would freak if I got caught trespassing.

Logan grinned, showing his cute dimple again, and took his seat in front of me. "We can ride anywhere as long as we don't bother the animals or run over any crops. I've worked this field before."

"You work at WyGas, run a ranch, *and* do other stuff?" I already knew the answer, but I didn't want him to know that I'd been talking about him.

"Yeah, I work part-time at Watson's when I can squeeze in some hours around school. I really don't mind it. Most of my bosses are all family friends, so it's almost like I'm my own boss."

He moved the ATV forward over the prickly-looking tall grass and I gingerly wrapped my arms around him again. He smelled like cinnamon and fresh, sweet hay.

"I was definitely wrong about you," Logan said. "The day we met, I had you pegged for a touristy buckle chaser."

"A what?"

"Buckle chaser. But it's no big. I was wrong."

"No, tell me," I said. "What does it mean?"

Logan increased the four-wheeler's speed and we zoomed toward a small hill covered in black rocks. "We call *aggressive* girls buckle chasers," he said. "You're not. I mean, I know we haven't been hanging out that long, but I can tell."

"Oh, God." Just when we had really started to get along, he had to ruin it with *that*. "You thought—" I started. "But I would never . . . forget it!"

I yanked my arms from around his waist and tried to hold on to the back of the four-wheeler. I thought we'd finished razzing each other from earlier.

"Brie—" Logan started.

"Do you expect every girl here to fall all over you, or what? Sorry if you were disappointed that I didn't try to make out with you two seconds after we met."

Minutes ago, we had been talking about man-eating bears and I'd been set to hike solo. Now that Logan had me alone in the middle of nowhere, he decided to tell me what he really thought.

"Put your arms back or you're going to fall off," he said. Ignoring him, I just stared at my camera case.

"No," I said. "If I touch you, watch out, that means I'm a belt chaser!"

"Buckle chaser," he said, his tone softening. "I didn't mean to offend you. Really. I was just surprised that you—"

I cut him off. "Didn't try to hit on you just because we're sitting like this? Do you think girls who aren't from around here find all cowboys irresistible?"

"I didn't say that," Logan said. "But a lot of tourist girls are the same. They think Lost Springs guys are backwoods idiots who do nothing but ride horses and kiss the visiting girls. People treat this place like Vegas. They get to leave and no one at home knows a thing."

"Well, I'm not one of those 'people.' You didn't even know me and you lumped me in that category."

"You didn't know me and you put me in the 'crazy horse protestor' category," Logan said.

"At least I was accurate!" I said. "Okay, maybe not the 'crazy' part, sorry. But you *are* a protestor. Why? What is it about the horses that makes you feel like you have to protest?"

Logan took a *long* pause. "The real answer is personal," he said. "It's only something that I tell my friends. The easy answer is one you'll find out if you stay on the ATV with me."

I sighed. "Okay, okay. Keep your secrets. But know that I would protest for my dad if I needed to."

"You don't," Logan said. "Your father made sure every possible piece of paper was signed before he got here. The Bureau of Land Management already gave him a thumbs-up, so he's good to go."

"Then why are you protesting?" I asked, shaking my head. "Just to show you're upset? What?"

"I don't know why each person is protesting," Logan said. "We're all there for different reasons. Everyone knows that we can't stop your father. For some of the townspeople, I think they would feel as though they let the horses down if they didn't at least show their support."

Logan fell silent. I didn't speak, either.

"It seems like if we want to make it through this ATV ride, we have to stop talking about our dads," I said.

"Agreed," Logan said. He opened up the gas more and we zipped over the long, weed-filled grass.

A few minutes later, he turned off the four-wheeler at the base of the black rocks and got off.

"C'mon," he said. "I want to show you something."

I shrugged, hopped off the ATV, and stepped behind him through the dewy grass. If only our entire exchange could float away in the gentle breeze.

CHAPTER SEVEN

When in doubt, let your horse do the thinkin'.

We walked around the base of the gentle hill and the black rocks choked the grass and weeds. Logan knelt down and felt the ground. He brushed aside a few rocks and exposed the rich brown dirt.

"Feel this," Logan said, motioning for me to bend down.

I stretched my hand forward and felt the spot where he'd touched.

"It's warm," I said, feeling the ground again. It was weird touching ground that was actually hot under my hands. It wasn't just warmed from the sun—it was a different, moist heat.

Logan nodded. "Now, remember what that felt like and come over here."

"What was that?" I asked, staring at the spot before jogging after Logan as he made his way across the loose rocks.

"You'll see," he said. I glanced at him out of the corner of my eye and watched him for a second. He looked around six foot one or two. In his side pocket, a pair of leather gloves peeked out, and what looked like the top of a pocketknife stuck out of his back pocket. I wondered if he got his arms so chiseled from weights or ranch work. A weird scent hit my nostrils, and I sniffed the air.

"What's that smell?" I asked. "It smells like rotten eggs. You're lucky this wasn't a date, or you would have so bombed."

Logan laughed. "I don't smell a thing. Must be you."

"Ha-ha," I said, holding my nose. "Really, what is it?"

"That would be sulfur." He slowed his stride and pushed his hat back on his head. No wonder no one moved to this town. They were gassed out.

"From what?" I asked.

"From this." He grinned and pointed to a smooth piece of land a few yards ahead that wasn't covered in rocks. It looked like gray mud from a spa.

We walked up to the patch of mud and I peered down at it.

"What am I supposed to be seeing— Oh!" I jumped. Bubbles popped in the mud. "No way!"

"It's a mud pot," Logan said. "Don't even try to get closer than this. The mud is hot enough to burn skin."

"That's what the sulfur smell was, huh?" I leaned a little closer and pulled my camera over my head.

"Yeah, it smells awful, but if you can stand it, it's amazing to see," Logan said as he ran his eyes across my face. I could see him taking me in, the way I'd done with him earlier. I clamped my teeth down on the inside of my cheek to keep from blushing.

The mud pots were out in the middle of nowhere. Like a treasure with no map. Behind us, the rocky hill shouldered acres of tall grass and flowers. If I looked straight over the mud pots, I could see the base of Blackheart Mountain.

I adjusted the camera without thinking—it was all like second nature. I pointed the lens toward the bubbles. I leaned in, balancing on my toes.

"Whoa," Logan said. I felt him move in and place a steadying, strong hand atop each of my hips. "I don't want to take you to the hospital with third-degree burns. Take your pictures. There's no rush this time. I don't have my truck to rev at you."

I zoomed in on the mud pot and tried to focus *myself*—not the camera. It was difficult with Logan's palms and fingers radiating heat through my jeans.

Blinking, I concentrated on the shots and got my focus back. Tried not to visualize his warm brown eyes and tan face. Thankfully, my no-boyfriends-until-college rule was firmly in place.

"Okay," I said, stepping back. "I got some great photos."

Logan grinned.

I followed him away from the mud pots and we got back on the ATV.

"Where are we going now?" I asked, wrapping my arms around his waist.

"Somewhere really special," he said. "It's not far."

We left the mud pots and the sulfur smell behind us as Logan eased the ATV up a slight hill. I could feel his washboard abs. *Don't even go there*, my nagging subconscious told me. I turned my face to the side and rested my right cheek gently on Logan's back. He didn't react, so I relaxed my neck muscles and let my head fully rest on him. The sun warmed my back.

Logan gave off a vibe that not many people had—he didn't talk only to prevent silence. He didn't make lulls in conversation feel awkward.

Logan slowed and turned off the ATV when we reached the hilltop. We climbed off the four-wheeler and into thick, emerald-green grass that came up to my knees.

"This view," I said. "Wow." The grass stretched across a plain that turned into gentle rolling hills in the distance. Hundreds, or maybe thousands, of reddish orange flowers created vibrant pops of color.

Logan stood beside me, his hands in the front pockets of his dark jeans. "I never get tired of coming here," he said.

"What are those flowers?" I asked. "They're so pretty. Your outfit sort of matches them, too."

"That was my goal this morning," Logan said. "I woke up and thought, okay. Today, I want to color-coordinate my T-shirt with the Indian paintbrushes."

I laughed.

"They're the state flower," Logan said.

We stood in comfortable silence for several minutes.

I held up my camera. "Do you mind if I take a few shots of this before we go?"

"No way," Logan said. "You need to be home any time soon?"

I shook my head. "Nope. Why?"

"If you want to stick around a little longer up here," Logan said, "there's something that usually happens . . ." He trailed off as he looked at his watch. ". . . in about a half hour to an hour."

I smiled. "Oh, really? What might this 'something' be?"

Logan took off his hat, tossing it onto the grass. "One of the most important things to me."

"I'll stick around," I said. "Are you going to tell me what's going to happen, or is it a secret?"

There was an impish twinkle in his eyes. "I think I'll make you wait and see," he said.

I turned on my camera and peered through the viewfinder. I wanted to take photos that would impress Mom.

"This is so—" I stopped talking. I'd been talking to air!

While I'd been focused on angles, lighting, and clarity, Logan had plopped onto the ground. Lying on his back, hands and cowboy hat beneath his head, he grinned up at me.

I giggled and pointed my camera at him. "I have to capture this!" I said. "I know you so much better now! Thank you for sharing this incredibly important act of lying in the grass with me."

Logan laughed. "That's right. Guess what? I'm feeling generous. I'll share the grass with you if you'd like to try this life-altering event."

I dropped my jaw, then put a hand on my cheek in jest. "Logan, you would share your field with *me*?"

"It was a very difficult decision," he said. "Ultimately, I decided that since you were new in town, it was the neighborly thing to do."

I laughed and removed the camera strap from around my neck. I rested the camera on the seat of the ATV.

I stood close, but not too close, to Logan, and lowered myself onto the ground. The grass wasn't sharp like I'd thought it would be—instead it made a soft bed as I lay on my back. Like Logan, I made a pillow with my hands.

"This is oddly comfortable," I said. "Mattress toppers should be filled with this. Obviously, someone needs to get working on an invention that would keep the grass alive."

"Obviously," Logan said. His tone was light and teasing. "I'll e-mail Serta the second we get back."

The ground was cool under my body, but the cloudless sky allowed the sun to warm us.

"I'm guessing that a guy who runs a company like your dad's moves a lot," Logan said. "Do you and your mom always move with him?"

I rolled onto my side, propping up my head with a hand. "Yes," I said. "I've got an older sister, Kate, and she's an entertainment TV reporter. But yeah, Mom and I always go."

"I can't imagine that life," Logan said.

I thought I detected a note of wistfulness in his voice.

"Where are some of the places you've been?" he continued.

"It's a *long* list," I said. "It would totally bore you."

Logan rolled onto his side and faced me. "I don't care how long the list is—it won't bore me. I *dream* about traveling."

"Where have you gone?" I asked. "Maybe we've been to some of the same places."

A hint of pink came to Logan's cheeks.

"I only left Wyoming once," he said. "I went to Montana to pick up a horse trailer."

"Are you going away for college?"

Logan shook his head. "I actually just graduated from Lost Springs High. I was able to take a test to graduate now instead of in May. This is only my second week not being in school."

"Wow, that's cool," I said. "Are you going to college now or later?"

"Neither. Family business. I can't go off to school and leave my little brother, Holden, and my dad."

"Is that what you want?" I asked. I studied his face, half expecting him to look exasperated or angry, even, that he was expected to carry on the family business.

Logan smiled—a genuine, real smile with no hint of anything but happiness. "Yeah, it is. I want to travel and see things, but I was never the go-off-to-college type. I've wanted to run a ranch since I was a kid."

"Would your dad freak if you wanted to go away to school?"

"No," Logan said. "He'd do exactly what he's doing now— take care of Holden and run things—he'd just have less help. But he wouldn't complain about it. He always wants me to do whatever makes me happy."

"I'm sorry you haven't been able to travel," I said. "But it has to feel good to accomplish so much with your family's ranch, yeah?"

"I'm definitely the right hand for the ranch," Logan said. "It's hard, but I used to get to take a couple weeks off school during the height of planting and harvesting seasons."

"The school let you do that?" I asked. "I've never heard of a school being that accommodating before."

"Lost Springs High has to let us out if we're working and our parents need help. So many families here grow produce, have dairy farms, raise cattle—we're a working town."

"What kind of farming does your family do?" As I spoke, I felt my muscles relax. Being in the bright sunlight with the gentlest of breezes was almost more relaxing than any spa treatment I'd ever had.

"Our ranch started with my great-granddad. It used to be a full working farm with cattle, horses, pigs, and produce. Now my dad and I only deal in produce. We split the work pretty evenly, but soon the labor will be divided among three people because my dad just hired a new hand."

"My family lived near a farm for six-ish months when I was ten," I said. "That's when I decided that I wanted to grow up and be a farmer because I'd get to be outside and work with animals all day."

Logan smiled. "I'm sure that's still your dream," he said, his tone teasing.

"It was, until I volunteered at my neighbor's place," I said. "I spent more time doing barn or field work than being with the animals." I plucked a leaf of grass, rolling it with my fingers. "I saw how hard everyone worked—even the little kids."

Logan smiled. "Holden is ten and he's the best kid. He gets up with me at four every morning and does extra chores without being told," he said.

"Aw," I said. "He must get his work ethic from you."

My brain started sending warning signals that I didn't need to be talking to the enemy. But something else stirred in me—I wanted to get to know him more. I was talking to Logan the Guy, not Logan the Protestor.

Logan bowed his head a little. "Thanks. I try to be a good example for him. He's helping me plant our summer crop of vegetables."

"It's March. You're planting for summer?" I asked. "Or, maybe you don't want to tell me. I have the *worst* luck with every plant on the planet. I don't want that to rub off on you."

Logan laughed. I liked it when he laughed. "I'll take my chances. We're planting peas, potatoes, spinach, and radishes."

"That's *insane*! Wow." I shook my head. "I love fresh veggies. You're going to regret that you gave me that list. I'll eat all your harvest before it gets to the market."

"If you can eat eight acres per vegetable, then they're all yours," he said. "You—" He stopped mid-sentence.

"What's—" I started, but Logan pressed his pointer finger to his lips.

Slowly, he got on his knees and peered down the gently sloping hill.

There was the sound of approaching thunder and the ground hummed. Both things I hadn't forgotten from yesterday.

"The mustangs are coming?" I asked. "Are they your surprise?"

"Yes," Logan said. "They're on their way. They usually come from the top of that hill." Logan pointed to a small hill that leveled off into a long stretch of plain.

I looked behind us at the ATV. Surely we could scare off the horses and get away on it.

"Um, I didn't get a chance to tell you," I said, whispering very fast. "But I've already seen the horses. They came onto my dad's property and almost ran me over."

Logan turned his head toward me. "They almost *ran you over*? How close did you get?" He sounded wistful. As if he wished he had been there.

"Close enough that tails stung my face; some were inches away when they swerved and avoided running into me."

"I'm sorry," Logan said. He reached over and touched my knee. "I know them. The horses. I'm sure they weren't trying to hurt you."

"I don't think they were at all," I said.

"The herd never comes this way," Logan said. "Don't be worried."

The rumble's intensity increased. I shot Logan a smile, nodding. Horses burst over the top of the hill. A robust chestnut led the way and the herd stayed tight together.

"The winds are in our favor today—they won't smell us and disappear."

"Look at all those colors," I said. "The lead chestnut is stunning."

"You've been around horses?" Logan asked.

"I took lessons on and off as a kid," I said. "I think they're pretty majestic animals."

Logan's gaze flickered from the horses to me. "Then you get it."

"What?" The lead horses began to slow from an energetic gallop to a lope. Finally the herd broke apart and the horses trotted to what seemed like favorite areas.

"You understand why I love them," Logan said. "You've trusted a thousand-pound animal with your life." He turned his gaze back to the horses. "Look at them."

The horses halted almost directly in front of us—there was only about a football field of hill and plain in between us and the horses. I watched foals frolic—letting out shrill little neighs and play-fighting each other. Most of the horses grazed and a few knelt onto the grass and rolled onto their backs, long legs kicking in the air as they wiggled on the ground.

I didn't know if a minute or an hour had passed when I caught myself looking at Logan. He was completely lost in the herd.

"Logan," I said. "What's going to happen to them? I mean, am I going to see you at my dad's site with other protestors?"

Logan looked at me. "No," he said. "The sheriff made it clear to everyone who was at your house that if we protested again there would be trouble. There's nothing we can do to stop your dad. Plus, that's the wrong place to put our energy—or so I've told my dad. We need to think about how to help the horses."

I licked my bottom lip. "Thank you. I don't want anything bad to happen to them, either."

"Just because I'm choosing to focus on the horses, though, it doesn't mean everyone else is doing the same. You may still see some protests at the site, so be prepared. But know that I'm not part of it." He turned his gaze in front of him and back to the horses. "The mustangs kind of saved someone in my life once. I owe it to them to help."

"How?" I asked.

"My mom left us five years ago."

"Oh," I said. I reached out a hand and touched his knee. "I'm so sorry."

"Thanks. She met some out-of-town guy and she wanted out of Lost Springs. She wanted to travel and this guy—*Brad*—was her ticket out."

"Logan," I said. "That is awful. I didn't mean for you to have to talk about that. You don't have to."

"I kind of do," he replied. "I have to tell you my story so you'll understand why I love those horses."

I nodded.

Logan plucked a piece of tall grass and swirled it around a few times before he began stripping it layer by layer.

"Holden was barely five when she left," Logan continued. His jaw tightened. "He cried every day because he wanted Mom. Or I'd find him bawling because he thought he had done something wrong that had made Mom leave."

He crushed the blade of grass between his pointer finger and thumb.

"So one day during winter break, Dad and I had been working a job at Pam's farm. If you hang around me long enough, you'll hear me talk about Pam a lot. When my mom split, Pam became a very important part of our—Holden's, my dad's, and my—lives." Logan smiled. "Like I was saying, Dad and I came home and crashed in the middle of the afternoon because we were so tired. I woke up to Dad yelling. Holden had left while we slept."

I covered my mouth with my hand. "Oh, my God."

"There were a few inches of snow on the ground, so Dad and I followed his tracks until they disappeared. We separated and soon it started snowing—hard. I thought I was going to throw up because that's how scared I was. Plus, all of Holden's winter gear was at home. He had gone out in sneakers, jeans, and a sweater."

My eyes were glued on Logan. His eyes were on the herd, but they had a faraway look, as if he was revisiting that winter.

"The sun just started to set and it was snowing so hard that I couldn't see much in front of me. I yelled Holden's name until my voice was gone. Then out of nowhere, a bay mare appeared. She had this look like she wanted something. She looked at me, then turned away and trotted off. Something inside me said to follow her.

"I ran after the mare," Logan said. "I saw red and blue peeking out from behind a pile of brush. This is the part that I can almost feel—it's still that real. I ran toward the brush and Holden was there. I picked him up and he was *warm*. We both were crying and I finally caught my breath and asked him how in the hell he had stayed warm."

In front of us, a stallion struck the ground with a gleaming black leg and let out a neigh that shattered the quiet of the land.

"He said that he had gotten lost in the woods and was trying to get home. Finally, he got so tired and scared that he sat down in the brush. He said a bay mare curled up in front of him and she let him put his arms around her for warmth. She only got up when she heard my voice."

I sucked in a breath. "Logan, oh my God. That is incredible."

"There's no other way he would have been warm and not suffering from frostbite if it hadn't been for the horse. I know how crazy it sounds," Logan said. "But I know that Holden's telling the truth. I've never been able to thank these horses enough for saving my brother. My dad feels the same way. That's a large part of the reason why he reacted the way he did the day before yesterday—he feels it's important to speak up on their behalf."

I looked over the herd again. The horses had a hold on him—something almost otherworldly. I hadn't understood his connection to the horses before. But now I could see the way looking at the herd lit up his face. Soon I would be partly to blame for taking that away.

CHAPTER EIGHT

Never walk when you can ride. And never stand
when you can sit.

I unwrapped the fluffy white towel and dropped it onto the wooden deck chair. It was barely sixty degrees outside, but the hot tub sounded perfect. I adjusted my turquoise bikini strap and stepped into the warm water. I lowered myself onto the seat, and water came up to my earlobes.

I'd spent the last three days working at Dad's job site. The starts of his jobs were always busiest—I'd been working from eight or nine in the morning to well after the sun set. Dad prided himself on finishing jobs ahead of schedule, and, with the rocky beginning here aside, this job was going well. Most of it. Dad had been a little shady about two phone calls that he got every day at ten a.m. and two p.m. He always stepped outside and when he came back in, the look on his face scared me enough to stay quiet.

I'd gotten brave one day and sneaked Dad's phone over to the card table between us. The phone rang and I lunged for it. Dad snapped at me to leave the phone alone. Every morning, there had been two or three people standing beside Dad's trailer with signs. Brody had offered to handle them from now on and Dad had agreed. I was glad—Brody was level-headed and could talk the protestors into leaving.

My fingers were about to press the jet button, when Mom's voice carried over the yard from her phone conversation. "Are you sure it's safe?" Mom said into the phone. "Don't lie to me." She paused and I strained to hear more. "Let Brody handle it, then. Is there someone else to take over? A job isn't worth . . ." Her voice trailed off and I couldn't hear her anymore. She put the phone in the back pocket of her jeans and returned to her garden. I started to call out to her, but changed my mind. She would tell me if it was serious.

I closed my eyes for a minute, grateful for the warm water relaxing my muscles. No more thinking about protestors. I wanted to think about things besides business today.

Mom had decided to start her first garden. We'd never had one before—it had never made sense to do one, since by the time the garden would bloom, we would move and someone else would get to enjoy the flowers.

But Mom decided to go for it this time, and planned to document the garden's growth and turn it into a photojournalism piece.

Photography was her first love, but she wanted to take writing classes to pen articles to accompany all her photos. She had tried talking me into a writing or photography class this summer. She knew I felt lost and wanted to find my "thing." My gut told me I wasn't going to find what I was looking for in a classroom.

Yesterday, during a break from working for Dad, I'd met Mom in town. Together, we had shopped for garden supplies. Everyone had looked at us, but no one had approached Mom or me. No one except the older woman who owned the store. She introduced herself to us and helped Mom find everything she needed for her garden. After a pleasant experience in town, I think Mom felt much better about me going into town by myself.

The sound of a hawk overhead jerked me out of my thoughts. I looked down at Mom and grinned. She was intently reading a bulb packet and muttering to herself. She stuck her hand in the hole she had dug, pulled out the bulb and turned it over. Like that poor plant had a chance of growing upside down. I laughed and twisted my hair into a knot, getting the dripping ends out of the water.

My phone rang on the table and I leaned over and swiped it off the stand.

"Kate!" I said into the phone, greeting my older sister.

"You're not lost in the wilderness, are you?" she asked. "If you are, I'm sorry to say I can't help you."

I laughed. "I never expected *you* to save me from the woods. But isn't LA like a concrete jungle?"

"I guess," she said. "I went to report on a star sighting at the Ivy and it was supposed to be an exclusive and all these other people from, like, *Entertainment Now* were there."

Disdain dripped from her voice when she said *Entertainment Now*. Competition among the networks was fierce. Last summer, she had visited us while she was on vacation and had yelled at me because I'd flicked on *EN* for five seconds. It wasn't my fault that only *EN* had the Sean Houston exclusive, but Kate didn't agree.

"Did you get the scoop anyway?" I asked, lazily swirling my fingers in the water. Mom was still planting and it seemed like she got the hang of it now. She was no longer flopping dirt from one freshly dug hole into the next.

A rush of voices flooded the background and that had to be the *Access* lot. Kate had told me stories of the dozens of people running around to meet the show's daily deadline. It was a pressure-packed job.

"Yeah, I got it," she said, sounding far away and suddenly distracted. "Listen, I've got to run, but tell Mom I got my vacation days changed. I can come visit you guys in July instead of waiting until Thanksgiving."

"Great!" I said, excited, since I hadn't seen her in months. "Miss you."

"Miss you and love you!" Kate said, hanging up.

I plunked the phone back on the table and half stood in the hot tub. The cool spring air gave me goose bumps and I sank back down in the water. "Mom!" I yelled.

She lifted her head and pulled off a dirty glove, shading her eyes. "What?"

"Kate's coming home before the holidays!" I called down to her. "She said she could come in July."

"Wonderful!" she said.

Even though it was mid-March, Mom would be thrilled from now until then. She'd start getting a room ready for Kate and would be buzzing around the house talking about how she missed having Kate at home.

After an hour of pruning in the warm water, I couldn't sit still any longer. I headed for my bathroom and hopped inside the glass shower, bikini and all. After I'd showered, I towel-dried my hair and let it hang loose at my shoulders.

Ever since my day with Logan, I'd sort of been keeping one ear open for a far-off sound of an ATV. I wasn't expecting him to pull up in my driveway—that was a definite *no* that we had established when he had offered to take me home that afternoon. It had been four days ago when he had dropped me off just before my driveway, and I had walked the short distance home. I'd been greeted by my parents and they had asked how my day had gone. I picked out a couple of things that I'd done with Logan and made it sound as though I had gone exploring by myself.

I pulled myself out of the memory and tugged a three-quarter-sleeve waffle knit shirt over my head and stepped into an airy peasant skirt. I dabbed on strawberry lip gloss and ran a bronzer over my cheekbones. My reflection wasn't half bad. My shoulder-length hair hung in dark waves around my shoulders and the bronzer made my green eyes pop.

Something swirled deep in my stomach. Again, it felt as though everyone had found their niche except me. Kate was on TV. Logan had horses. Mom had photography. Dad had work. This summer had to be different than before—I had to stop working for Dad in three-day sprints and start finding something that *I* was passionate about. If I wanted to find myself—as lame as that sounded—it wasn't going to happen while I sat in a hot tub.

CHAPTER NINE

A man is not born a cowboy. He becomes one.

Out of breath and trying not to look sweaty, I parked my bike outside of Watson's. I'd passed WyGas on the way and had lingered for a moment, looking for Logan's truck. But it wasn't there.

Inside Watson's, Amy bagged groceries at the register. *I live here now. This is the only grocery store in town.* Ignoring her, I went to the back of the store and got a Diet Coke. I waited until there wasn't anyone else in line before going up to the register.

"Just this," I said, thrusting a five at her.

Amy took the money and put the change back on my waiting open palm.

"Thanks," I said. I opened my drink and walked away.

"Um, Brie?" Amy called.

I put my hand on the exit door, ready to push it open, but turned around, facing her. "What?"

"I wanted to apologize again," Amy said. She tucked her black hair behind her ears. "I was a total bitch to you."

I stayed silent, just staring at her.

"I did a lot of thinking after that happened," Amy said. "Actually, you acted so much classier than I would have if somebody had talked like that about my dad," Amy continued. "If I were you, I probably would have hit me."

I almost smiled. Sincerity radiated through her voice and I could tell how sorry she was. This was her second apology. How many more times was I going to make her say that she was sorry? There was something about Amy that I couldn't help but like.

"Thanks," I said. "It was cool of you to apologize again."

"Are you doing anything now?"

I shook my head. "No, I was just going home."

"My shift was over ten minutes ago," Amy said. "I was just working until Casey got here to take over."

As if on cue, a curly-haired brunette jogged through Watson's automatic doors. She shook her head. "I'm so sorry, Amy! I'll stay late tomorrow."

"It's okay, Case," Amy said. "See you tomorrow."

Amy turned to me. "Do you want to get coffee or dessert or something and maybe talk?"

Her offer caught me off guard. I'd planned to slip in and out of Watson's.

"Sure," I said, finally.

Amy took off her Watson's smock and slung it over her shoulder. A cerulean-blue cross-body purse went on the other shoulder. "Do you like coffee?" she asked.

"I like it enough to think it should be added to the food chain," I said.

"Then I think you'll like Beans," she said. "It's not like the chain coffee shops that you're probably used to, though."

I shook my head. "I'm so *not* a coffee snob. I don't care whether it's instant coffee or Colombian beans—I just want the caffeine in my body."

Amy laughed. We crossed Main Street, which was—shocker—empty. Not a car visible in either direction.

We walked inside Beans and the coffee shop was just about the size of our kitchen. There were three small circular tables and square and rectangle ones along the window. All of them were filled, with the exception of one of the booths by the window.

We ordered, got our drinks—both skinny vanilla lattes—and snagged the free seats.

I took a sip of coffee, then another.

"Oh, this is some of the best coffee that I've ever had," I said. "I'm going to buy this place out!"

"So weird!" Amy said. "My mom says that I'm going to do that. She's also sure that I've stunted my growth. Since she's worrying about something as trivial as an inch or two of my height, I'm so an only child. Obviously."

"I've been the only child at home for the past few years, too. Well, kind of. My big sister, Kate, moved to LA several years ago and it's just been my dad, my mom, and me ever since. My parents are kind of the opposite in the parent department. My mom's a photographer and really into her career. Not in a bad way, she still pays plenty of attention to me. My da—"

I stopped and looked down at the table. I took sip after sip of coffee, trying not to look at Amy.

"Hey, I'll say it one more time—I really am sorry that I said those things to you. I thought about it a lot every day since then. I can't imagine how I would feel if people decided whether or not they like me based on my dad's job. He's a mechanic, by the way—I'm sure *plenty* of people would look down on that."

"We didn't come here to start a war. My dad will build the hotel, and before you know it we'll be gone and on to the next town."

Amy rested her chin on her upraised palm. "Have you ever lived in the South?"

"Like Kentucky, Tennessee, Florida—that South?" I asked. "Pretty much all of the South except for Mississippi and Arkansas, I think. Oh, not Alabama, either."

"Omigod! You are so lucky!" Amy's fair cheeks flushed and she almost bounced up and down in her seat. "I'm *obsessed* with the South and everything southern. You should see my room. I love scouring eBay for odd pieces that represent the South. I got these *amazing* wall decals that are—oh, wait." She rummaged through her purse on the bench and pulled out her phone. After a few clicks, she handed it to me.

"Wow!" I said, pinching the phone screen to zoom in on the space above her bed. "The black-and-white prints of fruit and southern hot spots are amazing. The Tennessee mountain range is a great one. Your room looks like a southern belle lives there."

Amy beamed. "Stop, you're just saying that."

"No, I'm not! Why would I lie?"

Amy's bedspread was a lace-lined baby blue. An empty bird-cage hung in the left-hand corner. She had a wrought-iron white headboard. Next to the top of the bed were white, shabby chic nightstands. They had matching lamps that were yellow glass.

I handed Amy back her phone. "So a few minutes ago, you said I was 'lucky' that I got to travel the South, but looking at your room—it looks like you've lived there until yesterday."

Amy shook her head. "Nope, I, um, I haven't been out of Wyoming."

I worked *really* hard not to let my shock at her lack of travel to *anywhere* show on my face. "Judging by your room, I would have guessed that you were a Kentucky or Louisiana transplant. But what really tipped me off was your voice."

"My voice?" Amy asked.

"Yeah, right away I heard the slightest southern twang. I can't place the state, but I know I've heard it before."

Amy covered her mouth with both hands. Her eyes got so wide it looked as if they were about to pop out of her sockets.

"Oh. My. God," Amy said, shaking her head. "I can't believe it. You—someone who has probably traveled almost everywhere on the planet—heard a twang in my voice!"

"Where did it come from?"

"I've sort of been listening to stuff on my iPod that actors use before a film so their voices are able to change from like a French accent to a New York one."

"Cool," I said, smiling. "You obviously want to go to college in the South."

"Yeees," Amy said. "I have to get out of Lost Springs. I love it, I do. But I want more than this. I especially want to try living in a place where I feel as though I should have been born and raised there. A place where I can visit an actual store instead of buying almost everything I own from eBay. A town with nearby shopping centers."

I liked this girl. Who would have known that I would meet someone here I would actually like hanging out with.

"Forget where you were born," Amy said. "Where do you think you *belong*?"

I opened my mouth and my jaw moved up and down, but nothing came out. I stared at Amy and shrugged. "I don't know where I belong," I said. "But I don't think it was at any of the places that I've lived."

"Can you tell me about them?" Amy asked.

"Sure."

That kicked off an hour-and-a-half conversation that had us wired from three coffees each by the time we finished chatting. We left the shop with plans to meet up again for coffee soon.

CHAPTER TEN

Never miss a good chance to shut up.

Logan's truck wasn't in the WyGas lot, but I leaned my bike against a metal rack and went inside anyway. Technically, I was on a "lunch break" from Dad's office—I was just choosing to spend it looking for Logan.

A guy with dark curls smiled at me from behind the counter. He looked around Kate's age.

"Hi," I said. Suddenly, I felt shy about asking my question. I picked up a packet of gum, pretending to be fascinated with the label. Half of me was scared the guy was a wildlife extremist, too, and would say something awful to me, and the other half was a little embarrassed to ask about Logan.

"Can I help you find anything?" the guy asked. Not an ounce of weirdness or anger in his tone. Whew.

"No. Well, um, maybe. Is Logan around?" I forced out the words before I changed my mind.

"He's off today. He's watching his little brother."

My shoulders sagged a little. This morning, I'd put extra time into choosing a cute yellow top and pleated white skirt. I would spend the rest of the day in cute clothes shut inside Dad's trailer.

"Okay, thanks," I said. "I'll come back another time." I put down the gum and headed for the door.

"Hey," the guy called after me. "Tell me your name and I'll tell you where to find Logan."

I turned slowly back to face him. "Brie."

"Nice to meet you." He reached out a hand to me. I walked back and took his hand. "I'm Jerry," he said. "You know where Black Creek is?"

"I don't," I said.

He motioned me over and used his finger to draw an invisible map on the counter. "Logan said he'd be taking Holden there today. Okay, go straight out of here and take the first right. You're going to follow a one-lane dirt road for about a mile and then you'll come to a clearing. Keep walking straight and you can't miss the creek."

"Thanks," I said. "I owe you one."

Jerry waved me out of WyGas. I climbed on my bike and yanked my skirt up over my knees, determined not to get it caught in the bike's chain. With Jerry's directions echoing in my head, I headed for Black Creek.

A short while later, I braked at a grassy, overgrown clearing that had to be the one Jerry had talked about. I laid my bike in the grass and followed what looked like a recently trampled path to Black Creek.

Clear, gently flowing water swept over the rocks, and the muted sunlight hit the creek bed in random places and made the rocks dazzle like black diamonds. The water was only a couple of feet deep and it looked like there were tracks on the other side. I kicked off my white flip-flops and held them in one hand. I dipped my toe in the water.

"Ahh!" The water was *freezing*! Tugging up my skirt, I thrust my feet into the water, stepping quickly over the sparkling rocks. "Ah! Ah! Cold!" I yelped to no one. When I got to the other side, I slid my chilly feet into my flip-flops and they squished as I followed the trail.

The forest was quiet except for the occasional bird. I tried not to let myself wonder about the bears, bobcats, and coyotes Logan had insisted inhabited the forest, but the sunlight cast strange shadows over the trees and I started eyeing each shadow with growing suspicion. If I didn't find Logan in five minutes, I was going home. Water splashed up ahead. *Please, please let that be Logan and not a fishing bear.* Dousing myself with jasmine body spray probably hadn't been the best idea. I tiptoed along Black Creek's bank and peered ahead, half expecting to see a ravenous bear.

Instead, it was Logan and a little boy who could have been Logan's younger twin, with the same flaxen blond hair, wide eyes, and golden skin. Holden covered his mouth with his hand as he laughed at Logan, who was balanced precariously on a small boulder and juggling three rocks. I'd come here with the intention to hang out with Logan. But now it felt like an intrusion on their family moment. *Logan doesn't get much time off to hang with his brother,* I said to myself. *You should have realized that before you came.*

I turned around to leave. As I started to walk away, my flip-flop caught on an upraised root and I tripped and fell on my knees. A few sticks cracked under my palms.

"Hello?" Logan called.

"It's Brie," I said, waving from my spot on the ground.

"Stay here," Logan said to Holden, who nodded and didn't move as Logan picked his way across the creek bed and jogged over to me. I sat on my butt and saw pebbles embedded in my knees. My poor skirt was streaked with dirt.

Logan knelt by my side. "Are you okay?" The concern in his voice made me forget about my minor scrapes.

"I'm fine. I just tripped. I was walking around," I said, waving an arm and trying to sound casual. I didn't want him to know that I'd tracked him down. "When I saw you and Holden, I didn't want to bother you. It looked like you two were having fun."

Logan pulled a blue handkerchief out of his pocket and bent down to swish it around in the creek water. He came back and brushed my hand away from my knee and motioned for me to stretch my legs out to him. Logan sat cross-legged on the ground and took both of my legs over his lap. He started wiping my knees. "So, you were just walking around Black Creek and you saw us, huh?" Logan asked, not looking up from my left knee.

"Yeah, coincidence, right?" I said, my voice was dangerously high.

"That's funny," Logan said, looking up at me. "Because *Jerry* texted me a while ago and said he gave some super-cute girl directions here."

"Oh, stupid boy code," I said, shaking my head. "Fine. I'm busted."

Logan grinned. "You were talking to Jerry about me?"

"No," I said, smiling. "I just asked him if you were working and he said you were watching Holden. I might have come here to see you, but when I saw you with Holden, I—"

"It's okay!" Logan cut me off, grinning. "You can talk to Jerry about me, but I'd like it more if you talked to me instead."

I looked away from him and down at my knees. Logan had managed to remove most of the gravel from my shallow scrapes. I was suddenly aware that my bare legs were strewn across his lap. My face felt like it was on fire as I tried to gracefully ease my legs off him and stand. Logan jumped up and offered me a hand.

I grasped his palm and let him help me. The warm feeling from his hand spread to my face.

"Is your brother okay over there?" I glanced over Logan's shoulder and saw Holden still in the same position—huddled on a rock. At that age, I would have been off exploring the woods. I wouldn't have listened to Kate at all.

"Holden? You okay?" Logan called.

"Yes," Holden said. His voice was soft.

"We're coming over," Logan said. He looked down at my knees. "Can you walk?"

"Oh, yeah," I said. "It's nothing but a flesh wound," I teased, quoting one of my favorite movies and wondering if Logan would get the reference.

"*Monty Python*," Logan exclaimed.

I nodded as we started to make our way over to Holden. "Right," I said. "I watch way too many movies."

Logan started to answer back until he looked at Holden's face. Holden's mouth was clamped tight and he wouldn't look at me. Great, I scared him with my bloody knees.

"Holden, it's okay," Logan said, leaving me to hop across the creek and crouch by his brother. "This is my friend Brie. She's new in town. Remember how scared you were to go to school on your first day because you were new? Brie's feeling like that, so let's make her comfortable, okay?"

Holden didn't say a word, he just nodded his head slowly.

Logan prodded him. "Okay?"

"Okay," Holden whispered. He lifted his chin that had been resting on his drawn-up knees.

Logan walked back to the creek, darted across and held my hand as I crossed.

"Sit here, Brie," Logan said, motioning to a rock covered with a plaid flannel blanket.

"Do your knees hurt?" Holden asked. He enunciated each word clearly.

"They did," I said. "Logan helped me and I'm okay now."

Holden nodded and stood. His tennis shoes were scuffed and his jeans looked worn. He had on a thin red T-shirt with a gray zip-up jacket. The clothes looked a size too big for his small body.

"Iodine," he said.

"What?" I asked.

"Put iodine on your knees so they don't get infected."

"Okay, I will. Thanks." He gave me a small smile and hopped off the rock. Maybe Logan had a future doctor on his hands.

"Why don't you grab the sandwiches from our backpack, Holden," Logan said.

Holden headed for a navy-colored backpack a few yards away.

"Your brother is really cute," I said. "And smart."

Logan's eyes were on his brother as he sat on the big rock next to me. "He's always been a precocious kid. Sorry for the look he gave you when you and I walked over."

"It's okay. I'm just glad I found you guys. We, um, haven't really talked or anything since . . ." I let my voice trail off. I didn't want to come across like one of those girls who counted hours since they last saw their boyfriends. And that wasn't how I felt, anyway. There was just something unexplainable about a pull that I felt to Logan. But I *had* to fight it. This was the guy who had revved his engine at me when we first met. The son of my family's biggest enemy. But . . . this was also the guy who took me four-wheeling and liked hearing about where I'd lived and how I got here. Talk about confusing.

"I've been a total jerk since our ATV ride," Logan said. "I should have texted or something. I mean, not that you were waiting for me to text."

"I wasn't," I said, shaking my head.

"This is the first time since then that I've been free of work in town or work at home," Logan said. He tipped his cowboy hat back and his eyes met mine. "Have you hiked along any of the trails we found the other day?"

"I've been too busy," I said. "You know, working for my dad."

The end of my sentence just stuck in the air. I felt as though it formed an invisible barrier between us.

"Have you thought through the things I said about the horses?" Logan asked.

I nodded. "Yes. But it's not like I can share them with my dad."

"I understand that," Logan said. "I really do. I've been talking to some of the locals and I'm trying to get an appointment to meet with someone from the local Bureau of Land Management. I want to ask their permission to move the horses from your dad's job site."

"That's perfect!" I said. "How soon can you get an appointment? Dad barks at everyone any time the horses show up. He has a call into the BLM, too, but he's not good at the waiting part. He got really pissed when his foreman told him that they had to talk to the BLM before moving the horses. The permits that he has don't cover moving the horses."

"I hope I get in before your dad does," Logan said. "I want those mustangs to stay around here and be as free as possible."

I started to respond, but Holden reached the rock and set down two brown bags.

Logan ripped open a bag and tossed me a wrapped sandwich. "We've got the McCoy special. Luckily for you, we always pack extra grub."

"And that would be?" I asked, peering at the package.

"Peanut butter and jelly sandwiches," Holden informed me, his eyes watching me as he unwrapped his sandwich.

"Ever had one?" Logan asked, winking.

"Oh, I don't know," I said. "Maybe once or twice."

Logan and Holden had already dug into their sandwiches. Holden watched Logan eat and then mimicked his big brother's large bites.

I took a bite of mine.

"Do you like it?" Holden asked.

"I *love* it," I said. "Next time, I'll make you guys my signature sandwich."

"What's that?" Logan said as he wiped peanut butter from the corner of his mouth.

"You'll have to wait and see," I said, taking a big bite. Logan opened the other bag and handed me a Sprite.

"Thanks," I said. I opened my soda and was about to take a sip when my phone rang. I plucked it out of the mini satchel that I'd been carrying.

"Brie? You okay?" Dad asked. Through the phone, I could hear the clicking of keys as he typed.

I checked the time on the phone. I'd been gone almost two hours.

"Sorry, Dad, I'm fine," I said. "I ran into one of my friends and I lost track of time."

"Okay, hon," Dad said. "Take the rest of the day off—I've got everything covered. Just be home for dinner."

"I will," I said.

I hung up and put the phone back.

"My dad," I explained. "Just checking on me."

"Can I go over there?" Holden asked Logan.

"Where?" Logan asked.

Holden pointed to a spot across the creek.

"Okay, just remember our brother pact," Logan said.

"We always have to be able to see each other," Holden said.

"You got it," Logan said, high-fiving his brother.

Holden smiled shyly at me as he got up.

Logan and I watched Holden navigate his way across the creek and crouch near a boulder.

"I did some reading online," I said. "About the horses."

I'd done more than just a casual search online. I'd spent hours and hours online when I was alone in my room late at night. I read articles about the fate of American mustang herds, and watched videos of the horses being corralled and shoved into trailers. There were even scarier videos of mustang cruelty that I didn't have the stomach to watch. Each night after work, I'd eat dinner before rushing upstairs to my laptop. I'd bookmarked site after site about the horses.

Logan nodded slowly. "What did you read?"

"A lot. But all the articles basically had the same conclusion—the wild horse population is in danger. They're running out of room because of . . ." I paused. "Um, because of businesses like my dad's."

"That's all true," Logan said. He stood and sat on a rock closer to me. "The issue isn't stopping your dad, like I told you. I promise that I don't want to do anything to cause problems in your family."

"I wish everyone could see this the way that you do," I said.

"What he's building, even though it is costing the horses room, is going to bring money into the town," Logan said. "Lost Springs is desperate for jobs and a cash infusion."

"What do you want to happen now for the horses?" I asked.

"It's kind of a waiting game," Logan said. "Everyone invested in the horses is watching how often the horses go to your dad's job site. If they stay away from the construction, then we have some time to think about what to do."

"And if they don't?" I asked.

"Then we'll have to find some land to temporarily corral them," Logan said, frowning. "It's not my first choice of options, but it *is* a solution that will keep them safe. Your dad isn't their only enemy. Other people have gone after them. The young ones are in danger from mountain lions to coyotes. Sick or injured mustangs are in danger, too. Even good, healthy horses have a lot stacked against them."

"What's your dream scenario?" I asked.

Logan was quiet for a moment. He glanced across the creek and watched Holden build a stick and rock fort.

"Ideally," he said, glancing back at me, "we find nearby land for them to be free and wild. We herd them to that space and they'll have everything they need and no reason to come back to your dad's site."

"You don't want to keep any of them?"

Logan smiled. "Maybe. I mean, I would have to get the BLM's permission first. It might be fun to have a few colts to tame."

"Have you ever worked with a wild horse before?"

Logan nodded. "One. My horse—LG—was a wild foal when I got him five years ago."

"LG," I said. "What does that stand for?"

"Don't laugh," Logan said, grinning. "But it's Logan's Gelding."

I nervously giggled. "Sorry, sorry!" I said. Logan's eyes were wide and he shook his head.

"I told you not to laugh!" Logan said. But he laughed with me.

"Do you name all your pets with your name?" I asked. "Is there a Logan's Dog, or a Logan's Cat?"

"Ha," Logan said, rolling his eyes but keeping a smile on his face.

"How did you get him?"

"One of my dad's friends was moving his cattle in for the winter when he found an abandoned foal. My dad took him and gave him to me. It was about two weeks after my mom left. Dad said I could keep him if I trained him."

"Wow," I said, my voice quiet. "That's amazing timing."

"I let Holden name him," Logan said. "Even though it's a silly name, I never thought of changing it. Every second that I wasn't working for my dad or in school, I was with LG. Wait until you meet him—you'll see how he follows me like a big dog."

"Aw, I can't wait," I said.

"You've been here, what?" Logan asked. "Two weeks?"

I nodded. "Something like that."

"I think it's time you were exposed to a little Western culture," Logan said. "Are you busy on Saturday?"

I blinked at him. It had been forever since someone had asked me that question.

"Um, no. I'm free." The words tumbled out.

"There's a fair not far from here," Logan said. "I go every year. It's a cruelty-free rodeo type of event. I'm competing in calf roping. I'm giving Amy a ride. It would be nice if you came."

"That sounds fun," I said. "I'd like to go."

I smiled at him, barely realizing that in the time we had been talking, Logan had moved closer and closer to me. He was close enough that I smelled cinnamon and sweet hay on his shirt. He placed a hand on my back and it sent little shock waves up and down my arms. I leaned closer to him and—

"Logan!"

I blinked, my body frozen for a moment. I snapped out of it and sat up straight. Logan sat up, too, pulling away from me and looking at Holden.

"What's up, bud?" Logan asked.

That was way too close! I told myself. *You were totally going to kiss him!* It was hard enough to keep pushing away my growing feelings for Logan. The last thing I needed was any physical component to complicate things more.

Despite everything I'd just told myself, I rubbed my thumb over my bottom lip, wondering how it would feel to be kissed by Logan.

CHAPTER ELEVEN

A man who's honest with himself will be honest with others.

Huffing and sweating, I shifted my backpack and glanced over at Mom. I *really* needed to bike more and add some incline to my workouts. We were hiking around the base of Blackheart Mountain. Amy had drawn me a map to a cavern where Mom could take photographs. I peered at the napkin Amy had used for the map and squinted to read her slanted handwriting.

Mom thought I spent my free time hanging out with Amy, which was partly true, but she didn't know anything about Logan. It felt weird to keep my friendship with him a secret from Mom. I'd always told her everything. I'd picked today to take Mom hiking and tell her about Logan since Saturday's festival was coming up.

Since our Black Creek picnic I'd seen Logan almost every day. I'd started going to WyGas for lunch and we would hang out. Or, I'd bike to Watson's if it was his day to be there. Yesterday, he'd ridden LG to his shift at WyGas. Meeting LG was like meeting a member of his family. Logan understood that I hadn't told my parents that we hung out together. Although it wasn't as though he had told his dad that we were spending time together, either.

When we couldn't find time to hang out, we texted. I really wished my phone had a cowboy hat emoticon. I visualized one beside Logan's name in my phone.

"Oh, Brie," Mom said, adjusting her neon green backpack with the hundred pockets that housed all her photography equipment. "Look at that."

A huge waterfall ran down the mountain and plunged sharply into a shallow pool below. A cloud of mist sprayed off the bottom and a couple of rainbows shimmered.

"Let's get a shot of this," I said.

We walked a few yards closer until the waterfall almost drowned out our voices. We set our backpacks on the ground. We each took out our tripods and carefully unfolded the legs. I screwed my camera to the top and peered at the LCD screen. I began clicking at the waterfall. I got shots of the falls, the bubbles below, and some of the fading rainbow. I checked my picture review feature and liked the color and angle of my shots.

Beside me, Mom clicked thoughtfully and moved the tripod around as she angled for the best light. "I think I've got it now," she said, yelling over the falls.

"Okay, let's keep walking." We packed up our cameras and equipment and I took one last glance at the waterfall. Lost Springs' nature amazed me more every day.

After a few more minutes of walking, I stopped and rechecked Amy's detailed map. "I think we're almost there," I said.

We stepped through a patch of waist-high grass that turned into weeds and then cleared to stone. We were now squarely along the base of the mountain and it got quieter the closer we got. At the same time, we spotted an opening in the side of the mountain.

"There it is!" I said. Thank God Amy's map was right. My hiking boots were giving me a blister and the backpack straps had started to dig into my shoulders.

"Where did you say you got those directions?" Mom said as she stepped up to the dark entrance.

"Amy."

We switched on our flashlights. Cool air trickled out of the cave and made my arm hair prickle uncomfortably. A sweatshirt would have been a good idea.

Mom reached into her pocket and pulled out a ball of yellow string. "Tie that to the tree over there," she said, pointing to a skinny tree next to me.

"This won't snap, will it?" I said.

"It's heavy duty," Mom promised. She yanked the string to prove it. "It'll hold."

I knotted the string around the tree and let the rope run through my hands. I'd learned how to tie knots thanks to some of Dad's crew.

The only time I'd ever been inside a cave before had been during a guided tour, complete with a lit path and handrails, at the Diamond Caverns in Kentucky. This way, unplanned and without a guide, was *so* much better.

Mom put a floodlight in one hand and her smaller flashlight in the other. "You can do the rope," she said.

"Oh, sure," I said. "Place the weight of our getting out safely on my shoulders."

I pulled on the rope again and we stepped into the gray-and-black entrance. I let out the string. As we moved away from the entrance, the sunshine weakened until the only light was from our flashlights.

"I'm going to flip on the floodlight now," Mom said. "I don't want you to trip." The powerful flashlight clicked on and a bright, white light overpowered the weaker yellow flashlight beams. The gray walls of the entrance to the cave morphed into a sandy brown color, and the cavern ceiling was about as high as ours at home. The brown walls were pitted and rough, and on the sides of the cave and above our heads, the ceiling jutted out at odd angles and contorted shapes.

"Amazing," Mom whispered.

"It really is," I agreed. Dad had to see this. No cell phone, no beeper, and no work. He'd probably panic and have Internet withdrawal.

The cave got cooler the farther we walked. The string kept trailing behind us as we wove our way toward what we hoped was an empty cavern.

"So," Mom said, peering behind a large rock where some sort of cricket had skittered. "Tell me about the guy."

"Guy?" I asked. "What makes you think there's a guy?"

Mom looked at me, her head tilted. "Sweetie, you're wearing skirts to work. You're spending extra time on your makeup and hair. I've never seen you so excited to finish dinner and be alone up in your room."

I blushed. Mom motioned for us to sit on the boulder near her.

"Okay," I said, finally. "There is a guy . . . I guess. Logan."

"Where did you meet him?" Mom asked.

"He was kind of the guy that I yelled at for revving at me our first day here," I said.

Mom laughed. Then, barely pausing to breathe, I told Mom everything about Logan. Every great thing. Every scary thing. *Everything.* Things I'd been afraid to even say out loud. I laid out all my thoughts about the mustangs and how Logan felt about them. How Logan was Jack's son.

"I don't want to be the family traitor," I said. "If Dad *ever* finds out that I've been hanging out with someone who's a giant supporter of the horses . . . I don't even want to imagine that lecture."

"I'm really touched that you care so much about your dad," Mom said. "But his problems with the horses are *his.* Not yours and not Logan's."

"Okay, but what if I really fall for him and then we move?"

"It would be hard," Mom said. "But isn't every good thing worth the risk of being hurt?"

I shrugged, not knowing what to say.

"I know that all the moving hasn't made it easy for you to make friends," Mom said. "That's something I think about constantly. But I am so happy that you have Amy here, and that you opened yourself up enough to like Logan."

"It wasn't your fault or Dad's that I didn't make more friends other places," I said. "That was my choice."

"Well, I'm so happy that you chose to share all that with me," Mom said.

I stood and hugged her. When I let go, she got up and we started walking again.

Mom tilted the flashlight toward the ceiling.

"Look, Brie," she said.

The low overhang started to vanish. We stepped forward into a massive cavern.

"Oh, my God." I twirled in a slow circle and looked around at the cavern. Razor-sharp stalactites hung from the ceiling at all angles. Some were pencil size and others were five feet wide. Water dripped off a stalactite in the center of the cavern and the minerals formed a twin stalagmite that jutted into the air.

The air smelled musty and the temperature had dropped at least another five degrees. The walls were covered in deep, dark crevices, rounded rock, and jagged rock.

Almost every few feet, the wall and ceiling surface varied. I'd only seen caverns like this in movies. It was like Tom Sawyer when he got lost with Becky in the cavern. In the center of the cavern ceiling, a small hole shed a tiny bit of light onto the floor. How was that possible so deep in the cave?

"This is gorgeous," Mom said, setting down her backpack and pulling out her camera and tripod. She set up the floodlight and it filled the cavern with light. "How did Amy decide to show you this?"

"I told her you were a photographer and she knew immediately where to go. She thought you'd love this place."

"I have to meet her," Mom said. "Editors are going to love this cave."

I followed her lead and brought out my camera and started snapping photos. I took dozens of shots of the ceiling, walls, and floor before walking over to a puddle. Something wiggled in the shallow water. "Mom! Come here!"

She peered over my shoulder. We stared at the whitish gray crustacean in the puddle. "It's a crayfish," she said. "A cave crayfish." The milky-white crayfish stuck its tiny pincers in the air and waved them threateningly as I bent down to take its picture. It looked like a ghost version of its normal reddish color.

Mom sat on a nearby boulder and glanced around. "I can't believe we're sitting in a cavern," she said. "It's just amazing."

I sat next to her on the rock and nodded. "Perfect," I whispered.

My head said "Show Amy the photos!" while my heart chimed in with "Show Logan!" I could see us in my room, both on our stomachs on my bed looking at my laptop. The thought of it made my heartbeat speed up. I looked down and there was a deep puddle next to my left foot. I hovered over it and smiled at my reflection. Whoever this new Brie was, I wanted her to stay a while.

CHAPTER TWELVE

Always ride the horse in the direction it's going.

I had twenty minutes to finish getting ready and meet Amy and Logan at WyGas. Saturday morning was clear and the perfect day to visit a fair. I'd been up half the night trying to decide what to wear. Finally, I'd settled on black combat boots, skinny jeans, an ivory long-sleeve shirt, and a jean jacket. I'd combed my shoulder-length hair into a ponytail and had used a curling iron on the ends. Makeup had been kept to a minimum.

I grabbed my orange faux-leather purse and hurried down the stairs.

"Bye!" I called to the kitchen, where Mom and Dad were having coffee and reading the paper. I'd already cleared the festival with Mom.

"Brie, wait," Dad said.

I sighed quietly, my hand on the doorknob.

I turned to face Dad. "Yes?" I asked.

"Listen, I know you already talked to Mom about going out now, but I could really use your help at work today," Dad said. "I'm leaving in a few minutes to head over there."

"Dad, my friend is waiting for me. I already told her I was coming since Mom said it was okay." I tried to keep any traces of annoyance out of my voice.

"Michael," Mom said as she walked into the foyer. "I'm free today. I did already tell Brie that she could go."

Dad crossed his arms. "Nicola—"

"I'll fill in for her today," Mom said, her tone light. "But you can't expect me to type ninety words a minute like Brie."

It seemed like hours passed before Dad nodded. "Okay," he said. "Go. But you missed a lot of time at work this week. The lunch breaks in town are over. Got it?"

I started to protest, but forced myself to smile and nod. I'd deal with that issue later. Right now, I needed to get out the door.

"Got it!" I chirped. "Bye!"

Before Dad changed his mind, I yanked open the screen door and pulled it shut behind me. I hurried to my bike and it felt like I didn't breathe until I got onto the road.

"Yay! You're here!" Amy exclaimed.

She and Logan stood by his truck in the WyGas parking lot. A small red trailer was attached to the truck.

"Love your sweater," I said to Amy. She'd paired a fuzzy red Fair Isle sweater with jeans and cowboy boots.

"Thanks! Two bucks on eBay," she said with a tone of satisfaction.

"You *are* the eBay queen," I said.

"You ready to go?" Logan asked, smiling at me. He looked *good* in a mustard-colored long-sleeve shirt that was just tight enough for me to make out his chiseled arms and abs.

"Ready!" I said.

Amy hopped into the cab, humming.

"I don't think she's excited at all," I said to Logan.

"Agreed," he said. "She's totally bummed."

I peered inside the trailer and LG was sleeping, his dark brown head down.

"I like your hair," Logan said. I looked away from the trailer and he was smiling at me.

"Thanks," I said, smiling.

We went around separate sides of the trailer—me to the passenger side and him to the driver's seat. I touched my ponytail and grinned. I climbed into the cab and sat next to Amy. There was a bag of candy on Amy's lap and she'd opened a can of root beer.

"Thanks for waiting, guys," I said. "Parental interrogation before I left."

"No way were Amy and I leaving without you," Logan said.

"We're seriously excited to take you to your first Western Outlaw Festival," Amy said, grinning.

"Wait, wait. A *what*?" I asked.

Logan and Amy laughed.

"I guess I didn't tell you *everything* about it," Logan said. He started the truck and eased it out of the lot. "It is a cruelty-free rodeo like I said, but it's also an 1800s Western Outlaw Festival."

"We go every year," Amy said. "I only missed one. I was six and had the chicken pox."

"Wow, that's dedication," I said, laughing.

"There's a steamboat, an old-fashioned shootout, and a rodeo," Amy said. "You're going to have so much fun."

"I can't wait," I said. "How far away is it?"

"Just fifteen minutes," Logan said. "I raided WyGas for candy and pop."

"Thanks," I said. "Are you going to win at calf roping?"

"Of course," he said. "I can't lose when it's your first time watching."

Amy elbowed me in the ribs, smirking. I shot her a what-are-you-doing-stop-it-now look back. Amy had told me more than a handful of times that she knew Logan liked me. I just kept responding that it didn't even matter if he did—I still felt weird about how attracted to him I was, even after my talk with Mom at the falls.

The ride to the fairgrounds went by fast. We laughed and sang along to the pop station the entire ride. Sun streamed inside the windshield and relaxed me even more.

I jumped out of Logan's truck when we reached the festival's parking lot. Trucks and trailers were parked at all angles and people were unloading horses and a couple had cattle in their trailers.

"Are all the horses here for the competition?" I asked Amy.

"Mostly," she said, tugging on a skinny red headband that held back her black bangs. "Some are going to be up for auction."

Amy stood on her tiptoes, shading her eyes against the sun.

"Logan," she said, "I think Bobby Farris just got here."

Logan grunted, muttering something I couldn't hear.

Amy grinned. "Aw, it's okay, Logan!"

"What's going on?" I asked.

"Logan's the calf-roping champ," Amy said. She patted Logan's back. "Three years in a row until he lost to Bobby Farris last year."

"Ouch," he said, faking hurt. "I think he cheated."

"How?" I asked, laughing.

"There were rumblings around the circuit that he knew the guy who owned the calves and he had them give his calf a little tranquilizer to slow him down," Logan said.

Amy snorted and rolled her eyes. *No way,* she mouthed to me.

"Do you need help?" she asked Logan.

"Nope," Logan said with a head shake. "I've got to register, get LG saddled, and warm him up. I ride in an hour."

Amy turned to me. "Want to go look around and then come back for Logan's ride?"

"Sure. Let's go." We waved to Logan and linked arms. Amy and I headed out of the parking lot and walked across the grassy field. Half a dozen red-and-white circus tents formed a backdrop for what looked like an 1800s Western town. Cowboys and cowgirls dressed in authentic outfits wandered the area and entered tents labeled *saloons* and other old-fashioned shops. Chuck wagons were parked around the lot and signs for pony rides, shootout reenactments, and horseshoe toss were stuck everywhere.

"Wow," I said. "This is great!"

"It's pretty cool," Amy agreed, dragging me toward a chuck wagon. "We need snacks and drinks for Logan's competition."

"Yeah, we kind of did blow through all the sodas and stuff that were supposed to be for the event on the way here."

A tall guy a few years older than us rubbed his hand over his whiskered face as he offered us a plate. "Want to try the jerky?" he asked us.

"Sure!" we said as we each took a small strip of the heavily peppered beef jerky off the plate and chewed for a second.

"We'll take some," Amy said. "And we need pop. Root beer okay with you, Brie?"

"Definitely," I said.

Amy got three glass-bottled root beers. We left the chuck wagon and swerved to the side as four horses pulling a stagecoach trotted through the street. People flooded into the tent with a canvas sign spray-painted with RIDE 'EM, ROPERS on the front.

Amy and I headed inside the dirt-floored tent and climbed up the metal bleachers to find empty seats. I looked around for Logan and spotted him smiling and laughing with a few guys. They stood by the side of the arena. Logan looked so comfortable and happy. Amy tugged on my arm and we sat on the bleachers. It was almost chilly in the shade.

We uncapped our sodas and touched them together.

"Cheers!" I said.

We took long drinks.

"Did you and Logan already make out?" Amy asked, turning slightly toward me. "Or is it only a matter of time?"

"Amy!" I said. "I need more sugar to answer that."

I took a long sip of root beer.

"Omigod!" she said. "You already did!"

"No. We haven't done anything. Not even one kiss. Almost, but we got interrupted."

In the arena in front of us, a couple of riders were working to guide a black bull into a smaller corral.

"Do you *want* to kiss him?" Amy asked.

I paused. "Yes. No. You know why that would be a problem."

"But maybe try to take moving out of the equation?" Amy offered. "And the McCoy versus Brooks thing."

I cocked my head, giving her a no-way-ever look.

"Okay, okay!" Amy said, putting up a hand. "Just go with me on this. Forget *everything* except for you and Logan. That's it. Would it make you happy right now to kiss him?"

"Yes," I said. The word sounded strange. "Yes," I said again.

Amy squealed and grabbed my arm. "Then maybe you should forget about the future," Amy said. "I know it's easier said than done. I know that. But you deserve to be happy *now*."

I nodded. "Maybe. But it would be at the expense of making my dad *unhappy*. We've always been pretty close. He wouldn't get over it if I told him that Logan and I were friends."

Amy leaned over, reached behind me, and draped an arm across my shoulders. She squeezed and let me go. Her hug was so sweet—it reminded me of Kate. I got out my phone, ready to take a million pics to send to her.

"All right, colts and fillies!" A loudspeaker crackled and static filled the tent. "Calf-roping is starting in this tent right now! Stay in your seats for half an hour of wild roping fun! Up first is Grady Harrison."

Amy and I looked at each other, then giggled. We sat tall in our seats so we could see every corner of the arena. The first cowboy loaded his horse into the chute and he waited for the signal. The rider nodded, and a brown-and-white calf shot out of the narrow enclosure and took off at a dead run down the arena. A cowboy in a red shirt broke out of the corral on a black horse and tore off after the calf. The calf zigzagged down the arena and tried to escape the cowboy's lasso.

"That calf is fast!" I said to Amy. No way would the cowboy be able to wrangle that one.

"Just watch!" Amy said, not taking her eyes off the arena.

The cowboy raised his lasso and swirled it above his head in several tight circles before letting it fly out of his hand. The rope sailed through the air and landed snugly over the calf's head. Before his horse had even stopped, the guy jumped to the ground and ran toward the calf. The horse halted and started slowly backing up as the guy wrestled the calf to the ground and took a thin short rope out of his mouth. He furiously wrapped the rope around the calf's hooves and then stood, raising his arms in victory.

"Time for Grady Harrison is twenty seconds," the announcer's voice boomed.

"Slow," Amy said, taking a sip of her root beer. "Logan's done better."

The cowboy released the calf, mounted his horse, and rode out of the arena.

"Next up is former champ Logan McCoy. Put your hands together, folks!"

I stood, clapping so hard my hands stung.

"Is Bobby Farris competing this year?" I asked Amy.

"I think so," she said.

I glued my eyes to the chute and watched Logan shift his weight in the saddle. He concentrated on the calf squirming in the chute next to him. The calf's gate was yanked open again and, like the one before it, the black calf zoomed out and raced forward. Logan and LG sped behind it. The calf didn't make it halfway down the arena before Logan's lasso had landed around its neck. Jumping to the ground, Logan raced toward the squirming animal and pulled it down. His hands moved so fast I couldn't see him tie the calf's four hooves together.

"Go, Logan!" I yelled as Amy clapped beside me.

Logan jumped to his feet and his eyes scanned the crowd. I waved and Logan saw me. He waved back, smiling.

I glanced at Amy and she grinned at me.

"What?" I asked, teasing.

"Somebody got a wave from a cowboy and her name is B-R-I-E!" Amy batted her mascara-coated lashes at me, flirting style.

I bumped her with my shoulder and we both started cracking up. I said a silent thank-you to Mom for intervening this morning so I could come.

"Time for Logan McCoy is thirteen seconds!" The crowd roared its approval and I had a feeling the other riders would have trouble beating Logan's time. Logan took off his hat, bowed, and waved it at the crowd.

After Logan, five more calf-ropers, including a newly chubby Bobby Farris—according to Amy—rode. None came within five seconds of Logan's time. I clapped hard while Logan accepted his trophy with a silver cowboy hat. He shook hands with a disgruntled-looking Bobby, who had come in third.

Amy and I waited by the gate as Logan led LG over. I jogged up to him and threw my arms around him. "You were great!" I said. *Oh, my God! What are you doing?* I yelled at myself.

I pulled away from Logan and didn't look at him when I awkwardly extracted myself from his hug. I stood behind Amy and pretended there was something interesting on the ground.

"Thank you," Logan said. Amy traded him a soda for his trophy.

While he drained his root beer, I tried to get my composure back. But I couldn't forget how it had felt when we had hugged. His strong arms around me had made me feel safe and, like, for that brief few seconds, I was special and important to him.

He started talking to Amy and their voices blended together and I didn't hear them as I took a deep breath. A shift had occurred. Something had happened that suddenly made it easier to breathe when I was around him. Something that made me want to say, *Sorry, Dad, but I am falling for this guy.* Something that made me regret our missed kiss in the woods near Black Creek.

We all walked away from the giant tent and back to the trailer.

"I got lucky Bobby decided to eat his feelings after his girlfriend dumped him," Logan said.

"Please," I said, whacking him gently on the arm. "You could have beaten him this year even without the extra pounds."

What was it about this place that was making me touchy-feely?

Logan removed the saddle from the now-cooler LG and replaced the bridle with a halter. "You guys ready for the show?"

Amy nodded vigorously. "You're going to love it, Brie. It's an old-fashioned shootout slash dinner theater. Wait until you see it."

"Will LG be okay?" I asked Logan.

"He'll be fine. The trailer is ventilated and it's shady over here. We'll just be a couple of hours and then we'll go."

"Okay." I emptied my soda and tossed the bottle into a recycling bin. There was something . . . liberating about being out of town. There was no more microscope. I wasn't looking over my shoulder for Dad. No one here knew me as the daughter of the man who was destroying the town. Here, I was nobody. I liked it. "On to the show!"

Less than ten minutes later, Logan, Amy, and I were seated at a rustic table with an oil lantern at the center. Along with the other diners, we sat inside an old barn that was turned into the meal spot. A wobbly stage had been erected at the front of the barn and everything inside was authentically Western.

Logan ordered us more root beer. Amy and I traded looks and struggled not to smirk as a cowgirl with huge boobs brought over three tin cups and a pitcher. She bent slowly over Logan's side of the table. She had stretched her shirt so far that the "Shootout Shack" lettering had cracked.

"Do you know what you'd like to order?" the waitress asked. The question was addressed to the group, but she hadn't stop smiling at Logan when she had asked it.

"I'd like a well-done cheeseburger, please," I said. "And no tomato."

"Same, but keep the tomato," Amy said.

"Burger with everything," Logan said. "Oh, actually, would you mind holding the onions?"

"Not a problem," she said, practically purring at him.

I peeked to make sure the waitress was out of earshot, then gave Amy the okay nod.

"Did you enjoy your side of boob?" Amy asked Logan.

Logan shook his head and picked up the pitcher. He poured soda into a cup and slid it to Amy, then did the same for me.

"I have no idea what you're talking about," he said. "She was perfectly nice."

"Perfectly nice with double *F*s!" Amy said.

I laughed.

"I'm glad you're here," Logan said. He bumped his shoulder gently against mine.

"Me, too," I said. This was our first official time going out. Not in a we're-together way but truly in a friends-going-out way. "Thank you for inviting me and driving. I'm going to help pay for the gas."

"Logan! Manners, manners," Amy said. "Aren't you glad that I'm here?"

He rolled his eyes to the ceiling, pretending to think. "Um, I *guess*."

Minutes later, the waitress set hot plates of food in front of each of us. She scurried off to the next table.

"I wonder when the show starts," I said, licking ketchup off my finger as it dripped from my burger.

A man in a black cowboy hat ran into the barn and zig-zagged around the tables. A blue bandanna covered his mouth and nose, and he waved a pistol in the air. "This is a holdup!" he yelled, and for a second, I almost believed him. Then I saw the orange tip on his fake gun.

"Oh Lord, help!" a waitress shrieked with pretend fear. The outlaw hid behind tables, rolled on the ground, and crawled on his hands and knees as he sneaked toward the stage, pretending as if he was hiding from the audience. Tables of people erupted with laughter as he tripped going up the stairs.

"I'll take you all hostage if you laugh at me," he joked with the crowd, breaking character for a moment. His heavy boots thudded on the wooden stage.

As we enjoyed our food, an old-fashioned shootout happened on stage. A wispy belle in a large, puffy yellow dress was kidnapped, men with guns dueled over the girl. The outlaw ended up choking out his last breath on stage. We were served homemade ice cream, and the actors left the stage to loud applause.

"I'm going to pee," Amy said. "Don't leave without me!"

I turned slightly toward Logan.

"Thanks again for asking me," I said. "This is one of the coolest things I've ever done."

"I'm really glad you came, Brie," Logan said. He reached a hand forward and placed warm fingers atop mine. "I've been going a little crazy since you found Holden and me in the woods."

"Crazy? Why?"

"Because I've been waiting for a chance to do this."

Logan leaned forward and touched his lips to mine. They were soft, like I had expected. He placed a hand on either side of my face. I kissed him back harder, wanting to take advantage of this moment.

We pulled apart and I was breathless. I dipped my head down, trying to recover. Logan cupped my chin underneath with his hand and raised my head until we were eye to eye.

"I know what you're going to do, what you'll think later," Logan said. "Don't."

"What are you talking about?"

"You'll go home and convince yourself that this was a mistake. That because you move every year or every six months—whatever—that you don't want to risk it."

"Risk what?" I asked softly.

"Falling for me. But you're too late." Logan kissed my lips with a featherweight touch. "You already have. Just like I've fallen for you."

I was speechless. I thought that this sort of thing only happened during cliché moments in rom-coms. But no. It was happening to me now.

"Sorry I took so long," Amy said, sliding back into her seat. She looked back and forth between Logan and me. "Is everything okay?" she asked.

I smiled. Under the table, I took Logan's hands, threading our fingers together. "Totally," I said, finding my voice.

"Let's beat the rush and get out of here," Logan said.

We stood and started weaving our way through the crowd. Amy reached for one of my hands and Logan held on to my other hand like he was afraid to lose me.

CHAPTER THIRTEEN

You won't criticize a man after you've walked a mile in his boots.

It had been a week since the rodeo and my first kiss with Logan. Since then, we had hung out as much as we could.

I used the time when my friends were at work to log hours for Dad. Logan, who got up at three in the morning (he promised that was what he did every year—he wasn't just getting up early for me) usually finished work around three or four every day, sometimes a little later, since it was prime planting time. Luckily for me, I didn't have set hours at the job site. I just had to stay long enough to finish whatever Dad needed done that day and then make headway on any long-term projects.

Every day this week, when the work day was over, I had hurried away before my dad could ask me where I was going. Anything to avoid lying to his face if I could help it. I could tell that Dad had been frustrated when my lunch break had lasted over two hours a couple of times last week, so I was forcing myself to limit Logan-time to after work. Well, after Logan's *first* job.

Our late afternoons and evenings were spent together talking, laughing, and making out at WyGas.

But today was Saturday, which meant no work for me. Logan and Jack traded days in the fields and it wasn't Logan's turn until tonight.

I'd met him a couple of hours ago, at nine, in the WyGas parking lot.

"So, you really like this?" Logan questioned, cocking his head and raising an eyebrow.

"I do," I said, taking a large sip of the suicide drink Logan had mixed for me. He'd made me turn away from him when he had filled a large plastic cup with various sodas. He'd stuffed them in a paper bag as he'd selected them from the fridge and had made me turn around when he popped the tops.

"Okay, so, it's WyGas tradition," Logan said. "If you can guess all the kinds of pop in the cup, you get them free for life."

"For life, huh," I said. "Wow. Okay." I took another sip.

"Definitely root beer," I said.

"That's one," Logan affirmed.

"Cream soda," I said.

Logan grinned and nodded. "Two for two!"

I took a couple of sips. The first two had been easy.

"Seven Up?" I asked.

Logan hung his head. "Oh, Brie Carter. Nooo free pop for you!"

I giggled, putting down the cup, and Logan lifted me onto the checkout counter. He stood between my knees, playing with my hair. It was down and around my shoulders.

"What else was in the drink?" I asked.

"Sprite and Coke."

"So close," I said.

"I don't know about that," Logan said. "But you get a gold star for effort."

I rolled my eyes. "A gold star. Lucky me."

He kissed me, then looked into my eyes. "Feel any better?"

I let out a sigh. "A little bit."

Logan kissed me again and this time the kiss deepened.

He stopped, looking back at my face. "How about now?"

"I think a few more times and I'll be okay," I said.

I ran my hands up his soft gray cotton tee and put a hand on either side of his face. The door jangled and an older woman stepped inside. I hopped off the counter and I knew my cheeks were pink. The same color they surely had been when I had told Amy about our kiss.

She had squealed loud enough for every person in the entire state to hear. Telling her had almost been a surreal experience. I had never been *that* girl. The kind who kissed a boy and had a friend who freaked out and wanted to hear every detail down to an almost re-creation of the scene. It actually felt pretty amazing.

Logan wasn't my first kiss. I'd been to parties before and had made out with a couple of randoms. But Logan was the first guy that I'd ever kissed who had meant something. Kissing him made me feel like all the girls in the movies that I had always rolled my eyes at, thinking there was no way being into another person was *that* amazing.

But it was. Logan and I could spend hours and hours just talking and telling each other about our pasts, presents, and what we hoped would be our futures. Even though we had only been together a week and neither of us had uttered the labels of "boyfriend" or "girlfriend," it felt to me like we were so much more than that.

The only weird part was that my dad knew nothing about things between Logan and me. Up until the rodeo, my parents had known almost everything going on in my life. Now there was this whole other world with Logan between us. I hadn't decided how and when I was going to bring them together.

Plus, the mustangs had been quiet for a while now, so things had been okay for Dad at work. That issue was tabled for the moment and it felt like a huge weight off my and Logan's shoulders. Logan had told me that the horses had left the plain behind for shade from the sun and cooler temperatures farther up the mountain. The horses weren't on Dad's time clock, though, and Logan estimated they wouldn't be on the mountain much longer.

"What time do you have to be at Watson's?" I asked.

Logan smiled and put the last travel bag of cheese curls on a rack facing the door. "I'm done after this," he said. He glanced up at the large wall clock. "I'm heading out in five."

"You are? You never skip work." This was usually the point where I planned to meet him back here tomorrow. I'd go hang out with Amy if she wasn't working or, if she was busy, I'd bike home.

"I decided to take the day off and go do something."

He had plans. And not with me.

"Oh," I said, trying not to sound disappointed. He *was* allowed to have a life. "Okay, I guess I'll head home."

"You could, but it would be cool if you came with me."

"Really?" I perked up. "Where?"

"You've been here, what? A month for sure."

I nodded. "I think almost exactly."

He leaned forward. He was close enough that I could smell that familiar Logan scent: cinnamon and sweet hay. "So, do you notice something practically everyone has that you don't?"

I frowned and thought about it. "Cattle?"

Logan laughed and took off his hat and placed it on my head. "True, but not what I was thinking. You don't have a cowboy hat."

"I don't, do I?" I reached up to touch his hat on my head. I felt proud to wear his hat. I wondered if this was how girls felt when they wore their boyfriends' letterman jackets. Not that Logan was my boyfriend.

"Let's go to the tack store and pick one out. I'll show you how to mold it so you don't look like a dude."

I helped him clear the counter and we greeted Jerry when he arrived for his shift. We headed for the tack shop. The sun warmed my back and I gently brushed my shoulder against Logan's. We grinned at each other. This felt so easy.

"I can't believe you've let me go all this time without a hat," I said, kicking a rock as we passed Watson's and headed down to the town's center. I looked both ways—always on the lookout for our Explorer.

"I know," he said, hanging his head. "I've done a horrible job introducing you to local culture."

I pushed his arm and he pushed me back.

"Oh, you did not just do that!" I barely got out the words before dissolving into laughter. I made a halfhearted swipe at him but only managed to touch my fingertips to his arm as he wriggled just out of my reach.

I stopped in the middle of the road—there wasn't a car to be seen—and stared at him. He charged at me from the side and grabbed me, throwing me over his shoulder.

"Logan!" I said through my laughter.

"Brie!" Logan said, echoing my tone.

"Put me down," I said, as we passed an upside-down post office.

"Nope." He kept walking as if I weighed nothing.

Finally, he plunked me down. He smiled at me. "Look at that—we're here!"

"Funny, I didn't realize I'd walked that far."

A wooden sign that read PAM'S TACK SHOP moved gently in the breeze. A life-size chipped horse, painted grape purple, stood next to the building's entrance.

"I'm happy you're meeting Pam," Logan said. "She's like a mom to Holden and me. She babysits him when I can't, and he loves her. She helped out a lot when my mom left."

"She sounds great." In the short time I'd been here, I'd learned family and community support in Lost Springs was everything.

Pam's shop was a small one-story building with a glass door and two large windows with cowboy and cowgirl mannequins dressed in full-blown Western wear complete with fringed suede chaps.

"I've never seen anyone around here dressed in anything like that," I said in a whisper, pointing to a red blouse splattered with gold horseshoes. It looked like something from a bad Western movie.

Logan made a face at the shirt. "No one around here buys it, but the out-of-towners love stuff like that. I think Pam has a hard time keeping that shirt in stock over the summer."

Logan pulled open the door and motioned for me to step in front of him.

"Thank you," I said.

I walked in front of him and the smell of leather and apple-flavored horse treats filled the air. Racks of Western saddles filled every corner of the tidy shop. Bridles hung on the walls, saddle pads were draped over wooden racks, and buckets were stacked in the far corner of the room.

A few strips of flypaper hung from the ceiling and a petite gray-haired woman was sweeping in the back of the shop.

"Hi, Pam," Logan called.

"Hey, hon," Pam said. She stopped sweeping and rested a tanned hand on top of the broom. She looked at me before turning her pale blue eyes to Logan. Pam's silver hair was pulled into a short ponytail and she was dressed in faded jeans and work boots.

Logan walked up to her and hugged her.

"Pam," Logan said, "this is Brie."

Pam reached out a hand. She clasped my hand firmly and put her other hand on top of mine.

"I'm so glad to meet you, Brie," Pam said. "This one has told me a lot about you."

Logan's face turned pink. "Is that a new brand of fly spray?" Logan asked, hurrying away from Pam and me. He picked up the bottle and read the label, staying away from us.

Pam released my hand and laughed quietly.

"I think you might have embarrassed him just a little bit," I said, grinning.

"Not quite enough yet," Pam said, winking at me. "Logan, honey! That's the good old spray. You've been using that same brand since you could walk."

There was silence from Logan's side of the store.

Pam and I laughed out loud.

"Go ahead and keep hiding," I said, my tone teasing.

"I'm glad you came in," Pam said, her eyes on me. "I want you to know that Logan told me where your heart is on the mustang issue."

Logan's head popped up from a different corner of the store. He walked over and stood behind us, massaging my shoulders.

"It's a really difficult situation," I said. "No matter what, it's still my dad. I don't like to see him attacked or vilified."

"I can't imagine being in your place," Pam said. "Want advice from someone who has lived on this planet many, many years?"

I nodded.

"Whatever you do, try to remember that it's not about picking sides. It's not your father over the horses. Or vice versa. It's what's right over what's wrong. That doesn't automatically mean your father's wrong. Evaluate each situation and decide on how to handle it by trusting your heart."

"Thank you, Pam," I said. "I appreciate the advice. I'm so glad you didn't automatically dislike me because of my dad's reputation in town."

Pam smiled. "I've only just met you, but you've got a good heart—I can tell. I'm glad you and Logan are in each other's lives."

I looked at Logan over my shoulder and he smiled down at me.

"Thanks for watching Holden last week," Logan said to Pam. "There was a fence break and some of the cattle got loose and headed for Vann's land. We had to get them before he called another town meeting." He huffed. Logan had told me stories about Vann—the McCoys' awful neighbor.

"Yeah, well," Pam said, picking up the broom. "Vann needs to act more like a neighbor and less like a dictator. His goats ravaged your dad's corn crop last year and Jack didn't threaten to have him fined for property destruction, now, did he?"

"Dad knew it was an accident, but Vann's still upset he didn't get the permit for the new barn he wanted to build," Logan said and shrugged. "I think he's plowed enough ground by now. He's ruined half of the forest behind his place anyway.

"I might call you in the next couple of days to give vaccinations to LG and some of the other horses if Dr. Dorsett isn't available," Logan said. He looked down at me. "Pam's a retired vet," he told me. "But she works more than she rests."

Pam smiled. "If I'm not birthing a calf out in the field or deworming the new goat herd, you'll find me here."

"She does it all," Logan said. "We've got a new vet, Dr. Dorsett, but he's not the most reliable guy. He's always on an 'emergency' call somewhere else."

Pam huffed. "That's the truth. So, aside from bringing Brie in for introductions, what are you both up to?" Pam asked.

"Brie doesn't have a cowboy hat," Logan said.

"Well, that's not acceptable!" Pam exclaimed with a wave of her hand. She pointed to the far left side of the store. "Have at it and make sure Logan breaks it in so you don't look like a dude."

I laughed. "That's what Logan said earlier!"

"We can't have new residents walking around looking like greenhorns," Pam said. "Especially the gals hanging out with the eligible bachelors of Lost Springs." She winked at Logan and the tips of his ears went red. It was beyond adorable.

"Let's go look," Logan said, leading me away from Pam.

"Aw, she didn't embarrass you, did she?" I pushed his arm with my hand.

Logan rolled his eyes and grinned. "No comment."

We stepped up to the rows of hats. Beige, black, white, navy. Tassels, feathers, beads. Every hat looked like the exact opposite of its neighbor, but I didn't see why picking one was such a big deal.

"How about that one?" I asked. There was a nice black hat on the rack in front of me.

"Black? No way," Logan said. "You want people to think you're an outlaw?"

"Umm . . . no?"

"Villains wore black hats in old movies. Now it's usually reserved for ranch owners and bosses. The top dogs wear black."

"Oh," I said. "No black, then." I didn't know a hat could say something like that. "How about you choose," I offered. "I don't want to accidentally choose a hat that says 'tourist' or 'boring.'"

Logan stepped up to the hat rack and stared carefully at the choices. He picked up a tan hat with a round top. "That doesn't look like yours," I said, looking at Logan's own hat. His hat had dents and creases in the top.

"This is an open crown hat," he explained. "It hasn't been shaped yet." He placed the hat gently on my head. *Focus, Brie!*

I told myself. *You're just buying a hat!* It was hard to concentrate on anything but Logan. He was inches away from me and I wanted to take my hands and touch the washboard abs that I knew existed under his loose T-shirt.

I peered at him from underneath the brim and our eyes met. I bit on the inside of my cheek—anything to keep back the cartoon hearts that I envisioned floating around my head when he got this close to me.

"I like this one," I said, glancing in the semi-warped mirror. The crown was rounded like a dome and the brim was straight.

"We have to shape it before you wear it in public," Logan said. His lips formed a small smirk.

I giggled. "I look like a Canadian Mountie!"

"We can fix it up if you want to come over to my house now," Logan said.

"Sure," I said slowly, trying to imagine what Logan's house was like. "Let me call home and check in."

"Okay," he said, taking my hat and heading for the front of the store. "I'm going to get this and then we'll go if you can."

"You're not paying for that," I said, shoving my hand in my pocket and feeling around for bills. "It's way too much."

Logan put his hand on my wrist and drew my hand out of my pocket. "I want to. It's only a hat."

"Are you sure?" I asked. His hand on my wrist left a lingering feeling like jumping into a cold pool and then slowly getting used to the water temperature.

"I'm *very* sure," he said.

I let Logan buy me the hat and I called home. Mom thanked me for checking in and told me to be home for dinner.

After good-byes to Pam, we headed back to WyGas to get Logan's pickup truck. I half wished Mom had said she'd needed me to come home. It would have stopped me from getting more invested in Logan. My stomach was in knots during the drive. I'd made similar mistakes before with girls that I'd befriended. I went to their houses, met their parents, played with their pets, and then real feelings of friendship developed. The closer I became to them, the harder it got to keep up a wall. Finally, when I ended up moving, it hurt so much that I swore to myself to never make friends again. That level of pain came from *friendships.* I couldn't imagine what leaving a potential relationship behind was going to feel like. Maybe that was why the only person in my phone's contacts list, aside from a few random Internet friends, was Kate.

Now we were headed down a bumpy road and I gripped the door handle for support.

"Sorry," Logan said when we bounced over a pothole. "If I go too slow, I'll get stuck." He gripped the steering wheel with both hands.

The road was muddy from day-old rain, and mud spurted up the truck's windows. On one side of the road, a green tractor was going down a defined row.

"What are they planting?" I asked, pointing out my window.

"Barley or oats," Logan said.

The truck hit another pothole and felt as though the tires were getting sucked into a deep mud puddle, and the truck strained to fight through the mud.

"Do you ever have trouble getting home?" I asked. It looked like the wrecked road would wash out after a decent storm.

Logan turned into a deep gravel driveway and glanced at me for a second. "Last year, we had a real gully washer."

"Pause. Define this 'gully washer.'" I grinned and made air quotes.

Logan laughed. "Sorry. It just means a ton of rain. When that happened, my dad had to drive through our neighbor's field, park the truck, and wade through knee-high water to get home."

"Something kind of like that happened to us in Belize," I said.

"Really?" Logan asked. "Tell me about it."

"You sure? I've told you so many stories about where I've lived. Aren't you sick of them by now?"

Logan leaned over and took my left hand. He squeezed it for a few seconds in his own warm, bigger palm. "I asked, didn't I? I promise that if I ever get bored with your stories, I won't ask you to share them."

I looked at him and wished I could pull out my phone and jot down every word he'd just said. Then again, I wasn't likely to forget.

"Okay," I said, smiling. "Well, my dad booked our first night there in a tourist resort. It was supposed to be this cutesy little place right off the main road in town. We got into town, asked for directions, and some old guy looked at us like we were nuts. We thought he just didn't understand where we wanted to go."

"Uh-oh," Logan said. "I can tell this is headed for trouble."

"Finally, we thanked the guy in *very* bad Spanish and started driving around. We found a sign for the resort that said 'welcome and park here' so we did and we followed signs that directed us to walk to the resort. The signs were wooden with words scribbled on them in, like, Sharpie. They kept popping up and said 'almost there' and 'keep going.' After ten of these signs we had walked at least a mile down a sticky jungle path before we found a bunch of canoes."

Logan shook his head. "Such a good kickoff to your stay."

"We had to take the canoes across a river and then we *finally* hit the resort ground. I was all sweaty and covered in bug bites. Plus, we had to trek back down to get to our car the next day." I stopped talking as a roof popped into view.

I looked through Logan's cracked windshield as we passed under a wooden sign straddling the driveway that said TRIPLE M RANCH. Horses, cattle, and sheep dotted the grassy knolls around a ranch house nestled in front of a weathered tall red barn.

"Logan, your ranch is beautiful!" I said.

"Thanks," he said. He kissed my hand and let it go. "I'm glad that you were able to come over."

An excited border collie appeared beside my window and barked at the truck. "Who's this?" I asked Logan, peering down at the dog.

"That's Squirrel," Logan said. "We got her as a pup and she's Holden's dog. Are you okay with dogs? I should have thought to ask. All our dogs are really friendly."

"I love dogs," I said. "I've only been wanting one for sixteen years." I grinned as Squirrel bounded up ahead. I didn't know where to look. There was *so* much land. "How'd she get her name?"

"Holden and Dad took Squirrel out on a hunting trip when Squirrel was a puppy. Squirrel found a nest full of baby squirrels in a tree hollow. She fetched a baby squirrel from the nest and carried it in her mouth like a puppy. Holden begged Dad to keep it, so we raised the baby squirrel and set it free."

"Oh, my God. I would so love a baby squirrel," I said, imagining the tiny gray face. "I like your dog already."

Logan smiled and eased the truck to a stop. "There are a lot more dogs to like."

His truck door was barely open when four or five—I couldn't tell in the flurry of fur—other dogs raced up to him, wagging their tails and barking. Logan waved me out of the truck.

"They're all harmless," he said.

"Hi, guys!" I said to them. I offered my hand to a curious Lab mix who eagerly licked it.

Logan walked over to my side of the truck with his dog posse behind him.

"Sit," Logan said firmly. All five dogs sat instantly and stared at Logan. They looked like mixed breeds. A few looked more like German shepherds, and Squirrel and another dog were border collies.

None of them moved.

"Wow," I said. "You're a dog whisperer, too."

"They have to be good," Logan said. "They're working dogs."

"Oh, right," I said. "Do they herd cattle and things like that?"

He nodded and stood behind a border collie and rubbed its black-and-white ears. "They're like an extra set of hands. They pitch in wherever Dad and I need help. This is Lara, that's Echo, next to her is Hudson, and on the end is Jane. Jane is my dad's old dog."

"Aw," I said. I walked over to Jane and bent down to rub her head. Jane had a few white hairs on her black face. "She's sweet." Kneeling, Logan was almost laughing as he tried to evade sloppy kisses from Squirrel.

"Watch out," Logan warned. "Don't spend too much time with Jane. She'll follow you home!"

"I'd take her home, but my dad would freak." Pets annoyed Dad even more than bad cell reception.

"So would my dad," Logan said with a laugh. He grabbed the bag with my hat off of the truck hood where he had placed it. "Ready to come in? Dad's working and Holden's at a friend's house."

"Sure." I glanced at the house as we made our way to the front door. Did I look as nervous as I felt?

Logan opened a patched screen door and twisted the doorknob.

I froze—shocked that no one was home and he had left the door unlocked. "You don't lock your door?" I asked. When we had lived in a cramped apartment in downtown DC, our door had four locks and two deadbolts. Ever since I could remember, I couldn't sleep at night without checking to be sure all the doors in the house were locked. Even if Mom swore she checked them, I had to do it myself. Borderline OCD, I know. Dad jokingly credited my security detail as the reason we'd never been robbed.

"Nah," he said, pushing the door open and allowing me to step in front of him. "Nobody locks their doors in Lost Springs. People aren't surprised if they wake up in the morning and their neighbor had left a note on the table because he borrowed a beer in the middle of the night."

"That's crazy. At least go for something like cheesecake."

I stepped through Logan's front door and walked into a shabby but spotless living room. "It's not fancy," Logan said as he kicked off his boots. "But it's home."

A light blue couch was in front of a TV old enough to have knobs on the sides to turn it on and off. Dozens of photos hung above the couch. There were pictures of Holden and one of a boy holding a large mouth bass.

"There you are," I said, pointing to the fishing picture.

Logan nodded, took my hat out of the bag, and put it on the counter. "Unfortunately. That was when the term 'bowl cut' really applied to my hair." I laughed and looked at the rest of the photos. There were none of his mom. Just Holden and Logan and Jack. I stared at a photo of Jack, smiling so wide, with his arms around a teensy Holden and a Logan who had two front teeth missing. I wondered if the photo had been taken by Logan's mom. Seeing Jack this way—not the man I'd come to know as my dad's arch nemesis—was strange.

I joined Logan in a large kitchen with dozens of cabinets. A few dirty pots were in the sink and there was no dishwasher or microwave.

"Is your dad one of those guys who hate modern technology?" I asked.

"No, he just never had a dishwasher installed. We had a microwave, but it got the brunt of Dad's anger the night my mom left."

"I'm so sorry," I said. "I didn't mean to bring that up."

"Stop, stop," Logan said with a smile. "It's okay."

Logan took two plastic glasses with moons on them out of a cabinet and opened the refrigerator door. He motioned me over. "Pop, juice, or water?"

"Pop, thanks." Even though I'd said "soda" all my life, I'd been influenced by Amy and Logan. I turned and looked out the kitchen window. The window looked right onto the farm lawn. Logan poured us each a full glass of Coke and grabbed a stainless steel pot from under the stove. I shot him a puzzled look. "Are we having tea, too?"

He filled the pot with water and turned the stove on high, flames licking the bottom of the pot. "We *could* have tea, but it's for your hat. We can't shape it without steam."

We sat at his round kitchen table, sipping our drinks and waiting for the water to boil.

I took a deep breath. "This week has been amazing," I said. "I don't know about you, but I don't know when I was this happy."

Logan put his hand on the table, palm up. I placed my right hand onto his.

"Whatever *this* is," I continued, "it doesn't feel like a summer fling to me. I don't want to freak you out, but I wanted to tell you that I think things with you are . . . *different*."

Logan squeezed my hand. "I wanted to say the same thing to you. I chickened out. Things with us kind of exploded so fast. I wasn't looking for this."

"Me neither," I said. "At all."

"I believe that. You have all these walls up. Like you're trying to protect yourself from getting hurt," Logan said. "I guess I'd do the same thing if I had your life."

"I'm scared," I said, my voice barely a whisper. "I really like you."

Logan leaned closer to me. His breath smelled like caramel. "Is this worth being scared?" He was so close, his lips almost brushed mine.

"Yes," I said. I tipped my chin forward, my lips on Logan's. I freed my hand from his and ran my hands up and down his back. I stood, keeping my head bent and my lips on Logan's, and managed to leave my chair and sit in his lap.

"I like you like this," he said, breathing a little hard. "I'm bringing you here more often."

We kissed, our tongues exploring each other's mouths. Logan wrapped his arms around me, pulling me even closer to him.

Whatever fear I had was quieted. I was over having my life dictated by when we would move. I was done not bonding with other people. I was just *done*.

A sizzling sound came from behind me. I jumped and turned to the stove.

"The pot's boiling over," Logan said. I hopped off his lap so that he could get up and remove the pot from the burner.

"Oops," I said, grinning. I stood and walked over to Logan. My knees felt bendy and pliable. I wasn't sure the smile was ever going to leave my face.

"Ready for your hat?" Logan asked.

"Yes, please!"

Logan pulled tongs out of a drawer and grasped my hat with them. He held it over the steam. "About thirty seconds for each side," he said. "Give or take a little."

"What can I do?" I asked.

Logan glanced around the kitchen. "Oh, open that drawer over there and get the can of Kahl Hat Stiffener. It's brown and has a horse on it."

"This drawer?" I asked. Logan nodded, so I pulled it open. Inside was a mess of tangled twine, keys to various machinery, and Kahl Hat Stiffener. I plucked the bottle from the drawer, shut it, and placed the bottle on the counter next to Logan.

He pulled the hat away from the pot and bent the rim. "Testing it out to see if it's flexible enough," he explained. "It's just right. Do you want to shape it?"

"You do it. I don't want to mess it up."

"Pressure!" he said. He sat back on his chair and put the hat in his lap. Immediately, he began folding and rolling the brim as he made a crease in the hat's crown.

"I can tell you've never done this before," I said, joking.

He was silent—all his concentration on my hat.

Thirty seconds later, the hat was back over the steam. Logan repeated the process and in less than ten minutes, the hat looked just like Logan's, minus the dents and dirt streaks.

"Wow," I said. "It looks great!"

He turned to me and placed the hat on my head. "No," he said softly, brushing my hair out of my eyes. "You make it look perfect."

CHAPTER FOURTEEN

Always drink upstream from the herd.

A couple of nights later, I was lying on my bed and twirling my cowboy hat. I flashed back to that night. Logan had dropped me off at the end of my driveway. I could have kept kissing him all night.

I'd been working hard at the job site recently, since Logan was busy in the field and I wanted to get and *stay* on Dad's good side. He was happily breezing through construction. The mustangs hadn't shown up in weeks, and Dad and his team were making great progress on the build.

My phone buzzed beside me and I picked it up. A tan cowboy hat, my new icon for Logan, was on my iPhone screen. I swiped the phone to answer and held it to my ear.

"Hey," I said. "What's up?"

"Just checking on my favorite girl while I'm on a break," Logan said.

"What are you doing?"

"Planting a few rows of potatoes."

Through the phone, I heard him open a can of soda.

"Are you tired?" I asked. "Can you stop soon?"

"I'm hot, but not too tired. I can quit when my dad gets home."

"Good. You need someone to *tell* you to take a break or you'll never stop."

"Well, I was thinking about taking Friday night off," Logan said. "How about dinner at my house? Holden has a sleepover and my dad will be in the field until at least midnight."

I smiled into the phone. "I'd love that. Can I bring anything?"

"Nope, just you."

We chatted for a few more minutes before hanging up. Once I'd ended the call, I typed a text.

Ames! Dinner at L's on Fri night! ☺

It took her seconds to write me back.

!! Dinner! OMG! So excited for u! <3

Yelling erupted downstairs and I jerked my head off my pillow. I dropped the hat on my chair and hurried down the hallway. "Mom?" I called. I found her pacing in the kitchen.

She put a finger to her lips, phone pressed tightly to her ear. "Come home when you're done," she said into the phone, then tapped the screen.

"What's wrong?" I asked. She slid into a kitchen chair and dropped her head for a second. "Is it Dad?"

She nodded. "Your father . . ." She paused. ". . . had an incident at work."

"Oh, my God, is he hurt?"

"No, sweetie. I'm sorry—I didn't mean to scare you. He's okay." Mom reached across the island and patted my hand. "Apparently, some guy has been harassing your father almost daily since the job started. Letters, e-mails, phone calls—showing up and only leaving when the sheriff would come."

"I thought that was over?" I asked. "Everyone knows that Dad's company didn't just start chopping trees without all the permits and stuff. The building is going up—do people really think they can still stop it?"

It felt like my insides were being ripped to shreds. All this time Logan had assured me that he'd spoken to everyone and that they had calmed down. This was *not* my version of calm!

Mom shrugged. "I don't know, honestly. I don't think this person's goal is to stop your dad, but rather to make the building experience as unpleasant as possible."

"What happened today?"

"Your dad didn't get into too much detail, hon. I guess the guy got in Dad's face and they had a screaming match."

I swallowed. "No physical fighting?"

"No," Mom said, rubbing her eyes with her fingers. "Brody stepped in before it came to blows."

"Oh, God."

"The man was pretty persistent and Dad may be in for a bit of trouble," Mom said. "Just be careful around town, okay?"

I nodded. "I will. Why is this guy so upset?"

Mom stood and started to make herself a cup of green tea. "Something about the mustangs."

"The horses have been *gone*. Dad never said a word about them when I was there. Nobody came by, either, when I was helping Dad. He's been keeping this from us?"

"Your dad and I will talk when he gets home. There's a lot he hasn't been telling me." Mom turned the stove up higher. "You need to be careful, Brie," Mom said. Tiny lines appeared on her forehead. She looked like she'd aged a couple of years in the past few minutes.

"I will."

After she'd made tea, Mom headed upstairs for a nap. I grabbed my phone and went out onto the front porch.

Logan answered on the first ring. "Hey, beautiful," he said.

I couldn't help but smile. "Hey, yourself. So, something kind of happened with my dad."

"What's going on?"

"I don't know very much, but some guy has been harassing him this entire time and my dad didn't tell me or my mom. It's not about the land. My dad just called a while ago and he told my mom that it was a fight over the horses."

"I'm sorry," Logan said.

"You didn't know about this, did you?" I asked, my voice shaking a little.

"Brie, of course not," Logan said. "You have to trust me. I would have told you."

"Why is anyone still fighting this?" I asked. "As far as I know, the horses haven't been near the job site in weeks. I'm waiting for my dad to get home so I can ask him if they've been back. I really just thought they had moved on somewhere else."

"Even if all that is true," Logan said, "remember, the horses are still losing ground. People here care about that."

The way he said "here" struck a weird chord inside me. "What you just said makes it sound like it's me and my family against you and the town all over again."

"I'm sorry," Logan said. "I didn't mean for it to come off that way. I promise."

"I *know* that I'm not an insider, Logan. I'm reminded of that constantly by little things every day, whether it's a tourist asking for directions that I can't give him, or old ladies stopping in mid-conversation and waiting until I'm *way* down the sidewalk before they start talking again, like I'm going to spill their secrets to someone."

"Brie, I admit—I have always been ready to jump into action if something popped up with the horses. But you're with me on that, right?"

"I want to help the horses, too," I said. "But I mean, I didn't know you were so on edge about the situation."

Logan sighed. "I'm sorry. I really mean it when I say that I don't know what's been going on with your dad. I also want you to know that you're as much a part of this town as anybody. You would be missed if you weren't here, Brie."

I held back tears at his last line and was quiet for a few seconds. "Okay," I said finally. "Thank you for talking to me about this. I'm going to wait for my dad and I'll talk to you later."

We said good night and I sank into one of the large wooden chairs and closed my eyes. A tiny part of me wondered if Logan was glad someone was still making noise about the horses' rights. Plus, everywhere he worked put him at almost all the best gossip sites in town. But I had to trust him. There was no way he would have known that this was going on the entire time and not told me.

I opened my eyes and watched fireflies dance in the night sky. I settled deep into my chair. I wasn't moving until Dad got home. I wanted to hear from him myself what was going on. I sighed. Maybe part of me, a part that I didn't want to acknowledge, had a tiny hint of doubt about what Logan had said.

CHAPTER FIFTEEN

Love a horse before you fall in love with a man.

Dad hadn't said much the night he had come home and found me waiting on the porch. In fact, he had been pretty quiet all week. At first, I'd tried to eavesdrop on Mom and Dad's conversations.

But my dad could handle his problems. Plus, I had been kind of distracted. There was Logan, obviously, and Amy had taken the week off from Watson's. She had planned our days almost from sunup to sundown to get the max out of her break.

We'd spent afternoons in her room chatting, reading gossip mags, and doing our nails. Then we'd spent an afternoon at Lost Springs Town Square Movie Theater, where we had each paid a dollar to watch two Audrey Hepburn movies—*Breakfast at Tiffany's* and *Funny Face*. Amy's time off had provided the perfect distraction until tonight's dinner at Logan's.

Logan was due at the end of the driveway any minute and I still had a straightening iron in one hand and only one shoe on.

It still didn't feel like the right time to tell Mom and Dad about Logan, so I'd told them I was having a girls' night out with Amy. Mom had brought up Logan once or twice since our trip to the falls, but I'd lied and said we were just friends.

"Wow, hon." Mom's voice jerked me out of my thoughts. She stood in my doorway, smiling. "You look so pretty."

"Thank you, Mom," I said. I slid my other foot into my other black peep-toe bootie.

I turned off the flat iron and squeezed a dab of finishing cream in my hands. I ran it through my hair.

"What's the plan tonight?" Mom asked.

"Amy and I didn't really set anything in concrete," I said. "We might go one town over for dinner and we'll probably see a movie."

I finished applying thickening mascara to my upper eyelashes. I dabbed peachy blush on my cheeks, white shadow in the corners of my eyes, and smoothed on a pink sheer gloss. Makeup was done.

"Okay, hon. Have fun and please keep your phone on. Text us if you're going to be home any later than one, okay?"

"I will, Mom. Love you."

"Love you, too."

I put my lip gloss and phone into the small fuchsia Coach purse that Kate had given me for Christmas.

In the mirror, my eyes swept over my reflection. I'd picked a soft-pink three-quarter-sleeve shirt that hugged my body and a pleated black skirt that hit just above my knees. A couple of bangles clinked on my wrist and a pair of skinny silver hoops hung from my ears. I adjusted my bra strap and stepped away from the mirror.

I practically ran for the door. I wanted Mom to stay where she was. I didn't want Mom to see me walking outside with no car waiting. It would send up tons of red flags that "Amy" was parked on the road.

When Logan's truck popped into view, I saw him leaning against the passenger door.

"Wow," Logan said, flicking his eyes up and down. "Brie, you look beautiful."

"Thank you," I said. "You look very handsome." He was missing his trademark hat and had paired dark blue jeans with a collared blue-and-white plaid shirt. His hair was neatly tousled.

"For you." He produced a bouquet of daisies.

"Aw," I said. I leaned forward and softly touched my lips to his. He put a hand on the small of my back.

Headlights appeared in the distance. "We should go," Logan said. "In case your dad decides to come home."

He opened the truck door for me and I climbed inside. He walked around the front and got into the driver's seat.

"Tonight is going to be great," Logan said.

With those words, my nerves immediately calmed. The second we stepped into Logan's house, the smell of pot roast, herb-flavored vegetables, and vanilla wafted through the air. He turned a knob on the stove and with a few clicks small flames shot up and encircled the pot.

"You made this?" I asked in surprise, peeking inside the oven.

"It's nothing," he said modestly, stirring something in the pot on the stove. "I cook for Holden all the time. Of course, he wouldn't eat this cranberry sauce I made, but I hope you like it."

"I'm sure I'll love it," I said, unzipping my booties and stepping beside him at the stove. "Can I help?"

"Take these," Logan said, placing a tray of dinner rolls in my hands, "and put them in the oven for nine minutes."

"Sure." I stuck the gooey masses in the oven and Logan kept stirring.

"Want to taste?" he asked, leaning toward me with the spoon. I nodded and cupped my hand under the wooden spoon as he directed it into my mouth. Warm cranberries filled my mouth. Logan grinned. "Good, huh?"

"Excellent," I agreed, wiping a bit of cranberry from my lower lip.

"Here." He leaned forward and gently touched my bottom lip with his thumb. I closed my eyes for a second when his thumb brushed my mouth. I stood still and brought my eyes up to meet his. Our lips touched. Soft at first and then harder. He tasted like cranberries—tart and sweet.

We gently pulled apart as the cranberries boiled and popped.

"We should fix those," I said quietly. Nodding silently, he stirred the berries while looking at me.

Forty-five minutes later, we had stuffed ourselves with cranberry sauce, tender beef roast in a savory thyme sauce, dinner rolls, mashed potatoes, and corn. Two vanilla candles burned at the table, their scent wafting around the room. I'd had one too many servings and wished my skirt had an elastic waistband.

"Tell me another one," I said to Logan, stretching back into my chair. We had been tossing around personal facts about each other for the past twenty minutes. So far I'd learned the following things: Logan was eighteen—I was embarrassed that I hadn't known that until tonight—wished he could draw but couldn't, and was the happiest when he was sleeping under the stars on Blackheart Mountain.

"Hmm . . ." He paused and thought for a second. "My last girlfriend was in sophomore year. We were together for eight months and that's my longest relationship."

"Why did you break up?" I asked.

"She broke up with me for working too much."

"That's not fair," I said. "You didn't *choose* to work all the hours—and jobs—that you do. You do it because you have to."

"True," he said, nodding. "When was your last relationship?"

"Eighth grade," I said. "I was with the guy for five months. Then it was time to move again—from North Carolina to Texas. We promised to stay in touch and have a long-distance relationship, but that lasted maybe two weeks. He wanted to see other people and I was over it."

"He lost out," Logan said, smiling.

"Um, the girls here lost out," I said. "How have you *not* had a girlfriend since sophomore year?"

"What makes me so irresistible?" Logan asked, grinning.

"You're a cowboy," I said slowly, tilting my head. Surely he didn't need me to explain this to him. But his face was blank. "Don't other girls find that appealing?"

Logan shook his head and smirked. "School is filled with guys like me. If you went to classes at LSH, you might think I'm one of the dorky ones." Yet, the way he was looking at me told me he didn't believe that.

I rolled my eyes. "Please. Don't even try to play that card." His foot brushed against mine under the table and all I wanted to do was kiss him. Again. A door slammed in the yard.

"Who's that?" I asked. Logan stood and peered out the window.

"It's my dad," he said. "We should probably clean up."

I piled plates on my arm. "Oh, my God. Logan! Only Amy knows that we're dating! I lied to my mom and it's obvious that my dad doesn't know. Should I sneak out a back door or something?"

Logan seemed to freeze for a second. "No," he said, snapping out of his thoughts. "You should meet him. I'd planned to tell him before tonight so that he wasn't surprised, but this is how it is."

I moved to the sink and helped Logan rinse the dishes, my hands shaking. I was about to face the man that had caused so much trouble when we had first arrived in town. The kitchen door opened.

"Hey, Dad," Logan said. I put down the dish towel, unsure for a second whether to smile or frown at the tall, tanned man with day-old stubble and short hair. "I didn't think you would be home this early."

His dad unlaced heavy work boots, leaving them by the door. "Trevor said he would finish up tonight," Mr. McCoy said.

"Dad." Logan took a step so he was beside me. He reached down and took my hand. "We haven't really had time to talk lately and I'm sorry to spring this on you. This is my girl-friend, Brie."

I smiled, nodding, and *whaat?!*

I looked at Logan, my eyes wide. I couldn't stop the smile that spread across my face. If Logan had saved the girlfriend card purposefully for this moment to shift my focus, he had done the perfect job.

"Hi," I said, stepping forward and offered him my slightly shaking hand. "I'm Brie. Um, Brie Carter."

Mr. McCoy stared at me for what felt like an hour. He hated me. He didn't like that I was in his house. Wait a second . . . he was *smiling*. He took my hand and pumped it warmly.

"Hi, Brie, I'm Jack, Logan's father. It's nice to meet you."

Panic whooshed out of me and I grinned back. "It's good to meet you, too, Mr. McCoy."

Was I selling out Dad by liking Mr. McCoy?

Logan's father shook his head. "None of that 'Mr.' or 'sir' stuff. Just call me Jack."

"Okay." I paused and struggled to say his first name. "Jack."

"Did you make a good roast, son?" he asked Logan as he peered into our empty pots. He placed a hand on Logan's shoulder.

"Sure did," Logan said, taking a covered plate out of the fridge. "I'll heat this for you."

"Thanks. I'm going to take a shower. I'll be back down to eat and share dessert with you kids, if that's okay. Brie, I want to get to know you better." Jack smiled as he headed out of the kitchen.

When I was sure Jack was gone, I turned to Logan and threw my arms around him. "Oh, my God. One of our parents knows we're dating. You called me your *girlfriend*."

"I think that title was way overdue," Logan said. "And my dad loved you."

"I blinded him with my awesomeness," I said, teasing. "He forgot that he probably has my dad's face on his dart board."

Logan laughed. He wrapped his arms around me, pulling me to him. "Just remember that even if he *does* bring up the horses—all is quiet at your dad's job site right now. Plus, you're here with me on a date. You didn't come to talk about the mustangs."

I nodded. "I completely agree. I'm with *you*. Not your dad."

CHAPTER SIXTEEN

A cowboy is a man with guts and a horse.

"So, you've really lived all over the place, huh?" Jack asked, smiling at me.

He wiped his mouth with a napkin after finishing the apple pie Logan had pulled out of the fridge for dessert. Jack really seemed interested in getting to know me and had asked a lot of thoughtful questions. His blue-gray eyes, though different from Logan's, had the same ability to make me feel as if I was the most important person in the room when I spoke.

"Yes," I said, sipping my water. "Oh, and a houseboat in Utah for a couple of months. We were on Lake Powell."

Jack laughed and shook his head. The three of us had been talking for over half an hour. The more time I spent with Jack, the more comfortable he made me. He had Logan's charm, serious side and funny side, and passion when he talked about his job. He worked his ranch during the day and did bookkeeping for a sheep farm down the road on the weekends. As if that wasn't enough, he also worked nights planting and harvesting seasonal crops. He valued hard work over everything else, but I caught him peeking at Logan and saw nothing but pride on his face. I thought of Holden and how beyond lucky he was to grow up with McCoy men.

Jack revealed that he'd only been a couple of states away from home, so, like Logan, he encouraged me to tell them stories about my different moves.

"What's one of your favorite places where you've lived?" Jack asked.

"Brooklyn," I said immediately. "I was around thirteen and was able to convince my parents to let me ride the train by myself a couple of times. I loved it there."

"What about Manhattan?" Logan asked.

I scrunched my nose. "It wasn't my favorite. Too busy and loud. Times Square was the worst! I think I *still* see neon lights sometimes from all the billboards that I saw there."

Logan grinned. "When my cousins came to visit us last year, they said they couldn't get the farm smell out of their hair for a week after staying with us."

We all laughed.

"Brie," Jack said. "I wanted to get to know you a little and I'm so glad that I did. You're a smart young lady and your parents should be very proud."

I looked down, then back at Jack. "Thank you."

"I think it's best for all of us to address the white elephant in the room," Jack said.

My smile slipped and my heart thudded in my chest.

"Dad," Logan said. "Do we have to do this *now*? Brie knows how you feel. And how I feel about the horses and the loss of land. She has no control over what her father or anyone does."

Under the table, I felt a hand touch mine. I unclenched my fist and held Logan's hand.

"Oh no, Brie," Jack said, looking at me. "Please don't think for a second that I don't like you because of your father's work. I know he didn't come to town with a hidden vendetta against the people who live here. Business is business—that I understand."

I nodded, staying silent.

"I don't have anything personal against your dad," Jack said. "I care about Lost Springs and the horses."

"Thank you," I said. "I respect your feelings and I do see your side of the issue." I looked at Logan and there was a tiny smile on his face. He gave me the slightest nod. "But Logan and I aren't involved in this. Logan and I aren't taking sides. Our side is the mustangs."

Jack took a sip of Coke from his glass and put it down in front of himself. He folded his hands on the table. "You are wise beyond your years. My son is very lucky to have met you."

I smiled, squeezing Logan's hand. I stayed for another half an hour or so and Jack didn't bring up the horses or the land again. He had said his piece and I'd said mine. Now that Logan and I were officially out as a couple, I had to tell my parents. I didn't want them to hear it, somehow, from anyone else.

Logan and I cleared the table and I said good night to Jack. Logan opened the truck's passenger door for me and we got back in his truck. The second our doors slammed shut, he was pulling me toward him. I twisted in the seat and in the pale moonlight, my mouth found his.

"You were so great," he said. He trailed kisses from my ear down my neck. I shivered and ran my fingers through his hair.

"I'm so relieved," I said, trying to catch my breath. Logan's feather-light kisses on the top of my shoulder made it nearly impossible. "I'm actually glad he came home early tonight," I managed to get out.

Logan looked at me and held both of my hands. "Me, too. I was so proud to introduce you to him. Honestly, 'proud' doesn't cover it. I can't tell you how great it is to have an amazing girlfriend like you."

"That was so sweet, thank you," I said. I kissed him lightly. "I'm so glad that your dad didn't look at me like someone from the enemy camp."

"He told you—he knows you have nothing to do with your dad's business."

"I just know my dad. It's not going to be as easy with him. I'll have to talk to him before you do. I'm too nervous for us to both be there."

Logan started his truck and circled the driveway and headed for the road.

"My only concern is you," Logan said. "I don't like the idea of you facing your dad alone."

"I know you'd be there if I asked you," I said. "But I *have* to do it this way. Especially now that someone stirred up trouble about the horses a few days ago."

We reached my driveway in what felt like seconds. Logan shifted into park and let the truck idle. He turned to face me.

"Whatever you decide—it's going to be okay," he said.

I looked into his eyes and the moonlight cast shadows on his face. It wasn't often that he didn't wear his hat. I leaned forward, kissed him, and ran my fingers through his hair.

We kissed for a little while before Logan's truck started to make angry sounds.

"Uh, I better let you get home," I said.

"I think you're right," Logan said as he leaned over and adjusted my necklace. "So, I'm going to be busy on Sunday."

Trying not to look disappointed, I nodded. "Oh," I said. "What's going on?"

"I've got to shear about five hundred sheep and Holden's too little to do much."

"Wow, five hundred," I said.

"I don't want you to feel pressured at all because it really is *tough* work, but do you want to come help?"

"Definitely!" I said. I'd never even seen a sheep up close. "What should I wear?"

Logan grinned. "I'd wear old jeans and a ratty T-shirt. You'll get oily when you hold them. Plus, it's supposed to be unseasonably warm tomorrow, I heard."

"I can really help you?" I wasn't afraid to, but I didn't want to disappoint Logan with my sheep-wrangling skills.

"Really," he confirmed. "Can you get over to my house around seven a.m.?"

I nodded. "I'll be there."

"Good." And with that, Logan kissed me again. The kiss made my face warm. Logan cupped his hand under my chin and his fingers were cool on my flushed skin. We pulled apart and I smiled at him.

"Bye," I said softly. My fingers fumbled on the door handle.
"Sunday." He smiled. "'Night."

Once in my room, I flipped on my lights. Logan could see the light from the road. He always waited until he knew I was safe inside. I opened the balcony door and stepped out. I watched his cracked taillight disappear down the stretch of road, and then I went into the living room. Mom and Dad were parked on the couch with the lights off as they watched some old Jane Allen flick.

"Hey, hon," Mom said, waving me over. She flipped on the lamp and got a glimpse of my face. "Good night with Amy, huh?" she asked with a smile.

"Great night. We had so much fun," I said. I settled on the recliner and laid the chair all the way back. If I tried to make it upstairs, my knees would buckle.

"Popcorn?" Dad asked, passing the bowl in my direction.

Wordlessly, I took the bowl of kettle corn and watched the movie. I barely heard the film's dialogue because I was too busy reliving tonight in my head. Old Brie, full of standoffishness and zero friends on speed dial had vanished. New Brie didn't think about moving, perpetually looking forward to the next adventure.

CHAPTER SEVENTEEN

Better for a man to wear out than rust out.

The sun peeked over Blackheart Mountain and I pedaled down Logan's driveway through the foggy morning. The mist was lifting, though, as the sun rose. It was nearly seven on Sunday and I was decked out in jeans with torn knees, an old pair of shoes, and a T-shirt with mud stains on it from the time I'd slipped into a creek in our Virginia backyard. My hair was in a high ponytail— as if I were channeling my inner cheerleader—and I was makeup free—quite a change from my first-date makeup routine.

My camera bag was slung across my shoulders—Mom had made me promise to take photos. I'd started to ease Logan into conversation over the weekend. I had talked to Mom a little bit more and told her that I was hanging out with Logan. I didn't get to the dating part. Yet. Mom was happy that I had Logan and even though I'd never asked, it was unspoken that Mom wasn't going to speak about him to Dad. I'd never have asked her to keep my boyfriend a secret, but I certainly wasn't going to argue with her *not* to.

That is, if I still had a boyfriend after Logan saw me without makeup.

I parked my bike in weedy grass by Logan's old barn and headed for the orange metal corral that held bleating sheep. The gray-and-whitish sheep were crammed into the dirt arena and barely had a few feet of moving space. Logan was in a smaller corral with a pair of clippers and boxes and *boxes* of trash bags.

"Hi, gorgeous!" he called when he saw me approaching. I snapped a photo of him smiling and waving against the backdrop of Blackheart Mountain with the sunlight beaming behind him. The light made him look glowy and gauzy—like he was on a soap opera. I sighed quietly to myself that he hadn't run screaming in the opposite direction at the sight of my face free of makeup.

"You started without me," I said, climbing between the fence boards and stepping inside the small corral.

Logan kissed my cheek and started to pull on his gloves. "Nah, I just got things ready. One by one, I'm going to drive a sheep from the pen through that chute and into this corral. You can help hold while I shear until you see how it's done and then you can try if you want."

"Okay, that sounds good," I said. "Are the sheep wild or gentle?"

Logan moved toward the chute and stood by the barrier he would lift so a sheep could enter the corral. "Most are gentle, but a few new ones haven't been sheared as much, so they're a little scared. They won't bite, though."

"I'll hold you to that." I was making it my mission to be the best partner he'd ever had. I hung my camera bag on a fence post and took the gloves Logan offered me.

"Can I feel their wool before I put these on?" I asked. "That okay?"

"Sure. Ready?"

"Let's do it." We smiled at each other and then looked into the corral. Logan pulled on the thick rope and the wooden gate rose. A sheep, seemingly eager to escape its crowded space, lumbered through the narrow chute and stepped into the corral. Logan jogged up to the corral and slid under the fence. He patted the sheep on the back and motioned for me to step up to the animal. I held out a hand to the sheep, and it allowed me to approach.

"Boy or girl?" I asked Logan.

After a quick peek below, he answered, "Boy." He slipped a thick rope around the sheep's neck and handed it to me. "Put your hand on the rope against his neck and he'll be still. If he starts to move, just tug on the rope and he'll listen. He's older, so he's a pro at this."

"Hi, boy," I said to the sheep, taking hold of the rope. I ran my hand across his back and was surprised at the oil that came off on my hands. "Wow, I had no idea they were this oily. What happens next with the wool?"

"Combing and washing," Logan said, turning on the clippers that buzzed loudly and caused him to raise his voice a notch. "We don't do that. We do the shearing and then send the wool to a farm down the road who takes it from there." He started at the sheep's neck and glided the clippers down the animal's back.

Tufts of cotton-like hair fell from the sheep and landed in a pile on the corral dirt. The sheep stood still and a minute later, Logan had almost half the wool off the sheep and onto the ground.

"You're fast," I said, concentrating on holding the now-antsy sheep still. He tugged against the rope and was stronger than I'd thought he could be.

"This is nothing," he said. "The local record is shearing an entire sheep in forty-five seconds. *That's* fast."

He sheared off the final puff of wool and helped me take off the rope. He guided the sheep into an empty pen. The animals probably felt naked after losing pounds of wool.

"Let's put this into a bag and we'll do the next one," Logan said, reaching for a garbage bag. We stuffed the slick wool into the bag, tied it shut, and Logan opened the chute for the next sheep.

"Where's Holden?" I asked, suddenly realizing the little boy wasn't around.

Logan secured the rope around the new sheep's neck. "It's his first day of day camp. He got me up this morning before five, ready to go with his backpack and everything."

"Aw. What a cutie."

"He'll do, I guess," Logan said, smiling.

"Holden's really lucky to have you, you know. He worships you. And your dad."

"Thanks, babe." Logan's smile reached his eyes. "He's lucky to have Pam, too." Logan clicked on the clippers and started on a new sheep. "I do what I can, but Dad and I aren't always there for him. Pam takes him out for a Mother's Day lunch every year and he began buying her a present each year. I think that helps."

"She's amazing," I said. "Does she have kids of her own?"

He wiped his forehead with his dirt-streaked wrist. "No, her only son died in a car accident about seven years ago. She was a single mom and the grief almost killed her."

"That's terrible," I said. "I couldn't even begin to imagine how she survived that."

"It has to be especially hard because the accident was just down the road. Her kid's truck spun out on black ice."

I shook my head, blinking fast so that I wouldn't get teary.

"I heard that Pam was going to leave Lost Springs because she couldn't stand to be here, but when my mom left, she started helping my dad with me and Holden."

"I've never met a woman like Pam," I said. "How could you lose a son and then sort of raise a thirteen-year-old and a five-year-old?"

"I have no idea," Logan said. "She's just always been there for us."

He pulled stuck wool out of the clipper blades. His smile peeked at me from under his cowboy hat. "Want to try?"

I reached out my hand and took the clippers. "Sure." Leaning over the sheep, I gently pressed the clippers to its head. Fuzz came right off as I made a stripe down its back, imitating the pattern that Logan had done with the other sheep. It took me ten times as long as it did Logan to shear the sheep, but he told me to do another one. I was determined to beat my time and soon, five sheep later, I got into a rhythm.

It was almost seven before I dragged my tired body through my back door. I was covered in dirt, oil, and tiny bits of wool. Logan and I had successfully sheared all five hundred sheep and when I got tired of holding the sheep still, we switched places. I turned out to be a whiz with the shears and Logan seemed impressed with my previously nonexistent shearing skills. We took a break around noon for lunch and Logan cooked a dozen ears of sweet corn and made turkey sandwiches. We laughed when butter ran down our arms, and the conversation flowed throughout lunch. We finished shearing and Logan tossed my bike into the back of his truck and drove me home. I'd protested that biking home would be fine, but he'd refused.

"Bye," I said, leaning into the driver's-side window and kissing him one more time.

"Bye," he replied, smiling. I hopped on my bike and he let the truck out of park. I biked up the driveway and all my muscles protested when I hopped off and walked it to the shed.

The second I stepped inside the house, I knew something was wrong. It was too quiet. "Mom?" I called. "Dad?" No TV was on and I didn't hear anyone. I walked upstairs and found Mom on my balcony. The door was partially open and a light wind blew into my bedroom.

"Mom? What's wrong? Are you okay?" I asked. My heart thumped like a jack rabbit. It was pounding so hard that I felt dizzy. I slid the door back more and stepped outside.

"I'm fine," she said, but the lines in her forehead said something else. She let out a big sigh and patted the wicker chair next to her. "Sit."

"Is Dad okay? Where is he?"

"He's fine," she said quickly. "But there's something you need to know."

"What?"

She pressed her lips together and reached for my hand. "Honey, how close are you and Logan?"

"Logan? What? Why?" I sputtered the questions.

She squeezed my hand. "Sweetie, your dad had someone show up at work again and bother him."

"Is he calling the cops? Is this guy dangerous, Mom?"

"Dad is going to file a restraining order, but that's not what I want to talk about. Brie, he just told me the name of the man who's been harassing him, and I think you should know . . ." Mom tilted her head and ran her fingers over her messy bun.

"No," I said, barely recognizing my own voice. "No. You're wrong! Dad's wrong!" A wave of nausea rolled over me.

"Honey, I'm sorry. But Jack McCoy has been bothering Dad since the job started. He knows there's nothing he can do to stop the development. But he's upset that the land is being taken away from the horses, so he's taking out his frustration on your dad."

"There's no way Logan knew about this," I said. "He would have stopped it. I just—we just—" I shook my head.

"I'm sorry, Brie." Mom reached over and hugged me. "Do you want to be alone for a little bit?"

I nodded. "Mom?" I asked before she walked away. "Where *is* Dad?"

"With Brody and the crew," she said. "There's no trouble right now." Mom reached over and put a hand on my knee. "The only reason I'm keeping the fact secret that you and Logan have been hanging out is that it will add to your father's stress."

I nodded. "Thanks, Mom. Sorry that I put you in this position."

Mom's eyes were gentle as she gave me a half smile.

I let her leave and I drew my knees to my chest and wrapped my arms around them. I didn't believe for a second that Logan knew anything about this. He wouldn't have let me sit across the table from his dad while knowing what was going on with *my* dad.

But what if he knew? The thought of Logan knowing and not being honest made me want to throw up. I had opened my heart to him. He was the first guy—the first person—I'd ever let get to know me this intimately. Almost everything in my heart screamed to call Logan and tell him what was going on. But the tiniest part of me said to pull back a bit. This wasn't my fight, but I felt like a traitor for having dessert with the person who had been making Dad's life hell. The great memory of that night turned sour.

I spent a long time on the balcony before going into my room, taking off my clothes, and hopping into a hot shower. Then I buried myself under the covers.

CHAPTER EIGHTEEN

No good man leaves spur marks on a horse.

For the next two mornings, I got up early and rode to the work site with Dad. He was quiet, never mentioning Jack McCoy.

I texted daily with Logan, but hadn't seen him since the day we sheared sheep. He kept asking if something was wrong, but I said no every time. I told him that Dad had come down on me about missing so much work, so I was going to be busy for a while. Fortunately, Logan was busy, too.

I talked to Amy almost every night before bed.

"Logan asked if you had said anything to me about him," she said. "You can't avoid him forever."

"I know. I need to have a face-to-face conversation about Jack, though, and I'm not sure I want to know the truth."

"If Logan confesses to knowing about what Jack has been doing . . . well, don't you think you need to know sooner rather than later?"

I was terrified Logan would admit that, though—that he would say those words and everything between us would be gone.

Mom knew something was up. She kept trying to convince me to go into the nearby city of Casper to go shopping. But I knew once she got me alone in the car, she'd ask a million questions. I'd talk for hours but end up with the same conclusion: I missed Logan more than I knew it was possible to miss someone. I was terrified that Logan had known about Jack all along, and finally, that I knew I couldn't keep avoiding Logan forever. What kind of relationship were we in, anyway, if he'd kept this from me?

Today, Dad and I were working in the office and he was making phone calls about what he had dubbed his "pest problem."

The mustangs were back. At first, the herd had seemed frightened by any movement or at the sight of the crew, but now they grazed about a hundred yards away from the trailer.

Now, after all the reading that I'd done and the conversations with Logan—I felt for the horses. We were in similar positions. Some people wanted my family out of town and Dad and his crew wanted the horses away from his site. The mustangs were constantly on the move just like me. The more I thought about my first encounter with them, the more it felt like that moment had been an initiation of sorts. As if the horses had seen me as being out of place and they wanted to connect with me.

I wished the horses would have stayed away, as much as I liked seeing them. The BLM hadn't told Dad much, according to him, but that they were backlogged from moving many herds of horses in other parts of the state. They would get to Dad when they could.

Dad was fired up again after the horses had grazed by his trailer overnight when everyone was gone. He had almost slipped on a muck pile outside the trailer door this morning—it was more than enough to get him moving on the horse issue.

"I told you, Marty," Dad said into the phone. "I need this taken care of this week. These horses are running all over the place and either you come and move them, or I'll have to call in a favor to take care of it." He hung up.

I didn't want to know what he meant. He wasn't someone who hated animals, but he wouldn't tolerate interference on site. Still there was no way—no way—Dad would ever hurt an animal.

"Dad?" I asked, shuffling the papers in front of me.

"What?"

"Isn't it . . . illegal to hurt horses?"

He peered at me from behind his desk and I turned my attention back to the copier.

"I don't want to hurt them, Brie, but the BLM can't stop me from protecting my land."

Normally, I'd go along with his plans to avoid an argument, but he couldn't just do whatever he wanted with or to the horses. Nausea settled into my stomach. Logan could talk for hours about these horses and never lose the smile on his face. LG had been part of the herd, and the gelding had saved Logan when his mom had left. I had to get Dad thinking about alternative plans.

"How about fences?" I suggested. "You could put some up until the construction is done. By then, the horses will probably be scared and they will likely move on to somewhere else."

"Brie, don't you think if I could have put up temporary

fences that they would have gone up the same day that you almost got trampled? I ran the numbers for plastic orange fencing, and the expense wasn't feasible."

"But if you hurt them, you could go to jail!" I protested. "And once Jack finds out—"

Dad cut me off with an angry wave of his hand. "How is Jack McCoy going to find out what we're doing? You're not friends with his kid, are you?" He jutted out his jaw.

"No. I mean, I know him . . . but just from the gas station and grocery store."

"Make sure you keep it that way," he said, getting up to grab paper from the printer. "I don't ever want to hear that you've been hanging around with McCoy's son."

The phone rang and I shut my mouth and turned away from him. He had to separate his business problems with Jack from his personal situation with Logan and me. If there still *was* a Logan and me.

"What?" Dad said, answering the phone. He listened for a few seconds. His face reddened and he took large strides as he made his way to the trailer door.

"What's wrong?" I asked.

"Brody said that idiot McCoy is headed up the road."

I felt a headache form between my eyes. "Why is he coming? Dad?"

"Stay out of this, Brie," Dad said, yanking open the trailer door and hurrying down the steps. "He's blatantly ignoring the pending restraining order. I don't have time for this."

Panic welled up inside me as I followed Dad out of the trailer. Suddenly, I realized what I wanted—what I *needed*—Logan. I needed him here to help defuse the situation. I had never *really* believed that Logan knew his dad had been coming to the site. But I had to stop trying to convince myself that he had.

I reached into the pocket of my jean shorts, my hands shaking as I groped for my phone.

I had no air—spots swam in front of my eyes as I tapped his face to call him.

"Brie," Logan answered immediately.

"Logan, I'm sorry!" I blurted out as I started sobbing. "I was all wrong. Everything is my fault." I gasped, trying to catch my breath.

"Brie, listen to me," Logan said. "Listen. Sit down if you're standing. Just sit down right now. Do it."

I obeyed, practically falling onto the lawn in front of the trailer.

"Where are you?" Logan asked. His voice was so calm and warm.

"I'm sitting. I'm in front of Dad's trailer," I said, barely able to get out the words. It felt like I was having a heart attack. Chills caused goose bumps on my bare legs, and my teeth started chattering.

It was as if I'd forgotten how to speak actual words.

"I can't—" Sobs stopped me mid-sentence and my heart pounded. I almost tried to call out for Dad, but he was too far away.

I managed to force air through my nose.

"You're going to be okay," Logan said. "Now, what's wrong?"

I took another breath, this time managing to almost fill

my lungs. I saw Jack's blue truck pull off the road and onto the driveway. I closed my eyes, not ready to see whatever was going to happen.

"Logan," I said. "Please come. Your dad is here and it's going to be so bad. Please—"

"I've been on my way from WyGas the moment you told me where you were. I'm pulling into the site driveway now. Everything is going to be okay."

Just as he said that, his truck turned off the road and started down the driveway.

"Omigod, you're really here!" A fresh wave of tears threatened to spill onto my cheeks.

"Stay where you are, don't get in the middle of this."

"I'm not staying away from you for another second," I said. I ended the call and stood—my legs a little shaky. I left the phone in the grass and broke into a jog. I kicked off my black ballet flats. The jog turned into a flat-out run.

"Brie? What the hell are you doing?" Dad called. But I kept running past him. I barely glanced at Jack's truck as I flew by. The door on the driver's side of Logan's truck opened and Logan got out and slammed it shut.

I threw myself at almost full speed into his open arms. I knocked him backward a few steps, but he didn't let go of me. I buried my nose in his neck and he bent down, sliding an arm under my knees and picking me up. I curled my body, clinging to him. He held me so tight.

"I love you," I said.

"Look at me," Logan said. I lifted my head up, my eyes connecting with his. "I love you, Brie."

I'd never said those words to someone. I *knew* he hadn't, either. Warmth from his body encircled me. He had picked me up as if I weighed nothing, and I felt so comfortable in his arms.

"I figured out you thought I might have known," Logan said.

"I was so wrong," I said. "I didn't know that I was trying to push you away."

"I want you to know that I didn't know what my dad had been doing. If I had, I would have asked him to stop. I never would have let you sit through dessert with him."

"I don't care about them," I said. "It's their fight. But I care about the horses."

"Me, too."

Logan squeezed me tighter for a moment, then carefully set me on the ground. He kissed my cheek and took one of my hands in his.

"You can wait in my truck," he said, looking down at me—his soft brown eyes searching my face.

"No way," I said. My breathing was back to normal and so was my heart rate. "I'm going with you."

Logan nodded, and kept my hand close to him as we walked up to Jack's truck.

In my dash to Logan and our conversation, I'd forgotten that Jack and my dad were nearby to witness everything. The moment that I'd barreled into Logan had put the world on pause.

I swallowed. Dad was going to call me out on my lie about not knowing Logan.

There he stood, arms crossed and his feet apart in a fighting stance. His face was a brilliant shade of red and he glared at me.

Jack, not too far away, had his hands in his pockets as he watched Logan and me approach.

"Go in the trailer," Dad snapped at me. "I can't even look at you right now."

"No," I said, surprising myself at how certain I sounded.

"I'm not asking you again, Brie," Dad said. His voice was low and controlled. Anger practically radiated off his body. "You lied to me. Minutes ago. You need to get in the trailer and think about how you're going to explain yourself."

I dropped Logan's hand and crossed my arms. "You know what, Dad? I can 'explain myself' right now. Logan is my boyfriend. I love him."

Dad threw his hands in the air and shook his head. "You're really confused, young lady. We haven't even been here a year! Not even six months! You don't 'love' anybody." He almost spat out the sentence.

"There isn't a time line for falling in love with someone," I said.

Dad shook his head and let out a laugh without an ounce of happiness. Jack was silent, his eyes soft as he looked at Logan and me.

"Logan and I don't have anything to do with your problem with Jack," I added. I had to get this out while I had the chance. "This is a fight between you two." I pointed at each of them. "But there's something at stake for us here, too. These horses are important to Logan, so that makes them important to me. I'm not saying that you deserve trouble. You are *my* dad and I will always stick up for you. But I won't put myself in the middle of this fight."

"Fine, Brie. Fine. We'll deal with this when we get home." Then Dad stepped up to Logan's dad and put his clean-shaven face inches from Jack's stubbly chin. "As for you, McCoy, I told you to stay off my property."

"I'm not here to fight," Jack said. His tone was calm. He stared at Dad and didn't back down. "I came here with an offer, actually. When I have time, please let my son and me move the horses. We'll contact the BLM and you won't have to do a thing."

Dad's head jerked back a fraction. I could tell that he had expected fighting words from Jack—not an offer to solve his problem.

Dad's fists clenched and I was afraid he was going to hit Jack. Jack pushed back his cowboy hat and waited for Dad to speak. I almost expected them to start circling each other. My head pounded and I fumbled for Logan's hand even though my palm was sweating.

"You know what, Jack," Dad said, spitting out his name. "Since my daughter is apparently in love with your son, I may as well say yes. I have new sod coming July first. The horses better be gone by then. *Long* gone."

Logan and I looked at Jack and I held my breath to see what he would say.

"Not a problem. Thank you," Jack said simply.

Dad turned to me. "Brie, let's go. Now. You're forbidden to contact Logan. Stay away from him. Say whatever you have to say to him, because your phone and computer are mine now. You won't be leaving the house except for coming here. No more trips to the gas station or grocery store."

I clenched my teeth and my mind raced as I tried to figure out the next move. I knew how Dad operated. He wasn't going to listen to anything I had to say. Arguing would only make him angrier. I had to play his game. And win.

I turned to face Logan and made sure he saw me wink at him. *Go with this*, I willed him. *Just play along.*

"Logan," I said. "I love you so much." I tried to sound like the lovesick teen that Dad thought I was.

"My dad is so wrong," I continued, making sure I was just loud enough for him to hear. "But this whole thing was kind of good."

"Brie? What are you talking about?" Logan's tone had the same perfect desperation that mine did.

I knew you'd get it, I thought.

"This isn't me," I said. "I don't know who I am like this. I love you, but what just happened did us a favor."

"Brie, no," Logan argued, playing along perfectly.

"I'm going to move soon—I don't know when—but I will. If you and I were still together, it would hurt so much worse then. You have to stay away from me."

"No," Logan said. "I love you."

"I can't keep loving you," I said, connecting my eyes with his to make sure he knew I was still lying. "It would be too painful later. Please leave me alone."

I spun on my heel and walked away from him. I passed Jack and my dad and kept my expression vacant. I picked up my discarded shoes, slipped them on, and walked up the trailer steps and pulled open the door. Only when it shut behind me did I collapse on the couch, putting my head in my hands.

I'd never done anything like that before. EVER. My chest and stomach hurt. Maybe I didn't *like* my dad at the moment, but I still loved him. *You're clearly showing your love for your dad since you just put on a giant production that was a total lie.* I curled up in a ball on the couch, squeezing my eyes shut while I waited for Dad to come back.

It was official: I had just become a traitor.

CHAPTER NINETEEN

You can scratch a cowboy out of your brand book,
but not out of your heart.

My "breakup" with Logan was puzzling Mom and Dad. They
still grilled me even though the showdown had been a week ago.

It would have been funny if I hadn't felt so nauseous constantly because I was living a complete lie. I was grounded and
only allowed to leave the house if I was going to the job site.
Dad's deadline to move the horses seemed to be approaching
faster and faster. I'd seen flashes of the horses through thick
trees at the back of the property, so Logan and Jack hadn't
moved them yet.

Today, Mom said Amy could come over, but I couldn't leave
the house. I'd even had to use Mom's phone to call her.

"Hey, prisoner," Amy said as she came into my room.

"Hello, visitor," I said.

Amy sat on my brown swivel chair and I sat up on my bed.
I had been lying down reading while I waited for her to come.

We were both in shorts and T-shirts and the door to my balcony was open.

"I think I might have something for you," Amy said quietly.

"Oh, really?" I said. I got up and closed the door to the balcony and quietly shut my bedroom door.

Smiling, Amy reached into her oversize brown satchel and pulled out a small pink cell phone, the present she'd promised me in her e-mail yesterday. (I'd been allowed to check e-mail once last night on the family PC.) She tossed it to me.

"Yeeees!" I said. "Thank you so much!"

"Please, you'd do the same for me."

"I would, and here." I rummaged through my purse and found twenty bucks. "This is enough, right?"

"More than enough," Amy said. "Thank *you*."

"Oh, the lengths you must go to when you have a secret boyfriend," I said, grinning.

"I already charged it for you," Amy said, her tone barely above a whisper, "and you have five hundred minutes. So go on, call him. You should, like, go over by your balcony, but don't go outside in case your mom is out there. I'm going to turn on your TV and talk to it."

I giggled. "I can tell you've done this before."

Amy shrugged, smiling. "Maybe once or twice."

I got up and tossed Amy my TV remote.

She turned on the TV and I dialed Logan's number. *Please answer!* I thought. *I know it's a strange number, but it's me!*

"Hello?"

"Logan!" I said.

Amy waved at me. "Shhh," she said, finger to her lips.

"Logan, oh, my God, it's me. I'm on a burner cell that Amy got for me so we could talk. If I hang up on you for no reason it's because my mom came into the room. Okay?"

"Got it," he said. "Hi." His tone was so soft and gentle. It made me miss him more. I wanted his arms around me, strong and tanned. I needed to smell his cinnamon and sweet hay scent.

"Hi. Are you busy?" I kept my voice low. I leaned my back against the wall next to my balcony door. I slid down so I was sitting on the carpet.

"Not for you. Walking to the alley behind Watson's right now." A door slammed and the background noise from the store vanished. "Okay. All clear here," Logan said.

"I miss you. So much," I said.

"You have no idea how much I miss you," Logan said. "I can't believe we're even talking right now."

"I know," I said. "How did it go with your dad when you got home?"

"I don't want to rub it in," Logan said. "But honestly, my dad was okay. We talked for a long time. He liked you so much when you guys met each other at dinner. He let me talk about you for, oh, a little while."

"What did you say?" I asked.

"I told him that I'd found an amazing girl who, when I first met her, irritated the crap out of me."

I laughed softly. "I know I did."

"But even after all that, there was something about this girl that was different. Something that I'd never felt about anyone else."

"Logan."

"I told him that I was pissed about how he had been treating your dad. I made sure he understood that I am *completely* on the side of the horses."

"How did Jack respond to that?"

"We argued a little at first. I finally got him to see that he wasn't accomplishing anything that he wanted to. Writing, calling, showing up and harassing your dad wasn't going to make him side with the horses. It just pissed him off. I think what really got my dad was when I told him that your dad took that anger home with him.

"I ended our talk by saying that no matter how busy my dad is, he *always* used to know every little thing that Holden and I were doing. But he had been so busy harassing someone that he never noticed that I'd not only met my dream girl, but I was in love with her."

"I love you," I said. "So much. Thank you for saying all that to your dad, Logan." I glanced at my bedroom door. "I better hang up since Mom is still practically on patrol. But I'll have this phone and this number. I can text from it, too. It's going to be under my mattress on silent, but you can call or text whenever you want."

"Okay," Logan said. "I'll see you *soon*."

"I hope so."

We said good-bye and I snapped the phone shut. I double-checked to make sure the ringer was off and got up. I smiled at Amy as I slid the phone under my mattress.

"So?" she asked, smiling. "How was it?"

I flopped onto my bed, lying on my back with my feet crossed in the air. "Perfect," I said. "Having a phone changes everything. But it also made me want to see him that much more."

"You will," Amy said.

We hung out until dinnertime and Amy headed home. She promised to come over the next day to keep me from dying of boredom.

I checked my phone before I went to bed.

Two new texts:

I'll be thinking abt u tonight.

And

Amy and I need to arrange a jailbreak for you.

I smiled and texted him back.

Thinking abt u too. And yes, get me out! ☺

The next morning, I dressed in jean shorts and a red tank top and came downstairs after Dad had left for work. He'd given me the day off. I had been shocked, but I *definitely* wasn't going to argue about it!

In the kitchen, I found Mom staring at her laptop screen.

"What're you working on?" I asked. She motioned me over and slipped her glasses up on top of her head.

"Cropping these photos." She pointed to the laptop. "They're just gorgeous, Brie."

I looked over her shoulder. They were the photos from the cave. Mom had snapped one of me grinning as I stood under a massive stalactite and next to a giant stalagmite. The intimate photos made me feel as if we were back in the cave.

"Hey, Mom?"

She looked up at me. "Why do I feel you're about to ask for a favor?"

"Because you have freaky Mom-radar," I said. "Can I meet Amy in town for coffee? Just for a couple of hours, max."

Mom sighed. She looked back at her screen and then at me.

"Amy. Coffee. Home. Deal?" she asked.

"Deal!" I said. "I promise! Thanks, Mom."

I grabbed the house phone off its cradle and dug into my pocket for the scrap of paper that Amy had written her number on last night. I didn't have my cell to speed dial it, and I had no idea what it was from memory.

The phone rang twice.

"Hello?" Amy answered.

"Hey," I said. "You busy this morning?"

"Nope. I don't have to be at work until two."

"Perfect. My mom said I could come into town and have coffee with you as long as I came home right after."

"That sounds great," Amy said. "I'll, um, make sure to let everyone know."

I almost broke out into a little dance in the kitchen. Amy was calling or texting Logan right now to tell him about coffee.

"Thanks, Ames," I said. "See you in a bit."

I hung up the phone and grabbed my purse.

"Brie?" Mom called.

I turned back to her and she held out something gold and shiny.

"I get my phone back?" I asked.

"Not really," Mom said. "You're getting it because you're going out. When you get home, it goes back in the drawer."

I didn't even try to argue. All I cared about was getting to Beans. "Okay. Thanks, Mom."

"Sweetie," Mom said.

I stopped mid-step and turned to face her.

"I don't necessarily agree with it, but do what Dad asked about Logan, okay? For now."

"Okay." I hated lying to my mom. She was the rational one in the family. If I told her what I was planning to do, she would probably try to help. I would ask her to let me see Logan, but I had *just* gotten permission to leave the house. It was way too soon to ask.

I'd have to convince Mom to let me see Logan, but I couldn't wait that long. The week that had already gone by was too much time. I owed Amy for all the minutes that I kept buying for the burner phone.

I headed out the door and grabbed my bike. I wasn't wasting another moment.

CHAPTER TWENTY

Minding one's own business is the best life insurance.

I spent almost every day for a week having coffee dates with Amy, which really meant coffee with Logan *and* Amy, who was there both because she was our friend and because Logan and I didn't want to get caught out alone. But last night I'd texted Amy and had invited her over for a girls' day. I wanted to spend more time with her and I also wanted to thank her for covering so often for Logan and me.

Mom had given me my phone back this morning and I didn't use it once in front of her. I'd set it on vibrate and had texted Logan the second I made it to my room.

Got my phone back!!!!!! ☺ I want to come have "coffee" but don't want to push it. Staying home today for girls' day w Amy. Miss u so much!

He texted me back within minutes.

So happy abt ur phone! Good idea to stay home at least for a couple days. I'm out in the field plowing with dad so my reception isn't great. I'll be out here until midnight at least. Miss u more!

The message made me smile. It felt like I had lost a limb when I'd been without *my* phone—the burner was great but not like mine. Tires crunched on gravel and I looked out to see Amy's car pull up to our house and, a few seconds later, a car door slammed.

I trotted to the end of the hallway and went down the stairs to the first level. Mom and I reached the door at the same time. Mom bumped me with her hip, reaching for the door. "I've got it," she said, grinning.

I bumped her back. *"I've* got it!" Giggling, I managed to unlock the door and open it.

"Amy," I said. "Hurry up and get in here so you can document this! My own mother is trying to hip check me practically out of the room." I darted away from Mom, running to the base of the staircase.

Amy came inside and broke out into laughter. I got a tiny running start and slid along the foyer floor in my socks and bumped right into Mom.

She grabbed me, wrapping her arms around my chest and drawing me close to her.

"Aw, my baby," she said. "I just love you so much!" She started planting big, noisy kisses on the top of my head.

"Mom!" I tried to wriggle away. "Stop it!" Even as I fought her, the hug felt good. I hated it when my mom and I weren't a hundred percent okay.

I heard a *click* and Amy lowered her phone. "Annnd, sending this photo to my FaceSpace album," she said.

"No, no!" I managed to slip out of Mom's arms and grab

Amy's phone. I looked at the screen. A happy face and *Your photo has been uploaded!* stared back at me. Amy had caught me trying to wriggle away from Mom as she kissed my head.

I handed Amy's phone back to her, shaking my head. "Just you wait. I'll get a pic of you when you're least expecting it."

Amy rolled her eyes and we all laughed.

"*Anyway,*" Mom said. "Hi, Amy."

Amy grinned. "Hi, Ms. Carter. Are you sure you don't want me to leave you two alone?"

No, no, I mouthed.

"You know that you're welcome here anytime, Amy," Mom said. "And what have I told you a million times?"

"Umm," Amy said. "Oh! Sorry, *Nicola.*"

"That's better," Mom said. "Have fun, girls!"

Amy and I headed for my room. Once inside, I gently closed the door. Amy put her tote bag on my purple recliner.

"You came prepared," I said, peering into her bag.

"Beyond prepared. Check this."

Amy reached into her bag and started putting items on my bed.

"We have," she said, "copies of every tabloid from Watson's, sunscreen, shades, an e-reader, hats, and a fully charged iPod with a 'tanning on the balcony' playlist."

I laughed. "This is awesome! I totally forgot—I made a giant pitcher of strawberry smoothies. Want some?"

Amy nodded. "Please!"

I left my room and went downstairs. I stopped just short of the kitchen once I heard Mom talking on the phone. I peeped around the corner.

"A thousand words by Monday," Mom said, her head bent as

she scribbled something on paper in front of her. "Thank you." I could hear the excitement in her voice. She hung up and I darted into the kitchen.

"Yay!" I said.

"Brie!" Mom spun around, a hand over her chest and wisps of brown hair flying. "You scared me!"

"That sounded exciting," I said as I went to the fridge and opened the freezer.

Mom smiled. "I got another writing job. An editor called me because he had seen my photographs of the cave that we explored. He wants more shots of the falls and an article about visiting this area."

"That's awesome, Mom. I'm so happy for you," I said. "Okay, Amy's waiting upstairs." I motioned with the pitcher of smoothies in hand.

"What are you girls up to?" Mom asked.

"Catching rays and reading gossip mags," I said.

Mom smiled. "That's great, sweetie. Here, take these cherries up for a snack. And don't get sunburned, okay?"

"We have tons of sunscreen," I promised.

I took the bowl, grabbed two red Solo cups, and a big spoon to stir the smoothies.

"How good does this look?" I asked Amy once I reached my room.

She took off the lid and looked inside. "It looks like it needs to be in my stomach."

Laughing, I poured cups for both of us.

We moved our stuff outside. The balcony was big enough for both of us to spread out and have side tables at each end.

"This was an awesome idea," Amy said. "Thanks for inviting me over." She shimmied out of her shorts and pulled her tank top over her head.

"Aw," I said. "That bikini is *so* cute!"

It was cherry red with tiny white polka dots.

"Thanks!" Amy said, smiling.

"Do I even want to know how much you paid for it, eBay queen?" I asked, smiling at her.

I adjusted my black string bikini and sat on my towel.

"It's Tara Salvadore," Amy said. "Brand-new. Retails for over two hundred and fifty dollars."

I let out a low whistle. "Fifty?"

Amy shook her head. "Fifteen. It would have been less, but I got in a bidding war with some idiot who drove up the price."

"Fifteen bucks. Geez, Amy. Shouldn't you be saving for college?"

We laughed and I took a sip of my smoothie.

"Wait, wait! We have to do a toast," Amy said. "Then sunscreen."

"Oops, sorry," I said. I held up my cup.

"To us for being friends and finding each other in this crazy thing called life."

"Definitely yes," I said.

"Finally, to having the best time of our lives! Cheers!"

Amy and I tapped our red cups together and I took a long drink. The temperature was perfect to be outside. It was in the mid-seventies and there were only a few wispy clouds.

"Would you?" I asked, holding up the bottle of Hawaiian Tropic sunscreen.

"Of course." Amy scooted over and rubbed sunscreen all over my back and along the tops of my shoulders.

We switched and I did the same for her, making sure to really cover her super-fair skin. Then we each coated our arms, chest, stomach, and legs.

"Want me to put on the playlist I made?" she asked.

"Yes!" I said. "I have mini speakers that I can grab from my room."

"Awesome," Amy said. "I'll wait on the music. I brought it for two reasons. The first is because you and I needed an amazing playlist for today."

"For sure," I said, rubbing my hands together to soak up excess sunscreen.

"Second, it is perfect for drowning us out when we talk about boys and stuff."

"That's super-smart about the music." I went and retrieved my speaker/dock combo. Seconds later, one of the hottest songs of the summer came out of the speakers.

"This is *so* perfect," I said, rolling onto my stomach.

"Agreed," Amy said. She lay on her stomach and turned her head toward me. "So! I totally admit I'm living vicariously through you," Amy said, biting into a cherry. "You know, since my love life is currently nonexistent."

I laughed. "It's really not all that exciting. The sneaking around gets old *so* fast, and we can't even go over to each other's houses."

"But you're with Logan," she said, sighing dramatically. "You're with the guy that all the girls—and some of the guys—drool over."

"I'm glad that I don't go to your school, then,'" I said, tossing another cherry at her. "Sounds like the mean girls would be after me."

Amy nodded. "That's pretty accurate. B., you could totally be one of them, though."

"I'm *mean*?!" I asked. "What are you talking about?"

"No! No, no!" Amy said, laughing a little. "I meant you could be one of the populars. You're pretty, smart, super-chic—stuff that makes an It Girl."

"This is why I'm so glad that I homeschool," I said. "I'm not really interested in being an It Girl. Well, an It Girl maybe, but not a mean one."

Amy tucked a stray lock of black hair behind her ear. "See. You should come to LSH."

"Nah. I'm not into all that drama. The girl wars and all the time stuck inside. I like the mobility and flexibility of homeschooling."

"You are a wanderer," Amy said, smiling.

I gasped. "I had no idea!"

She laughed. "It's fun to scour eBay all summer for back-to-school accessories. I've got a favorite seller who practically gives away tons of designer pieces. Mostly Jillian Benson. I *love* seeing the looks on the faces of this awful group of girls once they see my accessories. They must think that Watson's pays a *ton* because I'm able to have so many new pieces. I keep staggering certain dresses or statement necklaces so it looks like I'm getting new stuff every week."

"Shows how much they know, huh? You probably paid a dollar for a bracelet that they paid fifty for."

"Totally. I watch them whisper, 'How can *she* afford that necklace? Daddy said mine won't be here until October because they went on back order.'"

"Nice! You have the mean-girl voice totally down."

Her mouth gaped as she looked at me. "Seriously?"

"Ye-es," I confirmed. "Plus, since there is zero shopping in town, I bet everyone makes a big trip to the mall outside of town."

Amy nodded. "Yep. They do every year."

"I'd bet that two girls have shown up wearing the same shirt at least once."

"Except for me!" Amy said, grinning. "I go through the 'vintage' clothes online and buy stuff that has a hole in it or needs other minor TLC. That pretty much solidifies my chances of not having *one* shirt that anyone else does."

I propped my chin on my hands. "You've seen my wardrobe. It's not exactly full of designer brands."

"That's what makes a girl an individual," Amy said. "Who wants to be a billboard for some company? I mean, if Traci Reefer, *the* Traci—designer extraordinaire of TRNY—came to me and said that she'd pay me to wear shirts with her brand splashed all over them, I so would! But I'm not doing free advertising like a bunch of the girls *and* guys at school for the companies that practically every city in America has."

"So with you," I said.

Amy took a sip of her strawberry smoothie.

My phone lit up and vibrated. "It's Logan," I said. "One sec."

"I'm going to get a few pop, okay?" Amy said.

"Sure. Thanks."

She smiled and headed inside. We totally didn't need any soda. Amy was such a good friend.

"What's up?" I answered.

"Good and bad news," he said.

I took a deep breath. "Tell me."

"Bad news first. My dad got hurt. We're finishing up paperwork at the hospital, then going home."

"What? How? Is he going to be okay?"

"He's fine, but he'll be laid up for a few weeks. He was moving hay rolls with the tractor and he loaded one onto the truck and the ties broke. He tried to stop it from rolling off the truck, but he couldn't and sprained his back."

"Oh, thank God he wasn't seriously hurt," I said. "Are you okay to drive him home?"

"Oh, yeah," Logan said. "I already called Pam and she is going to take Holden so Dad can rest when we get home. I have to get back out in the field. The new guy—Trevor—took over for me until I returned."

"Anything I can do?" At least Jack had help. But since he was out of commission, it piled more work on Logan.

"Actually, yes," Logan said. "In a few days, I've got to move some of the cattle from our pastures up to the mountain range for the summer. I need another hand and so far, no one else is free to help and we can't afford to hire another person. Interested?"

"Of course," I said. "That sounds fun!"

Logan laughed. "It's fun for the first two hours. But we'll be moving twenty head of cattle up the mountain and it can be dangerous. We'd also have to spend the night."

Spend the night. Could I? Amy stepped back onto the balcony cradling four sodas in her arms.

"I want to help," I said firmly. "You'll protect me, right?" I said the last part in a teasing tone.

"Sure thing," Logan said with a laugh. "What about the sleepover?"

"I think I can pull it off with Amy," I said. "Thanks for the heads-up. It'll give me time to think of a good story to tell my parents."

"If you're sure. I'll meet you at WyGas on Saturday morning and we'll leave from there."

"What should I bring?"

"Layers of clothes," he said. "It'll get cold at night. And be sure to bring gloves, a coat, and a hat. I'll take care of the rest."

We said good-bye and I put down my phone.

"Need an alibi?" Amy asked, setting a can of Diet Coke in front of me.

"A big one. Logan and I are going camping on Saturday," I said, watching her eyes widen. "Jack threw out his back and has to rest. So we're moving cattle up Blackheart Mountain."

"He asked you to do that?" Amy's smile was replaced with a frown.

"Yeah, he asked if I wanted to do it. Obviously, I want to help him *and* spend time together."

"But Brie, it's *Blackheart Mountain*. It's dangerous! Experienced ranchers die up there every year. Herding cattle is tough, too. Are you sure?"

"Logan said I'll be fine," I said. "He'll make sure I'm safe. I trust him."

"I don't know," Amy said, twirling the straw in her soda. "I trust Logan, but the mountain is unpredictable, especially now. Storms pop up so fast . . ."

"It'll be fine," I said, waving my hand. There was no way I'd pass this up. "We're leaving on Saturday, so I'll be spending that night with you, aka Logan, okay?"

"Okay." Amy took a sip of her soda. "As long as you swear to be careful," she said, staring.

I opened my drink. "Promise!" We clinked cans and I shook my head.

"Oh, my God. I'm going to sleep over with a *guy*. With Logan. In a tent." Short sentences were all I could muster.

Amy laughed and scooted closer to me so we were sure no one could overhear.

"I'm betting a month's worth of eBay money that you'll be making out all night long and you'll forget about the cattle."

Rolling my eyes, I turned over on my back and shielded my eyes from the sun. "No comment!" I said, my tone teasing. "Okay, so it's time. Spill the details of Amy Banks's boy history."

Amy laughed.

"Okay, so first kiss was Aaron," Amy said. She told me all about her first sloppy kiss in fifth grade. As she talked, I couldn't stop my mind from wandering.

You're going to sleep over with Logan. Plus, big-time lies to Mom and Dad! My brain yelled at me.

After a few minutes, I managed to push away the thoughts and focus on Amy. I lost myself in Amy's stories and we giggled all afternoon.

I was sore from laughing so much when I waved good-bye to Amy. When her car disappeared, I pulled out my phone and texted Kate.

Can u talk? Kind of a big deal.

Are you ok? Call me!

Totally fine! Finding a private place to talk!

"Brie?" Mom called my name just as I had started to open the balcony door.

I put my phone away. "Yeah?" I called.

"I'm going for a walk, hon. I'll be back just before dinner, okay?"

"Okay, Mom." I tried to keep my tone even. When the door in the kitchen shut I plopped on the couch and looked at my phone. I didn't have much time before Dad got home, although he was often home long after dinnertime.

I pressed the number for Kate's speed dial. She picked up on the first ring.

"Are you okay?" she asked.

"Yes," I said. "I wasn't trying to scare you, but what I have to talk about is kind of urgent."

"Tell me."

I launched into a semi-edited summary of what had been going on and finally got to the invitation for an overnight trip up Blackheart Mountain. A trip without parents, on terrain that could be a little risky, and with Amy as the cover for my absence.

"Okay," Kate said, taking a deep breath. "I have to ask the tough questions now."

"Okay." My voice was barely audible.

"I want to preface my questions with this: really hear me when I say there is *no* and I mean *zero* judgment from me no matter what you tell me. You're my sister and I love you. You haven't said anything to me about being in love with Logan enough to take that big step. Have you two been together?"

"We haven't," I said. "Oh, I'm so glad I'm talking to you. You're the only person that I can be completely honest with who knows . . . you know. Stuff."

"Aw, B. You can always talk to me." Kate paused and I just knew that she was smiling on the other end. "So, do you *want* to?" Kate asked.

I paused. Did I? Yes. No. Ye—no. "Um, well. Yes. But actually no. I mean, well, maybe."

Kate burst into laughter and so did I. "Wow, Brie. That was the clearest answer *ever!*"

"I'm always that concise," I said, trying to catch my breath. "My final answer is: *not yet.*"

"He's been a thousand percent respectful of that, right?" Kate's tone was without laughter now.

"Always! He's never pressured me about anything. Ever."

"Good, then I don't need to bring a baseball bat."

"Kaaaate."

She laughed. "I've got to look out for my little sister. So, back to the big question: the sleepover." She sighed. "I can't say 'Yes! Go! Have an awesome time!' But I also can't tell you not to go. Is the trip dangerous?"

"Logan said it can be. But he's really experienced and he would never take me with him if he didn't think he could protect me."

"What's your cover story with the parents?" Kate asked.

I sat up on the couch and positioned myself so that I could hear one door and see another in case Mom came back from her walk. "I'm going to tell them that I'm sleeping over at Amy's for the weekend. Like it's supposed to be one long girly fest. Face masks, doing our nails, TV, junk food—all that kind of stuff."

"Okay, baby sis," Kate said, her tone a little less light. "I'd be a hypocrite to advise you to stay home. I spent the better half of my teenage years climbing in and out of my window at night."

I laughed. "Remember how when I caught you when I was little, you used to pay me not to tell Mom or Dad?"

Kate laughed. "I gave you enormous sums with quarters and dimes."

"That turned into five-dollar bills as I got older."

We both laughed. I stopped, hearing the back door open.

"Mom's home," I said quietly. "I'm so glad we got to catch up," I said in my normal tone. "I miss you."

"I miss you, too!" Kate said. "Be careful and don't think twice about calling or texting. Promise?"

"Promise."

"Pass the corn, please," I asked Dad. I'd pulled my hair back, half up and half down, and tried not to look as if I'd spent the better half of the day trying to figure out how to deceive my parents. I was *not* cut out for this—lies weren't part of my relationship with my parents. I kept telling myself that I was lying for a good reason—Logan—but that didn't stop the guilty feelings.

My sweaty fingers could barely grasp the corn dish. If they said no about the sleepover at Amy's, everything would be ruined. But I'd given them no reason to say no. Part of me desperately wanted to tell Mom what was going on, but that would put her in an awkward position. She'd either force me to tell Dad or she'd keep my secret. That wasn't fair for either of us. It was better for her if I kept this to myself. For now, anyway. I sneaked a look at Mom, sad that I was about to lie on a monumental scale to her. I just couldn't pass up this chance to help Logan and spend a weekend with him.

"How was work, Dad?" I asked, keeping my voice light. I didn't want to seem more interested than usual.

"Would have been better if those damn horses hadn't shown up," Dad grumbled.

Under the table, I clenched my hands into fists to keep from saying something that Dad wouldn't like. *Why did the horses have to pop up again now?* I thought to myself. *This is the worst timing ever.*

"Amy said she heard from a friend that Jack was making calls to find space to hold the horses just temporarily," I lied. I was going to need a notebook to keep my stories straight if this kept happening.

"Amy isn't friends with Logan, is she?" Dad asked.

"No," I said quickly. "They just work together sometimes."

Dad nodded and took a bite of his steak. "Oh."

It was now or never. "Speaking of Amy, she invited me over for a sleepover on Saturday. Can I go?"

"Are other kids coming over?" Mom asked, peering at me from down the table.

"Nope," I said, trying to sound casual. "Just Amy and me. We were going to watch movies and eat a bunch of junk food."

Mom's and Dad's eyes connected before they looked back at me. "No drinking?" Mom asked.

"No drinking," I said.

"Fine with me," Mom said, and Dad nodded his approval. The pepper steak barely slid down my throat and I couldn't sit still much longer. I was about to burst from excitement *and* lose my cool from the stress of all the lies that I'd just told. I kept my eyes down, afraid I'd give something away. "Dessert?" Mom asked, drawing my attention back to the meal.

"Definitely," I said with a smile. This was going to be the best weekend ever. Kind of. I swallowed, not able to dislodge the lump in my throat that had grown with each lie I'd told.

CHAPTER TWENTY-ONE

If a man allows you to ride his favorite horse,
he's paid you the highest compliment.

On Saturday I wanted to look camper-chic, so I left my tousled hair down with a few random skinny braids and put on jeans with a baby-doll T-shirt.

The forecast called for rain tomorrow. I hoped it was wrong and that Logan and I would have good weather as we made our way along Blackheart Mountain. I pulled out the backpack that had been hidden under my bed all week and peered inside at the contents, winter clothes that Logan swore I would need: two sweaters, a pair of jeans, gloves, and a hat. I tossed in a tube of mascara, a mini hairbrush, and lip gloss so I'd look semi-decent.

I put on my Converses and took one last look in the mirror. My normally pale-ish skin had a bronzed glow from spending time outside. I looked like a girl who was excited about solo time with her boyfriend. I grabbed my bag off my bed and walked into the living room.

"Mom?" I called. "I'm going to Amy's now!"

She appeared from the dining room, where she had been rearranging the lilies on the table. "Got everything?" she asked, nodding toward my backpack.

"Yep," I said, walking through the dining room and heading for the kitchen door. I'd never lied to her about something this big before. Sneaking around with Logan was different. This was a whole new level—I was climbing a mountain with the guy I had been forbidden to see. "I'll see you tomorrow."

"What time?" she asked. "Your dad and I want to go out to eat and we thought we could all try the new Italian place outside of town."

What time? I couldn't say *I don't know what time Logan and I will make it down the mountain.* "Six?" I asked, playing it safe.

"Six is fine," Mom said, kissing the top of my head. "Have fun and call me if you need something."

"I will."

I biked to WyGas. The plan was that I'd leave my bike there and Amy would pick it up after work and take it to her house. Logan and I had to drive to the McCoys' for supplies and to get our horses. I pedaled hard and looked at Blackheart Mountain—serene and vibrant against the clear sky. In a few hours, Logan and I would be up there.

I burst through the WyGas door and spotted Logan restocking the chip aisle. "Ready for me?" I asked with a grin. I pulled my sticky T-shirt away from my body. It was humid enough to make my eyelashes curl.

"I'm always ready for you," he said, placing his hand on the back of my head as he kissed me.

I wrapped my arms around him. "I'm so happy to see you," I said.

"Me, too. Give me two minutes and then we'll go."

"Okay. I'm going to grab a couple of Twizzlers for the road." Logan pulled the key for the cash register off his key chain and handed it to me before heading to the back of the store to grab his bag. I headed for the candy aisle and within minutes, my arms were loaded with more than the licorice. I unlocked the cash register, put money in, and slid the drawer closed. When Logan returned, I handed him the key.

"See you, Jerry," Logan called toward the back of the store. "We're taking off."

We hopped in Logan's truck and headed for Triple M.

The truck bounced along the road. Warm air flowed through the open windows, and I stuck my hand out into the sunlight.

"Is what we're doing really dangerous or really, really dangerous?" I asked Logan.

"It's only dangerous if you're not prepared. If a storm comes, we've got a shelter. If a mountain lion bothers us, I've got a gun. We're prepared. But that doesn't mean you have to do this." He looked at me for a second before directing his eyes back to the road. "Maybe you shouldn't."

"I'm doing it," I said. I was annoyed when my voice wobbled. He wasn't going to talk me out of it. "I just want to know what to expect."

"Well," he said, flipping on his blinker as we turned into

Triple M's driveway. "We're going to take the horses and guide the cattle on flat land for about five miles. Then, we'll start going up the mountain and go about a fourth of the way up before we hit flat land where the cattle will stay. They'll have water from the creek and shelter from trees. That means I don't check on them during the summer and fall. I just come up to get them right before winter."

"Do any ever die?" I asked.

He nodded. "Calves and sick cows are vulnerable to being picked off by coyotes and mountain lions. The herd does its best to protect its own, but that's really not enough."

"That's sad." I frowned and looked ahead to the barn.

"I know. But it's a circle of life kind of thing. That's just how it goes around here," Logan said.

"Speaking of sad, my dad was complaining about the horses again."

Logan took a deep breath. "There's nothing I can do for them yet. No one from the BLM has called me back. I'm just going to have to show up at their office once we get back."

He pulled the truck along the side of the barn that was hidden from the house and we got out. Logan pulled open the barn's silver door and I blinked as my eyes adjusted to the dark interior light. "Ever saddled a horse before?" he asked.

"A couple of times," I said, trying to sound nonchalant. I held back a grin. "I don't know if I remember everything."

"Well, let me saddle up LG and then I'll help you with your mare," he said as he patted a horse's black cheek. "You can pet her until I'm ready, if you want. Her name's Mazy."

I giggled under my breath as Logan walked a few stalls down to saddle his horse. I made sure he was gone before I opened a trunk in front of Mazy's stall and found everything I needed.

I started to tack up the small black-and-white appaloosa. She was sweet and batted long lashes at me while I slipped off her halter.

I looked around—the barn was huge, with tractors housed in the back and box stalls of various sizes lining the wall. Mazy easily took the bit and I fastened the bridle onto her head. The cotton saddle pad fit over her black back and with a grunt, I heaved the Western saddle on. After a quick check of the cinch and stirrup length, I took her reins in my hand and led her out of the stall.

We found Logan, and I hung over the half door. "Damn," I said with a serious tone. "How do you tack up a horse?"

"It's not hard," he said, not looking up from the saddle. LG stood quietly while Logan tightened the girth. "But—hey!" His mouth dropped as he glanced up at me and saw a fully ready Mazy standing behind me.

I smirked. "Looks like the greenhorn beat the cowboy."

Logan laughed and tipped his hat to me. "Where'd you learn to do that?"

"Belize," I said. "A lot of people rode horses on the beach or from work to home, so I picked it up."

"There's more about you than I know, isn't there?" Logan asked, cocking his head.

"Definitely," I said. "Now, do you need help?"

Logan mock rolled his eyes. "I'm going to watch out for

you from now on. Who knows what else you can do that you haven't told me about."

I stepped inside the stall and pressed my lips against his. "There are lots of things," I murmured. "Wait and see."

CHAPTER TWENTY-TWO

Most men are like a barbed-wire fence—they have their good points.

I held LG and Mazy by the barn's corner while Logan ran inside the house and told his dad he was going. "I'll tell him I found a guy from school to go with me," Logan said before he headed inside.

I petted Mazy's shoulder and stood in the rare silence at Triple M. We were really doing this. In a few hours, we would be halfway up a mountain with no cell signal, no adults, and no fast way to get down.

"You guys ready to go soon?" I asked the horses. They blinked at me, and LG rubbed his head on my arm.

Logan stepped out of the house, shut the screen door carefully, and jogged over to me. "Let's go!" he said, taking LG's reins and vaulting into the saddle. I copied him and we kicked the horses into a trot, our camping gear rattling in the saddle packs behind us.

"What first?" I said. I easily neck-reined Mazy with one hand and looked at Logan for guidance.

"We'll go to the pasture, gather up the cattle, and herd them down the driveway. Once they're all together, we'll take them across the road into the open field."

Logan turned his horse toward the pasture and I followed. The lead dogs, Jane and Lara, trotted along quietly beside us. Three other less experienced dogs were behind us. I repeated Logan's words in my head. I didn't want to do something wrong and let the cattle escape.

He opened the wooden gate and we rode through.

"What should I do?" I asked.

"I'm going to start herding them toward the gate. Stay beside the entrance and make sure they go out. Mazy knows what to do. She's an old pro, so let her do her work," Logan said. He smiled at me. "You're going to do great."

"I hope so," I said. I patted Mazy's neck. "I trust you, girl."

Logan squeezed LG into a fast lope and my breath caught at the way the horse ducked and cut in front of the cattle and herded them into an almost perfect line of black, white, and brown that headed for me and the gate.

"Jane! Here!" Logan gave a sharp whistle and pointed at the cattle. The dog zigged and zagged into the herd and within seconds, she had them moving. She growled at a few stubborn cows and they quickly joined the ranks of the cattle walking in line. Lara, needing no directions of her own, danced around the cattle with more speed than Jane, if that was even possible. Logan pulled up LG and watched Jane and Lara keep the cattle moving.

I grinned and called to Logan, "You don't need me and you know it!"

"Aw, don't say that!" His smile could have knocked me off Mazy's back.

"It's true," I said, shifting my weight in the saddle. "You could have done this by yourself. Jane and Lara are all the help you need."

Logan eased his horse next to me and left the dogs to their work. I could barely pull my eyes away from the dogs and cattle long enough to look at Logan.

"The dogs are good," he said, "but they won't keep me as warm as you."

I gave him a sideways glance. "Excuse me?"

"We have to share a tent," he said. I watched him—seeing him try to look serious but failing. "I only have one."

"One tent? Please." I rolled my eyes. "You camp all the time, so I doubt you only have one tent."

Logan nodded. "You got me. We probably have more tents, but I could only find one. I . . ." He paused and sighed. "I could sleep outside."

"Hmm." I pretended to think. "Nah, I'd rather you slept with me. In case a bear shows up or something."

I grinned and guided Mazy closer to him. We leaned over the space between us and tried to kiss, but Mazy decided it was time for a bite of grass and she yanked me away from Logan just as our lips touched. When I pulled up her head, she strained against the reins and arched her neck toward a clump of clover.

"Let's go," Logan said. He trotted his horse through the gate and I followed. "I'm going to be the point and you can be the drag."

"Huh? I don't speak cowboy!"

"Sorry. I'll be riding up front and you ride in the back and watch for stragglers."

"Okay," I said, slowing Mazy and letting the cattle follow Logan down the driveway. They fell into a quiet rhythm, plodding along as if they knew where they were headed, and Logan led them across the road and into the open field across from Triple M.

For three hours, I rode along at the back of the herd, listening to the cattle's hooves rustling in the tall grass and the occasional moo of protest when Jane or Lara got too close. Logan rode back to check on me every so often but he had to stay in the front to lead. I sighed with relief when Logan turned and headed toward me. The sun was beating down on us and sweat trickled under my cowboy hat. The temperature was probably in the low eighties, but it felt so much warmer.

"Hungry?" he asked. "Want to stop for lunch?"

"I'm starving."

"Okay, let's dismount by those trees and let the cattle graze."

Logan cantered up to a clump of scraggly fir trees and whistled at Jane and Lara. The dogs circled around the cattle and lumped them into a rough circle. The cattle began chewing up clumps of grass and a couple of them trickled a few yards away to a tiny stream.

I dismounted from Mazy's back and started unclipping the packs of food Logan had attached to my saddle.

Logan brought over two bottles of water and a blanket. He spread the checkered black-and-red blanket in the grass and I put the bags on the blanket. The trees shaded us as we sat down next to each other, legs stretched in front of us. I took off my hat and Logan removed his. Sweat darkened his hair to a golden amber shade.

"You doing okay?" he asked.

"I'm fine. Better than I thought." I pulled out two wrapped peanut butter and jelly sandwiches. I dug into mine. "I was worried that I would be more of a hindrance than help." I'd finished half my sandwich before Logan opened his. I gulped my bottle of water and poured some into my hand to splash on my face.

"You're not slowing us down at all. You've been great." Logan reached over and touched my cheek. "It's going to get a little harder soon. We will start going uphill, so you're going to be leaning forward."

"Okay," I said. "I can do it."

"I have no doubt." Logan leaned over and kissed me. His lips were soft on mine. I put a hand on his neck and kissed him deeper.

One of the horses let out a neigh that echoed, and I jumped, almost biting Logan's lip.

"Sorry! So sorry!" I said. I looked at the horses and Mazy was swishing her tail and her head was high. "Mazy scared me!"

"Bad girl," Logan called to Mazy. "Very bad!"

I laughed. "Poor Mazy," I said, giggling.

Logan looked over at me, watching me with soft eyes.

"You're beautiful," he said.

I smiled, looking down. "Thank you." I looked back up at him. "How far are we going tonight?" I asked. I finished my sandwich and opened a box of raisins.

"We should be able to get about half an hour away from the grazing ground. We'll ride until just before sunset and then we'll set up camp. If you're okay, it would be a good idea to keep going now."

"Sure," I said.

Logan put his hand on my back and rubbed slowly up and down. I looked over the ankle-high grass at the cattle grazing calmly. Logan had removed the bridles from the horses, trusting them not to wander off, and they were resting with one hoof cocked a few yards away. Blackheart Mountain looked *huge* from this angle.

"Relax for five more minutes with me?" I asked.

"Okay," he said, smiling.

Easing myself onto my back, I looked at the puffy clouds filling the blue sky. The shade had helped me cool down, but my jeans clung to my thighs. Too bad you couldn't ride in shorts. I patted the blanket with my hand and Logan flopped onto his back beside me.

"Pretty perfect, huh?" he asked.

"Almost," I said, raising myself up on one elbow and leaning over to look in his face. "We got interrupted before."

"Yes, we did."

He smiled and reached out to touch my hand. I leaned over him. We kissed until I was giddy. Resting on our sides, we looked at each other. I closed my eyes and relaxed in the shade.

While Logan had his eyes shut, I looked over at him. A wave of sadness hit—surprising me. It occurred to me that no matter how little thought I had given toward leaving Lost Springs, it was inevitably going to happen. How was I ever going to leave Logan? *Stop*, I told myself. *Be here. Now.* I took a deep breath and refocused my mind. After a few minutes, I let Logan pull me to my feet and we got ready to hit the trail again.

CHAPTER TWENTY-THREE

Horses are partners, not pets.

With a grateful sigh, I dismounted from Mazy and slipped off her bridle. "You're so good," I said to her. She leaned into my pat and huffed. I put a halter and lead line on her and tied her to a tree branch while Logan did the same to LG.

"You okay with this spot for tonight?" Logan asked, releasing the small pot and the bags of food from his saddle.

"This is great!" I said, looking around.

We'd reached our campsite for the night. We were within closing distance of the grazing ground, but it would be dark in a few hours and Logan didn't want to get stuck somewhere. He was afraid, too, that the horses would step in a pothole. The climb to get here had been exhausting. I hugged Mazy and then LG. They had been rock stars.

After Logan and I had left our lunch spot, the land started to go up an incline and we had to lean forward the entire ride.

I'd concentrated on the fact that we were going uphill and spent most of the time grasping the saddle horn or Mazy's mane. My stomach muscles were already sore from clenching and sitting in that odd position. Logan, Jane, and Lara had never faltered and they had kept the cattle moving easily up the gradual slant.

Logan signaled the dogs to round the cattle into a circle.

"Want to gather firewood or get the fishing gear?" he called to me.

"Firewood is fine," I said.

I started scanning the ground for dry twigs and small logs. We were in a flat part of the mountain with a rushing creek a few yards away. Logan had said the clearing was a frequent stop for other ranchers making this trek. There was a circle of rocks in the center of the clearing with a charred spot in the middle. Large, looming trees surrounded us and the only way up the mountain was a narrow path on the far side of the campground. I quickly gathered an armload of kindling and dumped it in the campfire circle.

Logan brought two buckets of water from the creek and set them near the fire pit, just in case.

"You up for fishing?" he asked as he untangled fishing wire and put together two crude poles from his bag. "It's okay if you need to rest."

"Totally up for it," I said, taking a pole and finishing threading the line. "What kind of fish are in the creek?"

Logan put lures on our hooks and we made our way to the river. "Mostly trout and a few cutthroats," he said. "They have a red slash on their throat. Ever fished before?"

I took a careful stance on the rocky riverbed and peered into the clear water.

"I've fished," I said. "Ocean fishing with my parents down by the Florida Keys. We rented a boat to catch swordfish and after eight hours, my dad finally caught one." I tossed my line into the water and huffed. "I was so annoyed that it wasn't on my line!"

"I bet," Logan said. "I've never even been to the ocean before." He cast his line and trolled it slowly through the water.

I kept my attention on my line as the bobber started to wiggle. "If you stare at the horizon long enough, you think you're looking at the end of the world."

"It sounds great," he said, "and you've got a bite!"

My bobber disappeared under the water and I gave my pole a couple of tugs and began reeling in my line.

"First fish!" I said, catching Logan's eye.

"Damn." He shook his head. "You beat me saddling the horses this morning and now this." He jiggled his line hopefully, but nothing was attached.

"Ha," I said, reeling the fish out of the water and holding it up for Logan to see. "What is it?"

"That's a brook trout," Logan said, running his finger along the fish's red stomach. The fish wriggled its dark gray body, which was spotted with bluish dots. "Good eating."

I removed the hook from the fish's mouth and tossed it in the water bucket Logan placed beside me.

"Your turn now," I said to Logan. "You better get the next one."

A tiny bead of sweat popped against Logan's forehead and he reeled in his line and tossed it back in the water. "Now I'm embarrassed," he said.

"Sorry." I rubbed his shoulder. "Girl of all trades, I guess."

Logan's bobber sank beneath the water and he reeled furiously on his line. "My manhood rests on this fish," he said. He walked so close to the creek's edge, he almost stepped into the water. He didn't take his gaze from the bobber. With a tug, he lifted the fish out of the water and pumped his fist in the air.

"Nice one," I said, pulling the line over so I could look at the fish. "You definitely got the cooler one." I pointed to the red slash on the fish's neck. Logan's pink-and-yellow cutthroat was twice the size of my trout.

"That's plenty to eat," Logan said. "I've got soup and chocolate chip cookies, too."

"Sounds good to me."

We headed for the campsite and Logan started the fire. While he cleaned the fish, I cooked a can of vegetable soup on the fire. Logan tossed the fish in a pan and within minutes, they were sizzled to golden-brown perfection.

In silence, we hungrily dug into our food. We were eating fresh fish on a mountain. No cell phones, no street noise, no parents, and no hiding our being together. It was just us and I loved it.

"Did you like it?" Logan asked, wiping his mouth with a napkin.

"Um, it was gone in three seconds. Loved it. Fish sticks are dead to me."

We rinsed our plates in the river and I froze. A sound came from the woods that sounded like a grunt and a moan.

"Logan," I said in a whisper. "What was that?" I stepped closer to him and put my plate on the ground.

"I don't know," he said. "Go back to the tent and I'll go take a look."

"No way!" I grabbed his arm. "You're not going to 'take a look' at anything."

He stared at me and his mouth was pressed into a thin line. "Brie, it could be a bear. Or a mountain lion. Go to the tent and I'll take the gun and look." His voice was low and almost commanding.

"I'm not staying alone," I argued. "I'm coming with you."

Logan tilted his head and his eyes narrowed for a second as if he was going to argue with me. "Fine," he said, "but if I tell you to run, swear you will."

"Promise." The sound came from the trees again. It was louder and longer this time. Logan jogged to the tent and pulled a rifle out of his oversize bag.

"It's safe, don't worry," he said. "I've been shooting with my dad since I was four." I looked at the gun, almost stunned by it. I'd only seen guns on TV and the movies. I didn't want to shoot anything.

Logan held the gun down by his side and we walked forward into the woods. Every branch or leaf I crunched made me jump a little. *Not a cougar, not a cougar*, I chanted in my head. We walked a few yards and didn't see or hear anything.

"I think it's gone," I said.

"Just a few more feet," he said, looking around us. "I need to be sure before we go back to camp."

We maneuvered through the dense forest and I tried to tread lightly on the dirt path.

Something moved in the tiny clearing up ahead.

"Logan," I said.

Logan raised his rifle and shook his head. He waved at me to stay where I was and he took a few steps forward. I felt like I was going to throw up.

I watched Logan's back and tried to make out the shape writhing on the ground. Logan took a few more steps and then his shoulders relaxed under his thin blue T-shirt. He let out an audible breath and lowered the rifle. When he turned to me, he put a finger to his lips.

Come here, he mouthed.

I tiptoed up behind him and looked at the ground in front of us. A black mare was lying on the ground, drenched in sweat and struggling. She let out several groans—clearly from pain. Her enormous stomach ballooned upward when she rolled onto her side.

"What's the matter?" I whispered to Logan.

"She's in labor," Logan said, not taking his eyes off the horse. "Something's wrong."

My stomach twisted. "Can we help her?"

The mare's heavy breathing filled the clearing, and the short grass around her had been flattened as if she'd stood and changed spots many times.

"We could try," he said, looking at me. "I've helped birth a couple of foals, but she's a wild mustang. She's not likely to let us near her."

I shook my head. We couldn't walk away and let the horse suffer or worse. "We have to try."

Logan put down the rifle and we took a few steps forward. The mare heard us the second we neared her and she lifted her head. Her black mane was stuck to her neck with bits of dirt and sweat. She rolled her eyes until the whites showed and Logan and I stopped.

"Easy, girl," Logan said softly, crouching down. I followed his lead and got down on my knees. "It's okay," he crooned to her.

She flared her nostrils and her sides heaved from her heavy breathing.

"Shhh," I said to her. "We're going to help you."

I inched closer and reached my hand toward her. "Brie," Logan warned, "she could bite."

My shoes scuffed the dirt as I crawled on my knees and got closer to the mare. I didn't let myself look her in the eye, so I didn't threaten her. She grunted and rolled her eyes as I got closer.

"It's okay," I said soothingly. "You're going to be fine." I kept my eyes on her and didn't even notice Logan crawling up beside me.

A contraction gripped her stomach and I forced myself not to look away. I placed a tentative hand on her swollen side and with a shuddering sigh of defeat, she dropped her head and rested.

Slowly, I inched up by her head and stroked her neck while Logan eased his way down by her tail and looked.

"What's wrong?" I said, stroking the mare and watching for a sign that she would snap at me or try to kick Logan.

He positioned himself far enough away from a possible flailing hoof, but close enough to see.

"The hooves are peeking through, but the foal must be stuck. She's probably been in labor for a while."

"We need to do something," I said. White foam spotted the mare's chest as contractions gripped her and she struggled to push out the foal.

Logan motioned for me to step away from her neck and stand by him. I squinted at the tiny black hooves peeking out and saw that with each contraction, the foal wasn't moving. "Is it . . ." It hurt to say it. "Alive?"

"I don't know," Logan said. "I'm going to help tug it out. I've done it before and as long as she doesn't struggle too much, I can do it. She *will* die if we don't help her to expel the foal."

"Are you sure you can do it?" I didn't want to hurt the mare or foal. He nodded and took off his shirt. "I don't want you to get hurt, either."

"I'll be okay. The legs are going to be slippery, so I need something to grab them with," he said, holding his T-shirt and inching closer to the mare. "And we've got to wrap her tail with something."

I took off my hoodie and gave it to him.

"Watch her legs while I do this," he said. I glued my eyes to the mare's back legs and was ready to yell if she moved to kick Logan. But the contractions had exhausted her. She didn't even try to lift her head to glance back at Logan. He quickly wrapped her tail as best he could with my red jacket and then covered his hands with his T-shirt.

"What should I do?" I asked. The mare's breathing was heavier by the second, and darkness started to bathe the woods.

"Sit by her head and keep her calm. If she starts to struggle, keep talking to her."

I nodded silently and took my position.

"When she has her next contraction," Logan said, "I'm going to tug very gently. The foal should slip out."

"I'm ready," I said. I put my hands on the mare's neck and tried to massage her. She let out a breath and another contraction rippled her stomach. Her four socks were dusty, but the small star on her forehead gleamed in the dusk.

"Hang on," Logan said, his voice tight and his forehead wrinkled. He took his T-shirt-wrapped hands and gripped the foal's legs. He watched the mare's stomach and when he thought the time looked right, he gave a firm but gentle tug on the foal's legs. The mare pushed harder than she had before and I rose up on my knees to see what was going on.

A tiny black nose emerged and a face started to slip out. Logan gave the foal's legs one more tug. The mare lifted her head as a strong contraction pushed the foal out up to its withers and then it slid onto the ground in a wet black mass.

In seconds, the foal writhed and snorted to clear its lungs. It was solid black without a speck of white.

"Oh," I said, biting my lip to keep from crying. But a couple of tears splashed onto the ground.

The foal was gorgeous even covered in the birth sac. The mare grunted and made whickering sounds to her foal. She gathered her legs under her and craned her neck to see the baby.

"Come on," Logan said to me.

He unwrapped the hoodie and motioned for me to step away from the mare and foal.

"We can't leave her now," I protested. "Don't we have to clean the umbilical cord or something?"

"We did more than enough," he said. "She's wild and she's probably had a few foals before this one. She can take it from here." The mare lurched forward and started to stand.

Logan motioned for me to follow him and we stood maybe ten or fifteen feet away.

"Can we watch from here for a few minutes?" I said.

"No," Logan said, shaking his head. "We need to get out of the clearing and back in the woods. She's still wild and she might feel threatened if we're too close to her foal."

"What if we watch from the woods for just a few seconds?" I asked.

Logan tilted his head. "Two minutes max," he said.

We both got down on our knees in some brush and dirt. I peeked through the leaves at the mare and her foal. It was getting darker by the minute, but I kept my eyes glued to the mom and newborn.

"You were amazing," I murmured to Logan as I watched the mare struggle to her feet and begin to lick her squirming foal. The foal snorted and it shook its entire body. The hair on its back stuck up in wet clumps.

"No, you were the amazing one," he said, kissing my cheek. "You saved a horse tonight."

"*We* did."

If I was honest with myself, after seeing this foal's birth, something had shifted in me. I realized that I hadn't cared about the horses as much as Logan did. I appreciated their beauty, and was grateful to them for the strength they had given Logan, but I hadn't been as emotionally invested in them as I thought I was. Even after all the research that I'd done.

Logan deeply cared for these animals, and his love for them made me see something in the mustangs. Something more than just horses. They were special, wild, and untouched by what was going on around them. But they were about to be moved, like I'd been a dozen times, and they had to go somewhere safe. My dad wasn't the one who could provide that for them if he went rogue and didn't wait for the BLM to step in.

I looked at the pair of horses, and the foal didn't waste any time attempting to struggle to its wobbly legs. It made several attempts to stand and finally locked its knees and shook as it fought to remain standing.

"It's a boy," Logan said, peeking sideways. He wrapped an arm around me as we stood together. The shadows began to fall across the woods.

"He's perfect," I said to Logan. "I think I get it now."

"Get what?" he said, shifting his arm around my waist so he could look at me.

The colt took a few tentative steps toward his mother before crumpling in a heap of legs. The mare nudged his back and seemed to encourage him to try again.

"I get why you and your dad are crazy about these horses. I guess I never really thought about what happened to animals when my dad takes over the land."

"Your dad's not the worst the town has seen, believe me," Logan said as we watched the foal take his first successful steps and try to nurse. "We had someone shooting horses in the middle of the day just because they trampled his crops."

"Oh, God. Did he get arrested?"

Logan nodded. "Served forty-five days on a plea bargain. My dad was furious with that sentence."

"I bet," I said. "Since your dad's injured, what's he going to do about the horses?"

"He can't do anything. But I can. Let's go back to camp and I'll tell you about it."

We turned to give the mother and foal privacy. Logan assured me they would be fine now and when we left, the foal was energetically nursing and swishing his wisp of a tail while the exhausted mare looked on.

I couldn't let Dad hurt the horses or move them where they weren't wanted. If I knew Dad like I thought I did, he wasn't going to wait for the BLM or anyone. I couldn't let that happen. Now this was *my* project. Mine and Logan's.

We wound our way through the woods to the campsite. It was almost black out, except for what was left of the fire.

"Spill," I said the second we got back to camp.

CHAPTER TWENTY-FOUR

A cowboy who says he's never been throwed ain't
telling the truth.

The campfire crackled when it hit a bit of green wood. A few sparks soared into the night. My face was warmed by the fire.

"Pam met with the BLM?" I asked, sure that I'd just heard Logan wrong.

We sat together next to each other on a weathered log. Our campfire spot had stones that made up a fire pit, and the ground nearby was free of grass and worn down to dirt.

Logan smiled. "I know—it's surreal for me, too. She had put in a favor for someone that she knew on the BLM board. She didn't tell me about the meeting because she wanted to make sure she was actually seen and they approved her plan."

"Which is?"

"Pam is giving the BLM thirty-five hundred acres of land plus an old barn to use. She wants the property to be a sanctuary for the mustangs that are near us. It's up to me to herd them to her land. The herd will still be free with that much room and they won't know that I'll be around making sure they're safe."

"So on all that land, they won't sense that they've been caught?" I asked.

Logan shook his head. "Doubtful. Roughly, they'll have seven miles to roam. This is such a dream scenario, Brie."

I gazed at the campfire, quiet. I tried to process what Logan had just told me, but it was too much.

"I don't know what to say. I can't even process it! And Pam can really take the whole herd? How will she afford the upkeep of the land and stuff?"

"You're right, it's a lot," Logan said. "Maybe we can break up the herd eventually . . . A few years ago a town not too far away started a private humane society and took stray cats and dogs off the streets and adopted them to new homes." He played with a stick and snapped off bits of the twig and tossed them into the fire.

"Is that possible for us?" I asked. "How hard would it be to tame some of the horses? Can you adopt out any of them? Like gentle them and hold an event?"

Logan looked at the stars and then back at me. "Depends. Some, like the older ones, probably won't ever let anyone ride them. But the young colts and fillies have a chance at being gentled. Doesn't mean they could be handled right away."

"We have to try. Logan, I can't let my dad's problem with your dad keep us from doing this. We'll hide it as long as we can. Hopefully, by the time Dad *does* finds out, we'll be so far along that he'll just let me keep going. We can do this. I know it."

Logan looked at me for a long time. "Let's get the bedrolls unpacked and we'll keep thinking," he finally said.

We left the fire burning and Logan erected a small red tent while I washed my face. I copied Logan as he released the ties that bound the rolled-up blankets and at the end of the blanket, a pillow popped out.

"How'd you get that so tight?" I asked. I couldn't even tell a pillow had been in the roll.

"Cowboy secret," Logan said. "Maybe I'll tell you sometime."

He grinned and we walked back out to the fire. It was completely dark now and the clear sky sparkled with thousands of glittery stars. I slipped my hand into Logan's.

"Ready to put out the fire and get in the tent?" He watched me swat at a mosquito that buzzed around my ear.

"Please."

Logan flicked on the battery-powered lantern and carefully doused the fire with a bucket of creek water. The horses slept a few yards away and the dogs watched over the cattle.

Nerves mixed with excitement stirred in my stomach.

Logan inched closer to me and tugged on the end of my sloppy ponytail. "We'll figure this out."

"I know."

Logan took off his hat and kissed my cheek, my nose, and my mouth. I kissed him back and wrapped an arm around his neck. We were in a tent with no parents for miles. It wasn't like I hadn't already thought about tonight. I wasn't worried for a second that Logan would be anything less than the perfect gentleman he always was.

He stayed outside of the tent while I'd changed into PJs—a thermal black V-neck and peach-colored leggings. I'd *agonized* over what pajamas to bring. Amy helped me go through my stash of pajamas. I'd tried on practically all of them and Amy had vetoed every single pair. She'd dragged me to a strip mall just outside of town and took me to a clothing store for people who lived and worked in the cold.

I'd balked at flannel and turned down thermal. Amy had shrugged and picked out two pairs of PJs that she liked. She paid for them and tossed the bag into my lap once we were back in her car.

"I'm *not* wearing this! Amy, I have to be *cute*! They still have the tags on them, so let's go get your money back." I'd started out of the car, stopping when she called my name.

"If you don't at least take a pair of those with you, then you have no alibi," she'd threatened.

Now I thanked Amy. I was going to buy her breakfast for this. Even in thermal PJs, I was chilly.

I left Logan alone to change. By the time I finished brushing my teeth, Logan was beside me—toothbrush in hand.

"You're in thermal, too!" I said. He was in a red thermal shirt and black pants.

"Yes, because it's cold out," Logan said, shaking his head at me. "You are oddly excited about my thermal pajamas."

"It's freezing out here," I said. "I can't believe how fast the temperature dropped."

He nodded, his mouth full of toothpaste. He tilted his head toward the tent. I hugged my arms to my body and took him up on his silent suggestion. While I waited for him to come into the warm tent, I checked my phone. No messages. But also no bars. *Please don't let anything happen that makes Mom or Dad need to call me*, I thought. Yawning, I put the phone away. It was barely nine and I was exhausted.

The tent doors flapped open and Logan crawled inside.

"It *is* cold," he said, zipping up the tent's door flaps.

"I bet I could distract you," I said. I grabbed his shirt collar, pulling him toward me. We starting kissing and I forgot all about my PJs.

He traced his fingers down my neck as we kissed. I had pictured this moment a thousand times before. All the time that we had been forced apart, I'd thought about kissing him all night long. I'd even shared some of my make-out session daydreams with Amy. I'd been putting on lip balm a zillion times a day trying to get pillowy soft lips.

"Your lips are so soft," Logan murmured as if on cue.

We kissed for what could have been five minutes or five hours. Finally, Logan lay down on top of his blanket and rolled onto his side so he faced me.

I scooted closer to him, pulling my pillow with me.

"This is the best trip ever," Logan said. He ran his hand up and down my arm and stopped to brush a stray hair from my face.

"It's definitely up there for me, too," I said.

Logan dropped his jaw. "You wound me. What trip topped this? I want to know."

"Oh, it was a trip with Mom and Dad," I started. Logan's eyebrows went together. "I got out of the car to . . . what was it?" I pretended to forget as I watched Logan squirm.

"Oh, right, I got out to photograph bison! This jerk revved his engine at me and I went over to his truck, ready to scream at him." I looked into Logan's eyes. "I took one look at him and he was way too hot for me to do that. So I called him a jerk instead."

"That was a great story," Logan said. "I'd like to hear exactly how hot this 'jerk' was."

"Shut up!" I said, kicking at him with my socked foot.

Logan picked up his cell phone. "Dispatcher, please send an officer to a tent on the mountains immediately. I'm being beaten up by my girlfriend."

"Logan! You big baby!" I carefully kicked him again and used my free arm to lightly punch his chest.

"I'm glad you think that's so funny," Logan said. In a quick move, one I barely saw, he had pinned down my hand and had his leg slung over mine. I wriggled and fought to get free.

"Logan!" I said, trying not to laugh. "Let me go! You totally ambushed me."

He laughed. That laugh that was deep in his chest and made me smile.

"You thought *that* was an ambush? Oh, Brie Carter. I'll have to show you what a real ambush is."

Logan shot forward, keeping my leg and hand pinned, and kissed my forehead. Then he quickly gave my right cheek a barely there kiss. He kissed the top of my nose, my other cheek, my chin, my mouth—all in rapid succession. I was laughing so hard that I was crying.

"*That* was an ambush," Logan said. He removed his leg and freed my hand.

I wiped under my eyes, thanking the makeup gods that I had used waterproof mascara today.

I rolled onto my stomach and looked at him. He had a satisfied smile on his face. He looked so young with hands beneath his head and elbows bent.

"Look at yourself," I said. "You think you won. You just wait."

"I hope I don't have to wait for this," Logan said. He pushed himself up onto his elbow and put a gentle hand behind my head.

His lips touched mine and I felt as if I'd finally found my place in the world.

CHAPTER TWENTY-FIVE

Talk slowly, think quickly.

Before the sun came up, Logan and I were dressed and had the horses saddled. I had woken up with Logan snuggling me. I hadn't wanted to wake him, but when I sat up, he rolled over and smiled at me. I grinned at him—his messy hair and sleepy eyes. As we had coffee, we watched the sun rise.

We crossed the creek and started the rest of the trip up Blackheart Mountain with the cattle carefully picking their way up the rocky incline. Logan led the herd from the front and I resumed my position in the back. I kept playing over every minute from last night in my head.

We had talked for hours about our plans for the horses and when we would throw a fundraiser. Logan wanted to work fast and get the horses moved. Once we got them settled, we would petition the town to let us host the event at the end of July. That date would also be in our favor because Kate would be coming to visit sometime in July. I'd never needed sister backup more than I would then. I wished that I could be hopeful that Dad would be pacified with the horses off his land and wouldn't care that I had been involved with moving them.

Logan figured that since it was mid-May, we would have enough time to get the horses off Dad's land well before his July first deadline, then have some time to look over the horses and make decisions about what each horse needed. It was also soon enough that we would hopefully raise some income to pay for the horses' keep.

Logan didn't think the horses would be ready for any kind of adoption event until early next year, so we settled on January as our target date. With Dad planning to move likely in April of next year, early in the year felt like a safe target.

After we brainstormed and filled a paper pad with ideas, we cuddled. I'd slid my blanket closer to Logan. He draped an arm over my side and I didn't have any memories after that.

The steep hill started to level off and Logan twisted around, pulling me out of my thoughts.

"Hold on to the horn. This part is steep. Over this next hill is the pasture."

"Okay!" I called. I leaned forward and gripped the Western saddle's horn with my hands. Mazy lurched forward and I squeezed my legs tighter around the saddle. "Should we get off and walk?" I asked.

"Too dangerous! Stay on!"

The cattle started to slow and the path up the mountain's side became narrower. I kept my eyes forward and didn't let myself look over the path's side into the steep drop-off into the trees below. Mazy's hoof slipped on a rock and she stumbled. Tightening my grip on the horn, I gritted my teeth. After a few more excruciating minutes, the incline started to level off and I sighed with relief. My death grip on the saddle relaxed and I leaned into a normal position.

Logan let Lara and Jane herd the cattle into the field and he cantered LG up to me.

"Interesting, huh? You'd never guess there was a flat plain after climbing as long as we did."

The flat ground had a creek rushing on the right side and lines of trees that would provide shade for the cattle in the hottest days of summer.

"No kidding," I said. "I thought I'd die back there!"

I grinned and watched the cattle eagerly spread out in the thick grass. Lara and Jane trotted back over to us and they seemed to know their job was done.

"It'll be much easier going down," he said. "Now that we don't have the cattle, we can take a different path. We'll get home quicker."

We plopped into the grass and started munching granola bars. The cattle settled down to graze while Jane and Lara rested in the shade.

"I survived my first cattle drive," I said, raising my bottle of water.

"And lost your greenhorn status," Logan said, clunking his bottle against mine.

CHAPTER TWENTY-SIX

You can take the cowboy out of the country, but you can't take the country out of the cowboy.

Hours later, Logan and I had made it safely back home and I'd raced through my back door just before six on Sunday evening. Mom, Dad, and I had a long dinner at the quaint new Italian place in the next town over.

They asked me a few questions about my night at Amy's. I successfully lied my way through it, feeling a twinge of guilt—particularly after my dad told me that things were well in hand at the job site and, if I wanted, I could take tomorrow off to hang with Amy again.

When we got home I launched myself onto my bed. I grabbed my phone and blinked, forcing my eyes open. I was so, so tired. After Logan had dropped me off at Amy's for my bike, he headed to work a shift in the field. He had superhuman powers.

I typed a text and sent it to Logan.

I can't stop thinking abt the trip. Thank you. <3

One message to Amy.

Will tell you everything! Can't wait but too tired. Talk tmrw! xx

When I woke up the next morning I went straight to the bathroom for ibuprofen. I had sore muscles on top of sore muscles from the ride.

Mom and Dad were both gone. Dad was at work and Mom had left a note that she was out scouting locations for a new set of photos.

I jumped on my bike, glanced at Logan's directions, and headed to Pam's. Logan was meeting me there and we were going to explain our plan to Pam. We needed her okay for the fundraiser and for a future adoption event.

Logan was waiting for me atop LG and holding Mazy's reins.

He dismounted to pull me gently to him, push back my cowboy hat, and kiss me.

"Hi," I said, my tone almost two octaves higher than usual.

Logan kissed me again.

"I'll give you a quick tour," he said.

He handed me Mazy's reins and I mounted. We did a quick loop around the near parts of the property. I fell in love with it.

Pam's place couldn't have been more perfect. She had a small farmhouse a few miles outside of town. She didn't have any pets aside from a couple of dogs, and there were several areas for us to work with the horses—two round pens and a fenced arena.

"That's where we need to get them," Logan said, pointing to a silver gate. I counted nine pencil-thin wires that were attached to wooden poles.

"What kind of fencing is that?" I asked him.

"It's called high-tensile fencing. Basically, you can have as many or as few wires as you want. The more wire—the higher the cost. You have to weigh the cost, though, against the idea of your horses, cattle—whatever—escaping by jumping the fence if the wire is too low or wiggling under it if the wires aren't placed right."

"So that fencing goes all around Pam's property?"

Logan chuckled. "Yep. Basically, once we've moved the mustangs, they won't be able to cross it to get back to their old grounds. They'll be safe. You're going to get a chance to see that for yourself." He laughed again.

"What's so funny?" I edged Mazy closer to LG so I could swat his arm.

"Pam hasn't used that land in a couple of years. So before we usher any horses into this space, you and I will need to ride the entire pasture fence line to check for broken or twisted wire."

I dropped the knotted reins on Mazy's neck. "You must be dreading spending all that time together while we do that," I said, trying to look serious.

Logan laughed again and tilted his head down, shaking it slowly. He did something to LG to make the gelding sidestep even closer to Mazy until my legs were almost against his. He let go of his reins, too, and leaned over, cupping a hand behind my head, guiding me close to him. I didn't need any encouragement.

The second our lips touched, a warm tingle started from my lips and worked its way down my body. LG and Mazy didn't move as our kisses became almost frantic. I tossed Logan's hat to the ground so I could touch his soft hair.

I pulled away from Logan and he stared at me, his chest moving up and down beneath his red T-shirt. I loved him in red. I slid my foot out of the right stirrup and swung my leg over Mazy's neck in a not-so-graceful fashion.

I got situated and reached my hands out to Logan.

"You want to kiss more?" he asked, winking at me. "I thought you were going to try to ride sidesaddle in that Western one."

I smiled. "I thought about it. But there's this really cute boy that I'd like to make out with instead."

Logan locked eyes with me and I could *feel* it—he wanted to kiss me.

I leaned toward him, balancing carefully on the saddle. It wasn't as easy as I'd thought to sit like this.

Logan ran his fingers through his sandy-blond hair, and dismounted to pick up his hat. He walked to my side.

I leaned down to him. "Before I let you kiss me again," I said, "you have to tell me what was so funny."

"Oh, right," Logan said, laughing. "I almost forgot about it. You fit in so well here that I sometimes forget that you aren't a local. Today, we're just checking out the house, the pens, and the immediate surroundings of the property. When we check the full fence line and there are two people, one person goes to the right and the other to the left. It would take way longer than necessary to go together." He looked at me. "Not that I don't want to ride with you," he spit out superfast.

I giggled. "Stop. I get it. Separate. When we do this, Mazy and I will be here waiting for you and LG to finish."

"Oh, really?"

We bantered back and forth as we rode. Our conversation was always flowing. Easy. Much like the early time I'd spent with Logan—we could also ride in silence and be happy. I never had to rack my brain for something to say.

We rode Mazy and LG down the driveway and I tried to picture the mustangs here. I wondered if they would like it. Would it become home to them? Or would they pine for the land around the job site? I felt a twinge of sympathy for what the horses were about to go through.

"We could use that arena for gentling the young ones," I said, nodding to one of the orange metal round pens near a bigger arena. A few yards away from the arena, a large barn with single stalls was just right to house the horses in extreme weather.

Pam had given us permission to come over any time we wanted. Before we left, we checked all the gates and walked part of the surrounding fence line to make sure none of the fences were broken or weak. Logan and I agreed to split up and each go in opposite directions on horseback to check *all* the fencing the next time we visited.

"Let's ride to the tack store and see if we can catch Pam there," Logan said. "Sound good?"

"Let's go!" I tapped my heels against Mazy and she surged into a smooth canter. We passed Logan and LG. "See you there!" I said.

"Hey! Aw, you asked for it!" Logan called.

Giggling, I let Mazy canter a little faster and hoofbeats pounded the grass behind me.

Logan and LG caught up to us and he smirked. "See *you* there!" he said. He let out the reins and LG switched to a gallop, leaving Mazy behind.

"Go get them, girl," I said, letting her charge after the boys.

Logan and I laughed almost the entire ride to Pam's.

We eased the horses to a walk for the last bit of the ride so they could cool off. Logan and I tied them in the shade behind Pam's store and he opened the door for me as we headed inside.

Pam was near her rack of Western saddles and speaking horse language that I didn't understand to a customer. She saw Logan and me and nodded a hello. We both smiled back and let her finish.

"Hi, guys," Pam said. She closed the cash register and flicked a bit of horsehair off the counter.

"We just came from your place, actually," Logan said. "I wanted to show everything to Brie."

"It's so amazing," I said. "I can't thank you enough for letting us use your space."

Pam smiled. "It's not as if you're using it to throw a giant party. What you kids are doing is a good thing."

"About that," Logan said. He took off his hat and placed it on the counter. "We have something to ask you."

Pam looked at Logan for a moment, then glanced at me. "All right," she said. "Let me hear it."

Logan and I talked Pam through our idea of herding the horses into her large pasture, holding back a few young ones, and working with them all fall. We would hold a fundraiser in July to raise money to cover the mustangs' general care. Next January, we would throw an adoption event—that is, if the town council approves our fundraiser.

"I'm going to stop you on one point," Pam said. "Logan, you know what Januarys are like here. You also know that it is going to take time to gentle these horses. I don't want to see any of them rushed off to a new home only to come back because they weren't ready to go in the first place."

"I agree," Logan said, nodding.

"I want you to wait until you've had the horses for a year before you hold any sort of adoption event. You can hold it next July," Pam said. "That's the first part. Now . . ." Pam looked at me. "Your dad has no idea that you are doing this with Logan, correct?"

I nodded. "Yes."

"Do you really understand, Brie, that these horses are *wild*?" Pam asked.

"I do—I know," I said. "I don't have any experience training horses, but Logan does. I want him to teach me."

Pam relaxed her stance. She looked at us for a few seconds and then nodded. "Okay, on one condition."

"Anything!" I said, squeezing Logan's hand.

Pam leaned over the counter to be closer to Logan and me as a customer stepped into the store. "The first time either of your fathers ask if you're doing something with the horses, you tell them. No lies. Just the truth. Got it?"

Logan and I looked at each other and then back at Pam. "Got it," we said in unison.

"We'll start rounding up the horses tomorrow," Logan said to Pam. She nodded, patted his shoulder, and walked over to help the customer.

"We're really doing this!" I said to Logan as we headed out of the tack shop.

Logan smiled. "Getting Pam on board was big. Now we've got to catch the horses. It would be best to move them in a quiet environment." He slipped his arm around my shoulder. "In case the horses are hanging around your dad's site tomorrow, is he going to be there?"

I thought for a minute. "Actually, no, I don't think so. He's supposed to be out of town meeting partners, and the guys have the day off."

"So, tomorrow it is," Logan said. "I'll bring Mazy and LG down by your driveway tomorrow morning. Then we'll ride over to Pam's to give the place one last quick look before we start herding."

"Anything I should know about moving horses that might be different from working with cattle?" I asked as we mounted our horses and moved them close together so we could hold hands.

"They're definitely smarter. And faster. One or two may get loose, but the trick is not to leave the main herd and dash off for one horse. They'll start to break apart if they have the chance. We want to keep them moving and if they want to gallop full speed—let them and it will tire them out. We'll go back for any stragglers after securing the majority of the herd."

Mazy and LG walked quietly and we reached Pam's place, where I'd left my bike.

"Tomorrow then," I said. I leaned over and kissed him. I dismounted and handed him Mazy's reins.

Logan waved and I watched him and the horses disappear back into the field. I'd have to double-check that there wouldn't be anything going on at the job site tomorrow. But what if we couldn't find the mustangs? We had *very* few chances to catch them since they had decided to visit the job site more and more. Our windows of time were small and limited by my dad.

Once I got home I started making a mental to-do list: contact someone about running a fundraiser, browse websites on taming wild mustangs, and call Amy and let her in on the plan. Everything was going to start happening tomorrow. This was big and risky and dangerous. I would be working side by side with Logan. I knew that as long as I followed his lead, I would be safe.

I tried to walk off the nerves that settled in my stomach. There were a lot of components to this plan. One of the biggest? Not getting caught even breathing the same air as Logan. Jack was still an "enemy" to Dad, and that meant Dad's dislike of McCoy men didn't stop with Jack.

CHAPTER TWENTY-SEVEN

Don't squat with your spurs on.

Early the next morning, Logan and I rode Mazy and LG to Pam's to give the place one last look before heading off to find the horses. Last night, I had casually asked Dad about his plans for today. He didn't give me much, but I knew he wasn't going to go to work until late afternoon—if at all—today.

Logan and I turned the horses away from Pam's and led them into a slow canter toward the job site. A couple of Pam's dogs ran behind us.

"No," I said to them. "Stay home."

"Let them come with us," Logan said. "They might be helpful."

As we got closer, it struck me how soon the hotel popped into view. I guess I hadn't been paying much attention to how quickly the job had progressed.

We reached the site within a few minutes and carefully walked down the driveway as we looked for any sign that someone from Dad's crew was here. But everything was quiet. The trailer was dark, none of the machines were moving, and no vehicles were in sight.

"All clear," I said as we craned our necks and started looking for the horses. We rode around the perimeter of the property and didn't see a horse anywhere.

"Let's wait over there," Logan said, pointing to a spot near the trailer where we could see the entire lot, but were semi-hidden.

After nearly two hours of waiting, we were sweating from the heat, and LG and Mazy were getting restless. "I don't think they're going to show," I moaned.

"We'll try again tomorrow, I guess," he said. "Ready to go?"

"Yeah. Let's come back." We nudged our horses forward and they had barely taken ten steps before we saw the herd, clumped together, emerging from the woods at an ambling walk. They raised their heads to look at us. LG let out a soft whicker and Logan tugged on the reins to silence him.

"What now?" I whispered. We couldn't lose them.

"Wait until they get into the open and then we're going to ride behind them and let the dogs help us. We'll move them the same way we came and if one breaks away from the group, let him go. Just keep your eye on the mass herd and stay on the right side."

"Okay. Let's go!"

I barely had time to take a deep breath before Mazy surged forward next to LG. This was it! The mustangs had a second lead on us as they galloped toward the opposite side of the lot. Mazy accelerated into an even faster gallop. Pam's dogs shot out in front of us and barked at the herd as they remained in a tight pack and headed in the right direction. The herd didn't break apart, but stuck together like they were protecting one another.

Logan charged around the left side and forced the horses to gallop down the lot driveway and they headed across the street and into the open field. Pam's border collies moved the rushing horses forward.

Logan dropped behind the herd and I tried to look at him and guide Mazy at the same time.

"Am I doing okay?" I shouted to him, hoping he could hear me above what sounded like a patch of moving thunder.

"You're good!" Logan yelled back, and then he bolted away again. He cut off a group of horses that were trying to break from the pack.

Logan guided the horses in the direction of Pam's house. After galloping for several minutes, the horses slowed to a quick canter. They stayed in a tight group and not one even tried to break away from the herd. I didn't drop my guard, though, and neither did Mazy. I could feel her muscles tensed beneath me as she was prepared to dart in whatever direction necessary.

We reached Pam's driveway in a few minutes and the horses surged through the open gate. Pam's dogs knew exactly what to do: one was stationed on either corner of the gate.

The horses all rushed at once and there was a chorus of angry squeals and a few horses threw back their heads, teeth bared and nipping at the closest horse to them. Logan took the coiled red cotton lead rope from around his saddle's horn and waved it in the air at them and they jolted forward again. I held my breath until the final horse made it into the pasture and Logan trotted LG to the gate and closed it with a satisfying *clank*.

I dismounted and dropped Mazy's reins to the ground and ran on shaky legs toward Logan, who had just dismounted and was loosening LG's girth.

I threw my arms around him and he spun me around. Laughing, we collapsed in the grass and lay on our backs.

"I can't believe that just happened," I said. "We *really* did it!"

"That we did, cowgirl," Logan said. He sat up and scooted over, lifting up my head and then lowering it into his lap. He took off my cowboy hat and ran his hand through my hair.

My eyes closed as Logan gently massaged my head. It may have been a small gesture to some, but it seemed intimate and so sweet to me. He did it without me even asking and I loved him for it. It was all the little pieces like that that made up Logan McCoy. The guy that I was in love with.

I put my hands over his, squeezed them for a moment, and then let go. I sat up and looked into his eyes.

"I love you, Logan."

"I love you, Brie," Logan said. He leaned forward and touched his lips to mine.

It felt as though I was on a Tilt-A-Whirl. The grass seemed to be spinning beneath me and the only solid thing to hold on to was Logan.

So I did. I wrapped my arms around him after we had stopped kissing and rested my head on his chest. The sun warmed my back and the light breeze kept it from being too hot. This moment was perfect. Finally, I let go of Logan and we stood, trying to see any of the horses.

"It was such a crazy melee that I forgot about the part where we were supposed to grab a few of the younger horses," I said.

"I did think about it, but then I decided getting the horses onto Pam's property was the most important thing."

"Agreed," I said. "We can track the herd anytime to get a few colts and fillies."

"That is going to be when the real work begins," Logan said, shifting his hat.

"I know." I slipped an arm around his waist. "We can do this." I'd have to read the dozen books about working with wild horses that I had ordered from Barnes & Noble last night. I'd made sure no bill for my e-books would go to my parents.

"Are you worried about your parents wanting to know where you are?" Logan asked as we straddled the wooden fence to watch the horses.

"Yes, but I've got Amy as a cover. The best thing, though, is that my older sister is coming home soon."

"Will she be here for our fundraiser?" Logan asked. "I mean, as long as the town council gives us permission."

"Not for the fundraiser, but she should be here a week or so before. As long as she doesn't change her schedule."

"We'll make this work," Logan said, kissing the top of my head. "We came this far."

"It's going to be tight to get everything done, isn't it?" I asked him.

He nodded. "We should start stockpiling coffee now."

CHAPTER TWENTY-EIGHT

Every jackass thinks he's got horse sense.

"It's *so* bad to say," I said to Logan, "but lying *does* get easier. I mean, I've been a model daughter. I'm doing chores, putting in hours at Dad's work site, keeping my room clean, and helping with dinner. Plus, they are both slammed with work, so they aren't paying much attention to me."

I was on my cell by the end of Dad's on-site trailer and I peeked around the corner to make sure he hadn't cracked open the door.

"That's good," Logan said. "Keep it that way—stay off his radar. That's pretty much what I'm doing at home."

"I *really* wish I could tell my dad and know that he would be fine with it," I said. "But he won't be. He won't look at it like, 'Oh, great. That problem was taken care of. Thank you!' No, that will *not* be the case. It will be all about how I lied this entire time about where I've been." I shook my head, frustrated. It drove me insane that Dad kind of did the whole cutting-off-his-nose-to-spite-his-face thing because he always had to be in control of *everything*.

"I'll let you go," Logan said. "Don't want you getting in trouble."

"Okay. See you in a little bit."

I hung up, putting my phone in the pocket of my jean cutoff shorts and heading toward the trailer steps. *Whoa.*

Um, when did the complex get exit *signs put on each floor?* I stared at the building—*really* stared at it. I knew the blueprint by heart. Four floors. Three residences per floor. One apartment for a live-in supervisor. An office for the manager. A front desk and welcome area. From the second floor up, each residence had a sliding glass door and a small balcony that could hold two chairs and a decent-size table. I knew the drill well enough—soon a decorator would come and furnish all the rooms. Dad's goal with extended-stay hotels was to make them feel like apartments to the guests. Next to the back of the building was a sauna, hot tub, and pool. The guys had almost finished the last piece of the complex—a quiet room with a fireplace, couches, and coffee and tea machines. It was meant to feel like a giant living room. I couldn't help but shake my head at the irony. Dad loved designing the quiet rooms, but was never able to stay in one for more than a few minutes before leaving to call someone.

A wave of panic hit my chest. *What if Dad is done early?* I asked myself. I took a few breaths. *It's not like you've been inside the building*, I reminded myself. *There's definitely a ton of work left to do inside. There's no way they could finish a complex this fast.* I shook my head at my irrational, panicky side. I went back into the cool trailer and sat behind one of the business laptops.

This morning, like every other morning for the past few weeks, I had gotten up at 4:45. I usually worked on stuff for Dad from then until 7:30 a.m., when he and I left to drive to the site. I'd gotten into a comfortable routine of doing as much of Dad's work in the morning as possible and then spending the time when I was on-site researching new articles about gentling and training of mustangs. Of course, I erased the computer's history every time I logged off. As far as I was concerned, it benefited both of us: Dad's work was always done on time and I got to use the super-fast Internet. While I was "working," I often texted Amy if she was home. If she was working at Watson's, then she texted me on her break. June was speeding by.

Amy had done lots of research about raising money, so I'd asked her to help me learn everything we needed to know about presenting a case to a town council and throwing a successful fundraiser in July.

"All done, Dad," I said from my spot at the mobile desk. It was just after noon.

His forehead wrinkled as he looked at me. "Hon, did you miss a few pages? I gave you a lot of changes to make."

"I don't think so," I said. I started paging through the papers just to pacify him. "The website was uploaded with content from this morning. Maybe check and see that it's all there?"

"Okay, give me a second." Dad typed a few words and then started scanning the screen.

His eyes scanned the site. Again. And again. And again.

"It's all there," he said, with a hint of gruffness in his tone. He smiled and pointed a pen at me. "What coffee are you drinking? I need a cup of that!"

"I'm not—" I started. "I mean, yeah, you *have* to try a cup. Beans added a secret recipe something or other coffee to their menu." I stood, slinging my orange cross-body bag over my head. "I'll grab you one on the way back from lunch. Oh, wait." I paused. "I finished the changes for the website." I put a finger to my temple. "I think that's all you told me to do today."

Smiling, I looked up at Dad. "The site looks great, Brie, thank you. Go have a good lunch." He smiled at me and turned his gaze back to the computer monitor.

"If you have more stuff for me to do, I don't want to waste time by going out for lunch," I said. I went through the motions of putting my purse back on the entryway card table and sitting back down, hand on the closed laptop lid. "Are you going to e-mail me a to-do list?" I asked Dad.

His mouth opened, then quickly shut. "Um, well," Dad started. The tips of his ears turned red like they always did when he was embarrassed. "You know what? I'm going to handle things for the rest of the day. You worked so hard, honey, to get all that stuff done *so* fast. You and I will get that amazing coffee from Beans tomorrow morning before we come to work."

"Thanks, Dad!" I said. "I'm off to Watson's." I was up and out the door before he could even think about changing his mind.

A short while later, I arrived at Pam's. Logan had managed to separate two horses from the herd last night. The young animals paced back and forth along the round steel pen's sides. They had worn tracks into the dirt from pacing.

"I feel so bad for them," I said, looking from the horses to Logan. "Should we let them go back to their moms? They're really little!"

"I know it's sad," Logan said. He whisked dust off LG's shoulder with a well-worn blue bristle brush. "It's all part of the process, though. They're both old enough to be weaned. They will stop pacing soon and before you know it, they'll be romping around and playing with each other."

I smiled and reached forward to run a hand down LG's cheek. "I hope that happens sooner rather than later."

"You have the kindest heart of anyone that I've ever met." Logan stepped in front of me, dropped the brush into the tack box, and wrapped his arms around me.

"You have the most passion of anyone that I've ever met." I stood on my tiptoes to touch my lips against his. His lips were soft and warm. I kissed him deeply and he pulled me closer.

I broke our lip-to-lip contact, giggling, thanks to LG. Logan turned around to face his horse.

"Really? That was the most *enormous* sigh that I've ever heard from you," Logan said, trying to sound stern but not able to keep a grin off his face. "Now, shh." Logan had his pointer finger pressed to his lips when he turned to me.

"Do-over?" I asked.

"Definitely."

After a brief make-out session, Logan and I turned our attention to the two young mustangs in the corral.

Logan had paired me with the stockier filly of the two—a chestnut. I moved a rubber currycomb in circles along her withers. Logan, a few yards away, spoke softly to the pretty paint filly that he was working with. She was backing up away from the fence, pulling on her blue lead rope. Logan tugged twice on the rope and the filly shook her head but stood still.

I concentrated on rubbing my filly's withers with the currycomb and watched over her shoulder as Logan continued to talk to his filly and grin as she listened to his commands. She was feisty and one of Logan's favorites. A week ago, she had almost kicked Logan when he'd tried to brush her flank. Now she got excited when Logan brought the brushes into the pasture. She was one of the first horses to trot up to us. I released my groomed filly into a side corral and helped Logan pick a few burrs out of his horse's tail.

My favorite, whom I had named Frogger, looked at me from across the pasture, pricked his ears toward me, and pawed the grass. He was just a bit older than the weanling fillies, and his bay coat shone brilliantly in the sun. He made me smile and he knew it. Frogger took two steps in my direction and let out a shrill neigh. That was one technique he used to get my attention. Another was pacing along the fence line and following my every move with his giant brown eyes.

"Hi to you, too!" I called to the colt. "See you later." Logan and I laughed when Frogger shook his head, sending his mane flying. "Sorry if you don't like it," I told him. "Go eat!" Frogger stood still and watched me work on the filly for a few more minutes before he lowered his head and went back to grazing.

A car roared up the driveway. I squinted to look past the barn and then I saw *it*. Black. SUV. Our Explorer. For a second, I thought that I was about to drop to the ground. I carefully untied the filly and slipped the breakaway halter off her head. She shook out her mane and lowered her head, taking a giant mouthful of grass.

Part of me wanted to hide. I looked around and it was too late. I was in the tiny corral just off to the front of the stable. The Explorer slammed to a halt, the driver's door opened and slammed shut so hard that I thought it rattled my teeth. Dad's face was already crimson as his shoes pounded against Pam's driveway.

"Brie," Logan said, jogging up to me. "Let me go talk to him. I'll explain what we've been doing."

"No," I said. Then Dad would yell at Logan. "I'll do it."

Dad marched up to me and gripped the wooden fence with his hands. "What the hell is going on? I went to Watson's and Amy was working," he shouted. The vein in the center of his forehead pulsed. "I was about to get her fired when she finally told me where I could find you. This place is far from Watson's—where you said you were going to be."

My chest ached for Amy. I'd never be able to apologize enough for what my dad had likely said to her.

I couldn't even explain this away. "Dad, I have a lot to tell you. First, as you've probably guessed now, is that I've been see-ing Logan."

"Since when?" Dad's voice rose with every word and the sun appropriately blazed behind him.

"Since you told me not to," I said.

"That's where you've been? With him?" Dad sputtered.

"Sir," Logan started, "it's not—"

"Shut up!" Dad interrupted.

I stepped away from Logan and faced Dad. "We haven't been doing anything wrong. We captured the mustangs and brought them here so they'd leave you alone, Dad. When we can, we come here and groom them. That's it."

"I don't care what you do with these horses," Dad said, his tone scaring Logan's filly. She shied and pulled on the lead rope. Logan whispered to her and stroked her neck. "You've been with *him*. Your mother and I told you to stay away from him."

"The horses needed us," I said. "Aren't you happy that we took them away from your job site? Logan and I want to gentle as many of the horses as we can. We want to hold an adoption event and find them homes by next summer."

"Next summer?" Dad asked, shaking his head. His volume level hadn't dropped at all. "You're not going to be near him"—he jabbed his finger toward Logan—"next summer. I can't believe this. Everyone here said to listen to the BLM. Looks like you both broke some major rules. Once they find out—"

"They already know, Dad," I said. I heard desperation creeping into my voice. *Pull it together, Brie. Don't get emotional now.*

Dad let out a half laugh and folded his arms. "Well, it's clear that the people here all stick to their own—I should have thought of that. No wonder I didn't get a call back from the BLM; good old Jack's son was working against me."

I felt as though I had gotten the wind knocked out of me. It was kind of like how it felt to be ice-skating one second and on my butt the next.

"Dad! We're trying to do something really good here! The statistics about mustang survival rates are scary. When their roaming lands are developed, they're shot or starved or shipped off to a totally new, foreign place. Don't you get it? *You're* the one forcing these horses to move, just like you're going to make me move!" I screamed the last sentence. Sweat beaded on the back of my neck. My head pounded and I choked back my nausea. I'd never yelled at Dad like this. We'd fought before, but nothing this intense.

Dad jerked his head back. "You stand there and say that to me when his father tried to make me lose this contract? This is such a betrayal, Brie."

"Betrayal? Don't you get it? It's not about that! I'm sorry about Jack, but I can't control him! Neither can Logan. Logan's amazing, Dad. You would know that if you gave him a chance."

I hated fighting, but I wasn't backing down. Logan stood still behind me and his breathing was heavy. He grabbed my hand from behind and squeezed it.

"I'm not discussing this anymore," Dad said. "Let's go. Now."

I released Logan's hand and ran to the Explorer, jumped into the backseat and slammed the door behind me. Dad couldn't do this. Not after the hours Logan and I had put into outlining every detail of how we would care for the herd that the BLM had entrusted with us. I'd make him understand. This couldn't be it. Logan called out something to Dad, and Dad turned back. Tensing, I put my hand on the door handle, ready to jump out and stop Dad from yelling at Logan. Logan started to talk, but I couldn't hear a word. He gestured toward the barn and pointed to the horse pasture. Dad didn't say anything—he just stared.

Logan stopped talking and Dad headed for the driver's seat. He got in and jammed the key into the ignition. Logan unclipped the lead line of his filly, and she trotted off to rejoin the herd of young horses. He stood there and watched as Dad turned around the SUV.

He tore down the driveway and jerked the steering wheel as we turned out onto the main road.

This fight hadn't been about Logan and me. It was because Dad hated Jack. But I didn't say a word and we spent the entire car ride in silence.

CHAPTER TWENTY-NINE

Go slower and get there quicker.

"Are you and your dad talking yet?" Amy asked. It was four days after the blowup at Pam's, and I was outside getting the mail when Amy called.

"Not a word," I said, pausing by the red mailbox. "He won't even look at me and I'm afraid to bring it up. I don't know what kind of magic my mom worked on him so I can keep my phone, though."

Amy sighed. "Don't question it. At least we have that. He *will* change his mind eventually, won't he?"

"I don't know. He's pretty stubborn. My mom's mad, too, but at least she's talking to me."

"Well, Logan and I are keeping the horses fed and groomed, don't worry. I have to say it one more time: I'm so sorry that I cracked, Brie."

"Stop apologizing—please. I would have done the same thing. I'm grateful to you for being there now and helping Logan when I can't."

I so wanted to be there! It was torture to tear myself away from the horses and from my daily visits with Logan. But Dad had stayed tough and showed no signs in relenting. Logan had wanted to come over and talk to him, but I knew that wasn't the right way to handle Dad. Any apologizing had to come from me.

"Don't worry, Brie," Amy said. "We're taking care of things now, but we'll help you figure out a way to convince your dad to let you see Logan again. Want to IM later and figure out something?"

"Definitely," I said. "Maybe around nine?"

"Perfect. Talk to you later."

I pocketed my phone and shuffled back up the driveway. I put the mail on the counter and went upstairs to my room. Flopping on my bed, I tried to think of something to say to convince Dad to let me see Logan. He had every right to be pissed that I'd lied to him, but he wasn't giving us any credit for doing something good. He had to change his mind. *But what if he didn't?*

CHAPTER THIRTY

It's the man who's the cowboy, not the outfit he wears.

"Are you and Dad speaking yet?" Mom asked me over breakfast. I was getting ready to go to work with Dad.

"Nope," I said.

"I'm not happy with you, either, Brie," she said, frowning at me. "I wish you'd trusted me to tell me what was going on. You *were* trying to do something good." We were in the kitchen, Mom slicing a banana into her oatmeal.

She was right. She'd never given me a reason not to trust her. "I'm sorry I lied about where I was. I should have told you. But is there any way Dad will let me see Logan?"

"I don't know," she said, shaking her head. "Do you want me to talk to him?"

"No, it's okay," I said. "I need to do it."

With that, I left the kitchen and headed for Dad's room. He was banging away on the keyboard and barely looked up when I entered the room.

"Dad . . ."

"I'm working," he said. "What?" Great. This was going to go so well.

I stayed in the doorway. "I'm sorry I lied. I shouldn't have, but it was for the horses and—"

Dad waved his hand in the air and slid the keyboard tray away from him. So he wasn't going to even let me explain. "Do you know where I was yesterday afternoon?"

"No."

"I went to see Jack McCoy." Oh, God. Jack was already injured—my eyes scanned Dad for any visible signs of an earlier fight. Signs that I could have missed yesterday. But he looked fine. "He told me what you and his kid have been up to," Dad continued. "He even offered to take me to see the horses. He said some lady named Pam was keeping an eye on you guys?"

"Yes," I said quickly. "That's where I had been going almost every day. She's a retired veterinarian and she helped us with the horses."

Dad nodded. "Jack and I"—he cleared his throat—"agreed that you kids were wrong for sneaking around. You shouldn't have lied."

I shifted from foot to foot. "I know. I'm sorry."

Dad shook his head and rested his chin on his hand. "Something could have happened. Those are wild horses and you could have been kicked or trampled and I'd have no idea where you were."

I just nodded. He was right.

Dad tapped his pen on the table. "Jack's upset with Logan, too. He thinks he should have known better, especially since he knows accidents happen around wild horses."

My shoulders sagged. "Okay," I said in a whisper and turned to walk out of his office.

"Brie." I stopped and turned around. "We also agreed that you and Logan were doing something good. You—in a *very* wrong way—were also trying to help get the horses off my job site. What kind of dad would I be if I didn't let you try to—what is it—*calm* a few . . ." Dad shrugged and I laughed. I reached his desk in three big strides and went behind it to hug him. He squeezed me tight, holding on for a beat before letting me go.

"It's called *gentling*," I said, still laughing.

Dad gave me a half smile. "Gentling, right. As I was trying to say, I'm not going to be the guy to tell his teenage daughter not to help creatures in need."

"Really? Dad!" I jumped up and down, then hugged him again.

He held me at arm's length and looked me in the eyes. "No more lying. None. You can still do this, but if you lie again, you're done. As in, no leaving the house until college."

"Promise!" I hugged him again and skipped to the door. "Thanks, Dad. And I'm sorry about lying."

"I know you are. Now get back to work and stop moping."

I ran down the hallway and took the stairs two at a time. I had to call Logan and Amy. The town meeting was happening in a few days and we had a full presentation to prepare!

CHAPTER THIRTY-ONE

Dudes dress up, but cowboys dress down.

The afternoon of the town meeting, Logan and I braced ourselves for opposition—Dad's hotel had gotten a handful of people on his side—horses be damned. Together, we walked inside the meeting room. I half expected Dad to change his mind and forbid me to go, but he didn't. Logan and I had spent the last couple of days practicing our pitch and we had it down. The meeting started at six thirty and we were one of the first inside the old-fashioned schoolhouse building.

Logan and I moved the podium to the front of the room and grasped our note cards. We'd memorized the pitch, but I worried nerves could cause a brain freeze.

As half the town trickled inside, Logan and I grabbed two wooden chairs near the front of the room. I rolled the note cards in my hands. Did the town come because of our idea or because they hoped to see Jack and Dad in a fistfight?

"We've got it," Logan whispered, squeezing my hand. "We can do this."

"I hope so," I said. "Is your dad coming?"

"Yep. Is yours?"

"I don't know," I said. "I doubt it. He'd said he had to work."

Lost Springs' mayor, Mr. Fletcher, took the podium and after a too-long speech about the town's current waste problem from the loose goat herd, he opened the floor for new business. Logan and I stood and made our way to the podium. My mouth was dry and I wondered if people could see me shaking.

"Good afternoon," Logan said clearly into the microphone. "I'm Logan McCoy and this is Brie Carter." He dipped his head toward me. "We'd like to take a couple minutes of your time to propose a plan to preserve the town's spirit and charm, and to help animals in need." I listened to Logan say his part of the speech and he sounded so poised. He knew every word of the pitch. "You know what," Logan said, stepping to the side of the podium, notes in hand. He tore them in half and dropped the pieces by his shoes. I clutched my papers, glad that I hadn't let Logan hold them.

"I was going to stand up here and tell you a crafted answer about why you should okay this. But I realized that if I love the mustangs as much as I claim to, I certainly don't need to read a rehearsed statement off a sheet of paper." Logan paused, looking down. Then he looked out across the room. "These horses have touched my life in a very personal way. When my mother walked out on my family and me, I was in a bad place. And so were my dad and little brother. I'm sure that most of you have seen me going back and forth between home and Watson's or home and WyGas on a gelding that looks as though he's calm enough to be a lesson horse. He was actually from a mustang herd a few years back. My dad saw that I was struggling without my mom. He gave me LG as a foal, and I didn't want to, but I instantly fell for him."

I took over.

"With the town's permission," I said, "Logan and I would like to hold a fundraiser at the end of July. As Logan mentioned, Pam Caldwell has donated her land as their permanent home. But as you know, keeping a herd is no easy task. All proceeds from the fundraiser would go toward the housing, feeding, and vet care of the herd of mustangs. Logan and I have been working with them for several weeks, gentling the younger horses. Many of them have shown so much promise in the short time that I can't imagine how well they'll be doing a year from now."

I paused, looking back at Logan. He smiled and I turned my attention back to the crowd.

"With Pam's recommendation, Logan and I wish to hold a mustang adoption event a year from now. But first, in the immediate future, a fundraiser. It would be a weekend event we would publicize, coordinate, and run."

My eye caught on someone slipping in the back door. Dad. I wasn't going to screw this up now, not with him watching. I took a breath and continued. "We're not asking for funds from the city, we're only asking the board to allow us to publicize the event around town. In addition to that, we would like permission to come back in front of you all a few months from now and discuss an adoption event. We appreciate you listening to us. Thank you for your time."

Logan and I headed back to our chairs. Gratefully, I slid into my seat and tried to gauge the mayor's reaction as he waddled up to the podium.

"Thank you, Mr. McCoy and Ms. Carter."

Please say yes! He had to agree. I grabbed Logan's hand.

"I read your proposal several times," the mayor continued, "and I found no reason why you should not be able to hold your event. Does anyone object?"

I looked behind me to see if any hands were raised. Seconds trickled by and no one raised a hand. Oh, my God, they were going to say yes!

The mayor nodded to us. "You have the town's permission. I think the cause is wonderful and if there's anything we can do to help, please don't hesitate to call my office." Applause started in the back of the room and grew.

"Logan!" I said, kissing him quickly. "We're really doing this!" We headed out of the crowded building and ran into Jack.

"Well done, son," he said, his eyes saying everything he didn't. Jack was dressed up, too, in khakis and a suit jacket. Damn, the McCoys cleaned up well.

"Thanks, Dad," Logan said, shaking his hand. "You interested in helping?"

"Sure," Jack agreed. "Let me know when the horses need shoes and I'll get a buddy of mine to do it for nothing."

I tried not to explode with happiness. Logan told Jack he was taking me out for a celebratory dinner and I glanced around for Dad. Did he already leave? He must have stayed just long enough for the speech.

I reached into my pocket for my phone to call Amy. She had to work and couldn't come to the meeting. My pockets were empty. I must have left my phone inside.

"I'll be right back," I told Logan as I hurried inside the empty building and looked around my chair for the phone.

"Gotcha," I said to no one when my fingers closed on the phone under my seat. I turned and almost smacked into Dad.

"God! You scared me!" I said, trying to return my heart to its normal rate. "What are you doing?"

He took a seat and rubbed his forehead with his hand. His face looked like it did when he'd lost a big job a couple of years ago. "I'm sorry."

I sat in the row in front of him and turned to face him. But I didn't say anything yet.

He put his head in his hands for a second and then looked back at me. "I'm sorry I gave you such a hard time about this. Your mom keeps reminding me that you kids weren't doing drugs or running around town. You were doing something good."

"I still lied," I said.

Dad shook his head. "Because of me. You lied because I told you to stay away from Logan." He paused. Minutes ticked by before he lifted his head to look at me. "I told you not to see Logan because of my issues with his father. It wasn't about not trusting you with a guy, Brie. I know that I can trust you to do what's right for you." He paused. "I wasn't being much of a man. It was wrong for me to expect you to share my grudge."

I'd never seen him like this. Humble, apologetic. He'd never apologized to me like this.

"It's okay," I said. "I'm sorry, too. This was just the first time I'd ever felt like I was doing something that mattered. It was even better because it was something that I loved. The horses have nothing to do with you or Mom and it makes me feel like I have something to do. Something to contribute."

"You haven't had many chances to do that, Brie. I know that. Moving doesn't get easier when you get older. I'm glad to see you love something so much." Dad reached over and put his hand on mine for a second.

Our eyes met and Dad gave me a half smile. I wished Mom was here to take a photo. Dad was looking *at* me for once, not through me. We were talking about things that had nothing to do with Mom's photographs or his business.

"You could help, too. If you want. But that's okay if you can't," I added quickly.

"I want to," he said. I got up and passed the row of chairs and turned into his aisle. I held out my hand. "Logan and I are going to dinner. Do you and Mom want to come? Logan's going to ask Jack, too."

He didn't hesitate to take my hand. "Let's call your mom." Hand in hand, just as Logan and I had left the building earlier, Dad and I headed outside and left the darkness of the schoolhouse behind.

CHAPTER THIRTY-TWO

Boots weren't made for walking.

The dinner with Jack, Mom, and Dad went better than I ever could have hoped. Mom and Dad met Logan, Jack, and me over at Bert's Steak House and we ate, talked, and laughed for a couple of hours. When we'd first sat down, the table was silent. But Logan started telling Jack and my parents about the horses, and that eased us into conversation.

There had even been a brief chat between Jack and Dad. When we were done, Dad and Jack shook hands.

Logan and I had taken two days after our town meeting to give the horses and ourselves a break. Jack had needed Logan's help with a few things around the ranch and Logan was working long hours.

Mom and I concentrated on readying the house for Kate's visit and putting together a guest bedroom for her. If I wasn't home, I spent lots of time with Amy and we worked on fundraiser stuff.

Since Kate was Hollywood savvy, I hoped she'd have a few tips for getting local media attention. Lost Springs didn't have an indie bookstore, so I hit the Lost Springs Library. I checked out dozens of books on publicity, marketing, business strategies—practically every book that I even thought could provide me one ounce of help.

"Mom," I called upstairs. "Can I talk to you for a sec?"

"Coming," she said. She took a seat next to me at the kitchen table. The table was covered with ideas for marketing and scraps of paper with ideas that Logan, Amy, and I had come up with.

"I think we need a website," I said. "Amy offered to put together the site—she knows *way* more than I do about web design—and I'm writing the content now."

"What kind of content?"

"Date of event, horses available, a few facts about mustangs, what we're seeking from sponsors. Things like that."

She took the paper and scanned it. "That sounds good," she said. "What can I do to help?"

I took back the paper. "I know you have that big spread to do for *Beautiful Homes*, but could you take a sort of head shot of each horse to put online?"

"Of course, hon!" She smiled and took my hand. "I'd love it. I've been taking so many pictures of plants and grass that I'm sick of it. Photographing horses will be a nice break."

"Can we do it this week?" I said.

"I should be done with my writing class assignments since that class is wrapping up and a magazine is sending a crew for

me for a new assignment on Wednesday. How about . . . Friday?"
She pulled her calendar off the counter.

"Perfect. Thanks, Mom."

I texted Amy.

Want to FaceTime while we work on horse stuff?

I flopped on the center of my floor, surrounded by papers, and my phone beeped.

Call me! ☺

I dialed Amy.

"Hey," I said, smiling as her face popped up on my phone screen.

"I'm glad we're FaceTiming," Amy said. "Don't get me wrong. This isn't like *work*-work. But it's still a kind of work and I'm glad to 'have' you around so we can talk and stuff."

"I totally know what you mean. And you're still coming over tomorrow, right?"

Amy nodded. "Yep. Is ten to ten thirty okay?"

"Oh, yeah," I said. "Whatever works for you. I'll be home all day. What are your hours at Watson's Friday?" I asked. "My mom is coming to the barn to photograph all the horses. We could swing by your house and pick you up depending on your schedule."

"I switched shifts with another girl," Amy said. "So I have Friday off."

"Awesome. I'm so excited. But please, please tell me if you want to take a real break, Ames. I know that the horse project is work. I wouldn't think twice if you said you wanted a day at home to chill or see your other friends."

"Please," Amy said. "This event is important to me. Even better—it's special to you and Logan. I want to help and support my friends."

"You're awesome," I said.

Amy tipped her head back and fanned her hair. "I know. I just radiate amazingness."

Giggling, we got to work.

CHAPTER THIRTY-THREE

Worry is like a rockin' horse. It's something to do that don't get you nowhere.

On Friday morning Amy, Mom, and I were in the Explorer on the way to Pam's.

I was twisted around in the front seat talking to Amy. "Logan had to stay home because Trevor forgot to rotate the cattle into a new pasture. Can you believe that guy?" I asked her, shaking my head.

"Jack is *so* firing him," Amy said. "That's not the first time he's messed up like that."

"Sweetie," Mom said, pushing her sunglasses to the top of her head. "Don't mean to interrupt, but where do I turn?"

"Oh, right!" I said. "Sorry."

Mom flipped on her right blinker.

"Oh, Mom, I'm sorry! I meant left!"

Mom gave me The Look.

"I was really saying 'oh, right,' like it just occurred to me that you haven't been to Pam's before," I said.

"You've talked about the horses so much," Mom said, "I felt like I'd met them all. Pam, too. You've been coming here for a while. I feel so *behind*."

She smiled, but it wasn't genuine. I could tell because the smile didn't make the few barely there lines around her eyes crease. The smile could fool Amy, but not me. Her feelings were hurt because of my lies. Guilt made me shrink a little into the car seat. Mom was used to knowing everything I did. She always got to know my friends—and by "know" I meant "heard about," because the friends were mostly people I met through my virtual classes during the school year. I was lucky to be a homeschooler with digital access to more traditional classes.

I wondered if Dad felt the same way. I'd invited him to come, but he was taking a work from home day to focus on home stuff like bills instead of job stuff. I realized that I hadn't asked Dad *anything* about his work lately. Usually, I knew at least as much as Brody and the crew.

Maybe this is how traditional families function, I thought. *Everyone's always off doing their own thing.*

"Pam should be at work," Amy said, jolting me out of my thoughts. "But you so have to meet her, Ms. C! You'll love her."

"That sounds like a plan," Mom said, looking in the rear-view mirror and smiling at Amy. "Amy, you and I see each other a lot, usually in passing, right?"

I turned in my seat so I could see Amy and Mom.

"Yes," Amy said, nodding. She tucked a lock of black hair behind her ear.

"Then why are you still calling me 'Ms. C'?" Mom asked, laughing.

I smiled. Amy had already told Mom about her southern obsession.

Amy and I giggled and it felt as though someone had pushed a refresh button on the mood surrounding us.

"You know why," Amy said, still laughing. "Because it's respectful. Especially for a southern belle."

I shook my head. "I do not know this person sitting in the backseat. She clearly needed at least a seventy-two-hour evaluation. This girl wants to live in the South so bad that she is pretending that Wyoming is Georgia."

That set Mom and me off—we laughed so hard that I had to wipe tears from my eyes.

"Oh, whatever!" Amy said, reaching forward and gently tugging on my ponytail. "I'm not speaking to either one of you." She put her nose in the air and looked out the window. I focused, looking out my window to gauge how close we were. The roadside grass was knee high and Mom tapped on the brakes as we went over a small bridge. The creek that ran under the road snaked through Pam's property. It provided constant fresh water to the herd.

"Daughter, since you're the only one speaking to me," Mom said. "Anything I need to know? I've never photographed horses before, let alone wild mustangs."

"The ones that you'll be photographing are the younger horses that we've done a *lot* of work with. They aren't spook-proof by any means, but they're not going to bite or kick anyone."

"The horses that *are* wild," Amy said, "are ones that we probably won't see."

"Ooooh!" I said, grinning and reaching around to poke her leg with my pointer finger. "She speaks!"

Amy swatted at my hand. "I realized that a polite young lady wouldn't give anyone the silent treatment."

We were still laughing when I pointed to Pam's driveway. Mom drove over a cattle guard and went slowly toward the barn.

"Wow," she said. "This property is huge!"

Amy and I jumped out of the SUV the second it rolled to a stop. Mom grabbed her camera bag and tripod.

This was the first chance the horses had to meet someone new. They only knew Logan, Amy, Pam, and me. What if one spooked? What if they *all* spooked? Mom reached my side and Amy came from the barn with a green bucket filled with a few handfuls of grain.

I let out a sharp whistle and a few of the youngest horses perked their heads and trotted up to the fence.

"Stand still," I said to Mom as Amy and I climbed into the pasture. "Let them get a look at you before you come in and maybe that will help so they don't spook."

Mom nodded, slowly sliding her arm holding the camera behind her.

"Hi, guys," I crooned. "You're all *so* gorgeous and clean! Who wants to get their picture taken?" I kept a singsong tone to my voice. Logan's spirited filly, whom Holden had named Sassy when we had told him about her, came over with her ears pointed forward. Amy scratched behind Sassy's ears and a muzzle bumped lightly against my back.

I knew who it was before I turned around.

"Frogger!" I said, giggling. The bay colt bobbed his head, looking proud of himself. "You got my attention, so I *guess* I'll pet you." I slowly put my arms around Frogger's dark neck and hugged him. He didn't move or fight to get away from me.

I let him go and he went over to Amy for his turn at the grain bucket.

Amy and I let the horses have a mouthful of grain and then motioned for Mom to come inside. She handed me her camera and then climbed the fence. The eight young horses around us didn't even blink when Mom stood up next to me.

"Wow, guys," I said. "We're all so impressed!"

Amy and I reached for each other's hand and squeezed, trading giant smiles.

"You both should be very, *very* proud of the job you've done," Mom said. "You realize that these horses are still very much wild, right?"

"I guess," Amy said. "I kind of forgot about how we got them once we started naming them and stuff."

I nodded. "They can be wild for however long they want as long as they suppress it until they're turned out in a big pasture to live out their golden years."

"I think there's a very real chance of that happening," Mom said.

"Thanks, Mom," I said. "Where do you want us to hold the horses?"

"Let's have you there by that patch of dandelions in the far end of the corral, facing away from the mountains," Mom said. "Do you guys like that angle?"

"I'm happy," I said, swatting at my knee. The flies made me regret my choice of cutoff jean shorts. Amy was swatting away at her own legs. Mom had been the smart one who had chosen jeans.

"I'm going to grab some hay to keep the other horses busy," I said. With fresh hay in hand, I shook out a few flakes onto the ground. The horses munched away while Mom took test shots and Amy and I fixed Sassy's long black mane.

"Do you want to hold her or should I?" Amy asked. She took a red halter that had been hanging on her shoulder and we quickly buckled it on the mare. She snapped a lead rope under the horse's chin.

"I don't mind taking her," I said.

Amy pulled her phone out of one of the back pockets in her shorts. "Say 'Amy rules!'"

I burst into laughter and *click*.

"Amy," I said, finally over my laugh-fit. "If I look bad and I even so much as *think* that you uploaded that to QuikPic . . ."

"Brie! Oh, my gosh," Amy said. "Your mom is ready and you're making her wait."

I tilted my head and started to yell back at Amy, but just in time remembered that I had a mustang at the end of a very short cotton rope.

Mom bent forward, her face near the camera. "These are going to look beautiful," Mom said. "Let me know when you're ready, Brie."

"Okay, I want to let out the rope a little so there will be a great shot of her without me being too close for good cropping." I let out the lead rope bit by bit. "Stay there, pretty girl. Just be still."

The filly stayed but looked at me. A brilliant white star peeked from under her forelock.

Amy clicked with her tongue a couple of times. It broke the filly's focus on me and she turned her head, looking dead on at Mom.

"That's a girl," Amy said. "Just keep looking at us. We're almost done with you."

"Got it," Mom said, looking up from her camera and trading grins with Amy and me. "Nice work, girls. I've got the easy job today."

"Please," Amy and I said in unison.

All three of us laughed. I praised the horse, then released her to join the others. A few lifted their heads, eyes filled with curiosity.

"One at a time, guys," I said. "You'll all get your picture taken. Don't worry."

The familiar sound of a certain truck's engine broke the quiet of our shoot. Well before he reached the barn, Logan cut the engine. He headed toward us, waving.

It was Amy's turn to hold one of the horses. She was at the corral gate, shooing the horses back so she could step inside.

"Hi, Ms. Carter," Logan said, smiling at my mom. He walked over to where I'd perched on the fence and ran a hand up and down my back. "Hi to you, too," he said.

I leaned down and gave him a quick kiss. "Everything okay?" I asked him.

"Now it is," Logan said. He didn't offer up anything else and I wasn't the type of girlfriend who always felt the need to pry info from her boyfriend. "How's the photo shoot?"

"Great," I said, watching while Amy held a buckskin colt for Mom. "They haven't gotten scared once."

Logan grinned. "That's good, because this place better be packed in a few weeks."

Mom took the final two shots and we dropped Amy off at home. Logan stayed behind at Pam's to start cleaning up the barn.

Later that night, Mom and I went over the pictures and chose the best one for each horse. Then, with Amy on the phone, I navigated the website and got the pictures posted online.

It was almost two in the morning when I felt a wave of exhaustion. I sat back in my desk chair and scrolled through the website.

"'Lost Springs Mustang Sponsorship,'" I read aloud. "'Browse our site to learn about available horses, dates, and how you can sponsor one this summer and take your horse home next year. One hundred percent of donations goes directly to the horses—not one will ever be euthanized unless its quality of life can't be improved. We will not give up on a single horse. If one is not adoptable for whatever reason, we will continue to care for it.'" The site listed Amy's cell as the contact number and Pam's address.

On the photo gallery page, Amy had helped me set up a photo album with the photos Mom had taken. Under each photo, a couple of sentences of description told potential adopters about each horse.

"'Santana,'" I read aloud. "'This gentle mare stands at fifteen hands high and is five or six years old. She's halter broken, leads well, and is ready for training.'"

Amy and I hoped, with lots of people home for the summer, those people would be browsing the web and feeling like sponsoring a horse or donating to our cause.

Logging off, I flopped onto my bed. I'd just closed my eyes when my phone buzzed beside me.

"I didn't wake you, did I?" Kate asked.

"No, I just finished some work for the fundraiser," I said.

"That's my sister," Kate said. "Planning ahead. Good girl. I can't wait to see you."

"Me, too," I said.

"You need to sleep. I was just calling to say hi and that I love you," Kate said. "I'm bringing a surprise, too."

"Surprise? What kind of surprise?"

"Bye, Brie. Talk later," Kate said, her tone mocking and playful.

"Kate! Wait! Tell me!" I pleaded, but the line went silent.

CHAPTER THIRTY-FOUR

Don't wear the same pair of boots every day. Variety not only spices up life, it prolongs it.

That evening, tiny bugs flew toward Logan's headlights as he parked his truck on Dad's lot. Dad had called and asked me to come. We had both been quiet on the ride over.

"Call me when you're done," Logan said, kissing me quickly. "I hope everything is okay."

"Me, too," I said. "He was cryptic on the phone. He just said to get over here and he wanted to talk. Thanks for the ride." I hopped out of the truck and waved to Logan as I walked over to the silver trailer. Lights from the inside made patches of light on the grass.

I climbed the stairs and opened the door.

"Hi," I said, tossing my purse on the sofa. "What's going on?" I asked Dad. He was bent over his computer, fingers clicking over the keyboard.

"One sec. Hold on."

I grabbed a mint from the jar on Dad's desk. The printer whirred and shot out a couple of neon-colored pages. Dad handed me a pink one.

"What's this?" I asked, taking it from him. A huff of surprise escaped from my lips. I read the flyer from top to bottom. Twice. *Fundraiser for wild mustangs! July 29 at 8 a.m. at 4249 High Falls Road, Lost Springs.* The flyer gave the time, website address, and a phone number. The flyer's border was the pictures Mom had taken and they had been downsized and tilted to be catchy.

"You've got to start advertising now," Dad said. "Is this flyer okay?"

"It's perfect! When did you do this?"

"I've been working on it for a couple of days. I told you I'd help, so here's the first step."

"This is great, Dad. Thanks." I hugged him.

"No matter what people say, I want to do this," he said, going back to his computer.

"What're you talking about?" I put down the flyer and sank into the couch.

"Some of the guys hear things when they're at the diner or bars," Dad said. "I guess, according to some people, if I help my daughter at all during your fundraiser, I'm doing it for my image."

"I'm sorry, Dad," I said. "That's not fair."

"I don't care what those people think because they aren't important to me. You are. I care what *you* think. What you think of me as your dad."

"I think you're doing okay," I said, my voice soft.

The trailer was quiet except for the whirr of the printer. Dad cleared his throat.

"Did you or Logan start a press release yet?" he asked.

Reaching into my book bag, I pulled out my spiral notebook. "I tried, but the library books on publicity were confusing."

"Then let's do it now." He motioned me over to the computer and I pulled up an empty chair.

Dad reached for his phone and dialed Mom. "Hey, hon, Brie and I are working on her horse project. Want to come over? Good. See you in a few minutes."

Dad and I were sitting in his office working on *my* project. That was a first. Mom pulled up a few minutes later and we studied the marketing books. We munched on Chex Mix and downed some of the Red Bulls in Dad's mini-fridge. The countdown to the event was on!

CHAPTER THIRTY-FIVE

A man on foot is not a man at all.

The next day, I straightened an already straight pillow on the couch. I was alone in the house and Mom and Dad were on their way back from the airport with Kate. I was so excited to see her that I was going stir crazy!

Tires crunched on gravel. Doors slammed and I ran from the living room and skidded to the front door.

I reached for the handle just as it started to open.

"Hi!"

"Kate!" I squealed. I threw my arms around her California-tanned body.

"Brie!" She grabbed my wrists and held me at arm's length. "You look great!"

Kate took my hand and twirled me in a circle. We laughed and squeezed hands. When she spun me back around to face her, I realized she'd changed, too. Her hair was a soft shade of honey blond, and blue contacts made her once-green eyes pop against her tan skin.

"Both my girls look beautiful," Mom said, her smile stretching across her face. She motioned for Dad to follow her with Kate's bags and I slung my arm across my sister's waist. Kate was wearing low-slung jeans and a preppy, but pretty, sparkly white sweater.

"You have the boyfriend glow," Kate said, bumping me playfully with her hip. "You're going to share every little detail. I'm the press—I have to know!"

Laughing, I led her toward the guest room. "I'll tell you later," I said. "It'll take a while."

"I bet," she said, quieting down as we neared the bedroom door. Mom busily directed Dad where to put Kate's bags and I had a vision of her turning down the bed and placing a mint on Kate's pillow. Mom loved it when we were all together. It was a rare occurrence these days when we weren't separated from my older sister. We were a family again and Lost Springs was home.

It didn't take long to get Kate settled. She wasn't an LA drama queen about her clothing—she was photographed in tabloids and said to have amazing taste in clothes. Kate never told her secret, though. She shopped only at thrift stores and went outside of Hollywood to a Goodwill store, where she bought designer pants for $2.99. Kate always kept an eye out for photography things, purses, and candles, for Mom and me.

With Mom and Dad safely out of hearing distance, she pulled me onto her bed and the sisterly chat-fest began. She knew bits and pieces about Logan and the mustangs from what I'd told her on the phone, but telling her in person was so much more fun.

"How did this happen?" Kate asked. "I live in LA and can't find a decent guy. You move *here* and find a cowboy!"

Laughing, we shifted on the bed. "You'll find one," I said. "Wait till a big celeb stops by the set and try to snag him."

"Oh, yeah, right," Kate said, rolling her eyes. "I tried to flirt with Collin Chang last month and he completely blew me off. Actors." Kate shook her head, then sat up super-straight. She looked at me sideways.

"What?" I asked.

"Something," she said. "What haven't you told me?"

I shrugged. "I don't know."

Kate stared at me.

"What are you doing?" I asked, laughing.

"You're in love with him, aren't you?"

"Oh, my God! How did you—"

"It's a gift," Kate said, smiling. She rubbed my arm. "He feels the same way?"

I nodded. "Yeah, he does."

Kate was always able to do that. She could be goofy one minute and serious and big-sisterly the next. Sometimes I forgot she was eight years older than me, but when she acted like this, it reminded me I could tell her anything and she'd give me good advice.

"Love is a big, scary, wonderful thing," Kate said as she stretched her legs onto the sage-green bedspread. "You can always talk to me anytime."

I grinned. "Oh, I know. I'll tell you more later."

"Deal!" Kate shook my hand and laughed. "Anyway, what press do you have for the event?"

I counted them off on my fingers. "We've got the local paper and radio. Maybe the Lost Springs TV station will cover it, if we're lucky. The radio is a one-man gig run out of some guy's basement, but at least it's something."

Kate nodded and ran her fingers through her long hair. "You're almost like a new sister."

"What do you mean?"

"The old Brie didn't have the sparkle the new Brie has. You always went along with whatever Mom or Dad did and never had your own thing. I've never seen you care about something like this before."

So she did notice. I'd noticed the change, too. After months of being around Logan and being here, I'd finally found something I cared about. Maybe I'd always been a closet horse person.

"It's different," I said, taking a Sephora lip gloss from her purse and opening it. "I'm not doing photography like Mom or business like Dad."

"I'm proud of you," Kate said. "I ran off to Hollywood to cover celebs with road rage and you're saving horses. How bad does that make me look?"

"Please," I scoffed. "You'd still be Mom's favorite if you raged with them. She loves you."

Kate grinned and pulled a box out of her closet. "She'll love me more once I give her this kick-ass camera bag. It's from the new Dooney & Bourke line for the working woman."

"It's gorgeous!" Carefully, I took the bag and turned it over in my hand. The pliable bag was a glossy black with Dooney & Bourke's signature logo emblazoned on the side.

"After we finish our Carter-Brooks reunion, you're taking me to meet Logan and see the horses, right?"

"Promise," I said.

"Dinner, girls!" Mom called from downstairs. Kate and I eyed each other and leaped to our feet, tearing off down the hallway to be the first one in the kitchen, like we had done when we were kids. It felt good to be a family.

CHAPTER THIRTY-SIX

Never work for a man with electricity in his barn.
You'll be up all night.

Because Kate had absolutely refused to bike to Pam's in the heat, she'd borrowed the Explorer and was driving us there. While we had been getting ready to leave, Kate had reminded me that we needed to leave at least half an hour early to "beat traffic." Her brain was still stuck in LA. The only traffic here that could delay us pretty much fell to tractors.

I rubbed my eyes, still a little sleepy. Kate and I had been up most of the night talking until we had passed out. Kate had wanted to know everything about Logan. I worried, at first, about boring her. But she assured me that if she was over boy talk, she would tell me. She was the perfect big sister—telling her had been so much fun. I was glad I'd saved so much about Logan for her visit, because talking over the phone wouldn't have been half as fun.

I shifted my eyes to my sister, then back to the road. I ran my hands down the royal-purple fitted tank top Kate had insisted

I wear. The front was covered in rows of small purple sequins. She had ignored my protests that dressing up for the barn was insane. I hadn't been able to stop her from wearing a navy blue dress with teensy polka dots and a Peter Pan collar.

I'd gone to Mom and Dad, like I was ten, complaining that we hadn't left yet because Kate was putting "beachy waves" in her hair. They had seemed amused and told me to just go with the flow.

"What's the bag for?" I asked, peering into the backseat as we headed for Pam's.

Kate shook her head and kept her eyes on the road. I'd never noticed how many potholes there were. "You'll see. It's a surprise."

"I've heard that before," I said. "It won't scare the horses, will it?"

She rolled her eyes and guided the SUV into Pam's driveway. "Don't worry so much. Just chill."

"Fine," I grumbled, getting out of the car and trying to make it to the backseat before she did. Triumphantly, she snatched the bag away from my fingers and she bounced up and down as we headed for the barn.

We stepped inside and found Logan bent over one of the colt's hooves, studying the work Jack's friend had done a few days ago. We'd decided not to shoe them, but to trim their hooves instead. The shoes would have been too much of an adjustment for some of the older horses, since they'd never been shod.

"Hey," he said, his head popping up from the opposite site of the gray horse as soon as he saw us. "You must be Kate."

"Yep, and you better be the guy dating my sister, because you're gorgeous."

"Kate!" I shouted, jabbing her in the ribs. Logan blushed from his neck to his ears and he cleared his throat before turning his attention back to the horse.

"Nice to meet you," he said, his face hidden by the gray horse's shoulder.

I stayed on the opposite side of the gray. I felt so dumb in the middle of the barn in my sparkly shirt.

Logan reappeared, head cocked. He crossed his arms and let them rest on the gray's back.

"Is this going to be a thing from now on?" he asked. "Do we have to dress up every day before we come here?"

"Shut up," I said, rolling my eyes and trying not to grin.

"I doubt that you really want me to 'shut up,' since I was going to say that you look beautiful."

I shook my head. "Thank you. I didn't want to wear this top—it's new and Kate got it for me and it's totally fancy. But she insisted that I had to wear it or she wasn't coming."

"Funny," Logan said, starting around the hindquarters of the horse and coming toward me. "Kate dictated half my wardrobe this morning, too."

He stepped into full view. He shrugged off a Carhartt jacket, revealing a black polo. Logan took off his cowboy hat, and underneath, his usually tousled hair was combed neatly.

"What?" I shook my head. "Logan, you look amazing. I was wondering why you had on a jacket when it's so hot outside. But what is going on? Kate!"

Kate slowly made her way toward us. She peered into the stalls and nodded at the fresh paint, recently swept floors, and cleaned-up aisles that Logan, Amy, and I had done to get ready for the event.

"Now," she said, her voice carrying down the long aisle. "I'll need to lead a horse, Logan, you can shoot, and I'll interview Brie." She clasped her hands together. "We all look so great! Aren't you glad that I told you to dress up?" Kate looked at me, smiling.

"Interview?" I asked.

Kate jangled the mystery bag and set it on top of a trunk near us. "I don't get to see you a lot, Brie. You're my sister and I want to do something nice for you. First, I want to shoot a segment directed at *Star Access*. Then we'll start over and shoot a few minutes of footage about your event. I'll overnight the tapes to a friend of mine who will submit them to local and statewide news channels as well as a few national shows."

LA smog had ruined my sister's brain.

"Kate." I talked as if she were a little kid. "*Access* won't care about a teensy event like this. It probably won't even make the local news. We don't have celebrities."

Kate ignored me and continued to lay out the equipment. "No, but with me anchoring the pieces, you'll get attention. I'm not enough, of course, so that's why we're going to amp up the drama and make this an emotional segment."

Logan and I shot glances back and forth and he shrugged. "We *are* already dressed and here."

Kate's determined face told me I wouldn't be able to argue with her. She already had Logan's attention with her video camera and sound equipment.

"Logan's going to shoot it," she said, placing the camera in his hands. He held the camera with outstretched arms as if he were afraid of breaking it. "Don't drop that, because I had to beg the camera operator to borrow it and he'll be *so* fired if something happens to it." Kate looked at the camera, pressed a button, and an orange light started blinking. "Okay, so here's what to do," Kate told Logan.

While they worked together, I caught Frogger and brought the colt inside to groom him before he went on camera. I swapped the dusty brown halter on his head for a bright blue one. He stamped a front leg, scattering flies.

"Aw, poor guy," I said. I bent down and rummaged through the trunk of grooming supplies. "Here we go!" I sprayed the colt with fly spray, then continued to groom him.

It took Kate less than fifteen minutes to get Logan used to the camera, teach him how to operate it, and select a location for the shoot. She picked the opening of the barn, with the gorgeous field and backdrop of the mountains in view if we left the big sliding door open.

She practiced a couple of questions with me and the more she asked, the more I realized she wasn't trying to make it into a glitzy over-dramatic Hollywood piece. She was trying to get the word out about our event, and Kate *always* knew what to say to get attention.

I showed her how to lead Frogger and it felt like my chest puffed out with pride as I watched the horse that I'd trained with Logan follow my sister like a giant, gentle dog.

"Ready?" Kate called to Logan.

I jogged a few yards back so I was out of the way.

"Ready," Logan said.

"Count it down," Kate said, stroking Frogger's neck.

"Five, four, three, two, one . . . ," Logan said, nodding at Kate at the "one."

"Wild, neglected horses, two teens who love them, and a race against the clock. Welcome to *Star Access*; I'm Kate Carter."

I stood back and watched Kate in action. She spun the story in a Hollywood-esque way that pleaded for national media attention for our cause. Kate asked me to lead Frogger in a circle, then come next to her for a few questions.

"What's your goal for this event, Brie?" Kate asked.

"To raise money so that we're able to ready adoptable horses for homes next summer *and* care for horses that will call our property their forever home. We would be incredibly grateful for any help."

Kate addressed the camera again. "So, there you have it. Come join us on July twenty-ninth, and save a horse!" Kate gave the event information again and signed off.

With a satisfied grin, Kate nodded to Logan to turn off the camera.

"Now," Kate said. "No guarantees the tape will ever make it on air, especially since it's not typical *Access* material, but we've definitely got a shot with the local stations."

Logan thanked Kate and helped her pack up the equipment. Kate promised to have someone edit the tape and send it out.

"Thank you," I said, wrapping my arms around her in a tight hug. "This was the best present."

Kate hugged me back. "It'll be even better when we get media here. Can I take you guys out for brunch?"

"That would be great," I said.

Logan nodded in agreement. "Let me turn this guy out." He took Frogger outside to the pasture.

Kate flashed me a grin. "You better keep this guy."

If only she knew how much I wanted to, and how afraid I was it wouldn't happen.

CHAPTER THIRTY-SEVEN

*If you're in this business to make money, you better
have your head examined.*

Kate's visit and planning for the fundraiser gave me little time
for anything else. Mom and Dad spent some solo time with
Kate while I did work for the event. I wanted to spend more time
with Kate, but every free second was needed to figure out last-
minute fundraiser details.

The local media had latched on to Kate's tape, and we were
lined up for TV, radio, and newspaper interviews. Logan, pulling me aside last night, had confessed he was somewhat camera
shy, and had asked if I wouldn't mind doing the interviews. It
was adorable that he was shy in front of cameras. I'd told him I
didn't mind doing the TV stuff.

Kate left for LA on the red-eye last night and it had been hard
to see her go.

"You'll visit again soon, right?" I asked.

"Wherever you are, you know I'll come," she said, kissing me on the cheek and waving good-bye as Mom and Dad drove her to the airport.

Now the event was only five days away, and Logan and I had to put up flyers around town, then pick up Holden and take him with us to Pam's. Jack was busy with a landowner's meeting today. Logan and I were taking Holden to see the horses.

The clock just hit nine in the morning as I biked to WyGas. Logan and I were splitting a stack of flyers. "I'll go west," I said. "If you go east."

Logan took the stack and walked me out the door. "Let's meet back here in an hour, okay?"

"Deal."

We both headed off through town. I dropped flyers at the drugstore, farm supply, post office, and bakery. Out on the street, I handed flyers to anyone who walked by. At the furniture repair store, I rang the silver bell on the counter. "Rodney? You here?"

"Hold on, hold on," a gruff voice called from the back of the store. A round-faced man with furniture polish streaks on his face stepped into view. "Oh, it's you, Miss Carter," he said, his voice losing its edge as his face creaked into a smile.

"Sorry to bother you, Rodney, but could you post this flyer in your window?" Rodney was an old friend of Jack's and I didn't think he'd turn me down.

He held out his hand and studied the flyer when I handed it to him. "Of course. Right in my display window."

"Great! You coming?"

"Wouldn't miss it. Might sponsor a horse myself. Got a little lonely around home when Rodney Jr. got married."

"I'll look for you," I said. "See you there." Heading outside of the store, I checked my watch and an hour had already passed. There were a few flyers left, so I passed them out to people shopping and headed to meet Logan.

This was phase one of a dozen.

"Careful, that's Oscar the Grouch," Logan said to Holden, causing the boy to giggle. We'd picked up Holden and had brought him with us to Pam's.

"Why does he have that name?" Holden asked, taking a few steps back from the stall he'd started to peer into.

The black mustang had his back to us and faced the stall corner. We'd tried treats, grain with molasses, and even other horses to get Oscar's attention, but he refused to lose his swept-back ears and wild eyes. Logan had blindfolded him to get him into a stall because he'd needed to be checked out by Pam. Each horse, no matter whether we thought they had gentling potential, got a thorough checkup. I hadn't been here when Pam had checked him out, but Logan had said tranquilizers had been involved.

"Because he's so grumpy, he hasn't let us pet him yet," Logan said.

"Oh," Holden said, hanging on Logan's every word. It wasn't the first time we had brought him here. Holden loved it. He'd helped us groom a couple of the gentle yearlings, and the horses brought out an animated side of him.

"I'm going to grab a fresh bucket of water," Logan said, slipping off his gloves. "And then we can get ready to leave."

Logan headed outside to the water pump and I walked down to Frogger's stall. He pricked a white-tipped ear to me and came up to the stall door. Frogger was one of seven horses inside the barn, while the rest who hadn't adjusted yet to being indoors were out in the pasture. We tossed them hay every day.

I stroked his muzzle. Thanks to Kate's *Access* piece, he was famous around town as the movie star horse. Several people had already contacted us, wanting to sponsor Frogger.

In addition to people who wanted to help, we were also getting lots of calls from other TV shows and newspapers. Logan had taken on most of the print interviews and I'd been doing some by phone and scheduling in-person sessions with news crews coming to Lost Springs.

I wished I could keep Frogger, but it wasn't a reality.

I left Frogger and headed back down the aisle. Blinking against the strong outdoor light, I saw Holden petting a dark muzzle. At the same moment, Logan came inside with the water bucket.

We both stopped.

Holden was gently stroking Oscar's muzzle as the horse leaned his head over the stall door. Water from Logan's bucket sloshed over the side and splashed against the pavement.

"Holden," I said in a whisper. White-hot fear flashed in my chest. An image of Oscar taking a chunk out of Holden's arm flashed through my mind. "Put your hand down slowly and back away."

"Right now," Logan added.

"He's a good boy," Holden said, smiling up at Oscar.

Holden turned and walked away from the stall. Oscar didn't retreat into his corner. Instead, he kept his head poked outside the stall and watched us all. The whites had receded from his eyes and his lower lip wasn't flapping from fear.

Slowly, Logan walked forward and grabbed Holden from behind.

"You scared me, kid! If you're going to come here, you've got to listen." Logan hugged Holden before putting him down.

"Okay, sorry," Holden said softly. He frowned and sat on a hay bale near an empty stall.

"Hey, Holden," I said. "We got scared, but you helped Oscar. Look, he's not so grouchy anymore."

Holden looked over at the horse and smiled. "He's happy now," Holden said.

Logan ruffled Holden's hair and mouthed *Thank you* to me.

"Let's call it a day, guys," I said, putting my arm around Logan's waist. "We've got an interview to prep for."

We left the horses napping and eating in their stalls and headed to Logan's truck. Logan and I held hands as Holden trotted ahead. A pinto colt lifted his head with a mouthful of grass and neighed at Holden. Holden laughed and waved at the colt. We were all laughing when we climbed into Logan's truck.

CHAPTER THIRTY-EIGHT

Only fools or gamblers walk behind strange horses.

"And now back to *Inside the Issue*. I'm Trista Todd and we're here in little Lost Springs, Wyoming. With us today is Brie Carter, a teenage horse tamer and animal activist. Welcome, Brie."

Smiling at Trista, I nodded. "Thank you. I'm glad to be here." Trista and I sat in director's chairs in the mustang pasture with Blackheart Mountain behind us.

The event was four days away and Logan and I were working from sunup until two or three in the morning.

Today, Mom and Dad had come with me. They wanted to watch my first TV interview with someone who wasn't Kate. Off camera, Mom and Dad smiled while Logan gave me a thumbs-up.

The woman's blond hair had bad black roots and her face was caked with a pound of foundation. "So, Brie, tell us about the event this weekend. Whose idea was it?"

"The event is a fundraiser for mustangs who have been displaced. My partner, Logan McCoy, and I started the event because thousands of mustangs are moved, slaughtered, and abused every year in our country."

Trista shook her head. "That's so cruel. Now, what are you looking for in potential sponsors?"

I sat a little straighter. These questions weren't hard. "We need people who understand these are still *wild* animals," I said. "We've halter-broken most of them, but we need adopters who are willing to sponsor a horse. That means, if someone comes and sees a horse they like, they'll leave their name on a contact sheet. Next summer, we will hold an adoption event. People who have their name on a list will get first dibs at adopting their sponsored horse. The sponsorship doesn't mean the horse belongs to them—it just moves them ahead of the line if they do want to adopt next summer. The horses are all ages and they have different comfort levels with people."

"Wonderful, just wonderful," Trista cooed, a smile plastered on her face. Maybe I should consider a career in TV. Every question she asked made me want to talk more.

"Thank you," I said. "We just want people to come out, see the horses, and consider donating to our cause. These horses need all the support they can get."

"Let's talk about your partner for a second. What's your relationship with Logan?"

"We're dating," I said with a tiny smile.

Trista grinned through her red lipstick. "Ah! Young love! How long have you been together?"

"Sorry," I said. "I'd like to stick to talking about the horses."

Oh, my God. This is only the first interview of the day. Three more left! They better not all be like this.

"Okay, okay, no more boyfriend questions," she said, patting me on the arm. "Now, a couple of minutes ago, Brie, you mentioned these horses had been displaced."

I nodded. "Yes, that's absolutely correct."

"Well, we did a little research before we came. Isn't it true that your father, Michael Brooks, is a land developer?"

"Yes," I said slowly. "He is."

Trista's smile engulfed her entire face as the camera moved closer to us. "Then isn't it correct to say that your father drove these horses off the Lost Springs land?"

"No—"

Trista cut me off. "But Brie, we know he's a developer and he wanted these horses off his land. We had several anonymous people step forward and go on the record to say that your father threatened to quote 'kill the horses' if they didn't leave his property. How do you explain this?"

I clenched my jaw and looked at Dad. I half expected Dad to shove aside the camera guy and defend himself.

"My father," I started quickly, "would never hurt the horses. He was frustrated with them being on his land and he wanted to move them, but he'd never hurt them."

Trista raised her eyebrows. "Then, Ms. Carter, how do you explain the anonymous witnesses? They all claim your father—"

Leaning forward, I looked Trista in the eyes. "Those witnesses don't like my father because he's a land developer. But that's not the issue we sat down to discuss, is it, Trista?" I asked, smiling. "We came to talk about the horses, and if you want to draw attention away from our cause and make up stories, then I'm done here."

Pulling my eyes away from Trista, I flicked them to Dad. He just stared. *Love you*, he mouthed. Smiling, I glanced back at the reporter.

"So, um, tell our viewers again the date of the event," Trista said, turning pink and shuffling through papers on her lap.

"It's this Saturday in Lost Springs. You can see the horses starting at eight and we hope to see you there."

"Thank you, Brie, and on the bottom of your screen, we're flashing the website and phone number to call. Stay with us and we'll be right back."

The cameraman signaled we were finished and I expelled a breath. Trista hopped out of the chair and stalked off toward her *Inside the Issue* van without saying a word.

"Thank you, ma'am," Logan called after her. Trista stiffened at his words but kept walking toward her trailer. Mom, Dad, Logan, and I smothered our laughter.

One down. Three to go.

CHAPTER THIRTY-NINE

When you get to the end of your rope, tie a knot and hang on.

"Two days until the fundraiser," I said, bursting into the kitchen. Mom and Dad were seated at the counter and without looking at them, I grabbed two pieces of bread out of the fridge and started making a turkey sandwich. "Logan and I did three newspaper interviews today and we've got another one tomorrow. After that, we'll be at Pam's practically every minute." They still hadn't said a word. Mom's chin was rested on her hand and Dad stirred his coffee without looking at the cup. "What's wrong?"

Mom reached over the counter and patted my hand. "Nothing's wrong. Can you sit for a minute?"

"Is it Kate? Is she okay?"

Dad shook his head. "Kate's fine. But we need to talk."

Something had happened. Dad forehead was scrunched and Mom wouldn't look me in the eye. "Brody and the crew have been working hard," Dad said. "The job is going to be finished soon. Last night, I got an offer from a big company that needs help rebuilding."

"Where?" I asked.

"San Diego," Mom said. "They need help from those wild-fires a while back." I nodded, but I felt a dozen emotions at once. Anger, sadness, hope, understanding—those were just some of the ones I could identify. My chest felt like it had been stabbed with a red-hot poker.

"I guess it's good you found out early for once," I said slowly. "Now you have plenty of time to find a place in California."

Mom looked down at the counter. "For this job, they're going to need us sooner, sweetie."

"What? Like March?"

Dad stood and put his coffee cup in the sink. "Brie, I'm sorry. We're moving during the second week of August."

"No! What? Mom!" I slammed my hands on the counter and stared at my parents. I'd never been this angry or shocked in my entire life. This couldn't be happening. Not now. Not with the fundraiser and with Logan. I hadn't even prepared for moving in the spring. How could I deal with this in two weeks? "It's practically here already," I yelled. "You totally sprang this on me. That wasn't a warning."

Mom and Dad looked at each other out of the corner of their eyes. I wasn't the one who had outbursts—that was Dad. But how could they do this *now*? Two weeks. That was nothing. In fourteen days, I'd be in California. What was Logan going to do? He hadn't planned on caring for the horses by himself until at least the spring.

"We're so sorry, Brie," Mom said. "We wish we could stay until the spring like we had planned, but this is a great opportunity for Dad. We couldn't risk missing it."

Then it felt like all the air went out of me. I didn't scream, argue, or cry. I just sat there. This wasn't the first time we'd moved early. A couple of years ago, we had stayed in a rented house for two weeks before Dad had been called to another site.

But this was so different. I had Logan, Amy, and the horses. Lost Springs felt more like home than anywhere we'd ever lived. But Mom would say wherever we were as a family was what made a home.

"What about Logan and the horses?" I said, my voice low.

"You'll still be here for the fundraiser," Mom said in a forcibly brighter tone. "You and Logan can talk on the phone, e-mail, and when we drive through Wyoming again, you can stop in and see him."

I couldn't listen anymore. It was too much. After coming here, finding Logan, and putting everything into rescuing the horses, I wasn't ready to let go. I'd made the mistake of falling in love with Logan and now the thought of moving was sickening. Would anything ever feel good again? No guy was like Logan. Leaving my sandwich on the counter, I stumbled out of the kitchen and shut myself in my room.

"Amy," I said, the second she answered her phone. She was the best friend I'd had in a long time. I didn't want to leave her.

"What's wrong?" she said. "You sound weird."

"I'm moving."

"I know. In, like, next spring or summer."

I paced around my room. "Two weeks."

"Brie! Oh, my God, when did you find out?"

"Just now," I said, rubbing my forehead. "My dad's job is going to be finished early. We're going to San Diego."

"Oh, no. What did Logan say?"

Tears stung my eyes and I could barely breathe. "He doesn't know. I can't tell him now. Not with the event so close."

"Brie, you need to tell him now. He's going to know something's wrong."

I shook my head, even though she couldn't see. "No. I'm not telling him until after the fundraiser. That has to be perfect. I'll act like nothing's wrong."

"Brie—"

"Promise you won't tell him."

Amy sighed. "I don't like it, but I promise."

We talked for a while and I hung up and crawled into bed. I cried until all the tears were gone. There was no way I would tell Logan now, not with our event so close. I wasn't going to ruin it for Logan or the horses. My sobs drowned out Mom and Dad's voices downstairs. This was the last time I'd cry until our SUV pulled away from Lost Springs. My remaining days here weren't going to be a waste.

CHAPTER FORTY

You can't tell a horse's gait until he's broken.

The fundraiser had been in full swing for an hour and, so far, not one of the eleven mustangs had kicked, bitten, or even shied. They proved even wild mustangs could be gentled to some degree in a short amount of time. Logan and I had held our breaths when the gates opened, but now we were like proud parents of our horses.

"So, Mr. Miller," I said, taking the older man's arm and steering him toward a dun colt. "This colt is one of the first we gentled. He's halter broken, leads well, and lets you pick his hooves. Isn't that great for the short amount of time we've had him?"

"It is," Mr. Miller said. He pushed back his tan cowboy hat. "Will he let me touch him?"

"Yes, sir," I said.

I held my breath as Mr. Miller reached down to feel the colt's legs. Thanks to endless hours of training, the colt didn't flinch when the man's gloved hands ran up and down his legs.

"Good boy," I whispered.

Mr. Miller nodded and smiled. "I'll write you a check for two grand and you put this guy under my name. I'm looking forward to seeing him next summer. He'll have grown up more by then. My grandson's been looking for something to gentle and this colt will be a good project for him next summer. He's not ready to start with a foal, so a horse that's had some hands-on work will be just what he needs."

Two grand. Two grand for a green mustang colt!

"Thank you, sir," I said, offering him my hand—Dad would love that. "Amy will get you an adoption packet."

A local attorney had offered to make a contract for our event that stated when someone adopted a horse next summer, the owner would properly care for the adopted horse, and wouldn't have the horse sent to a slaughter farm or subject it to any cruel treatment.

Mr. Miller followed me over to Amy, who was handling the paperwork area. It had been nonstop for her all morning, too. The press must have worked, since people were here when we opened Pam's gate.

Pam's pastures, driveway, and main barn were full with people walking around and looking at the horses. It looked as if all of Lost Springs had showed up just to see what Logan and I had put together.

The weather was cooperating, too. It wasn't dreadfully hot or too humid.

"All right," Mr. Miller said a few minutes later. "There you go." He signed the check and handed it to Amy. She put it in the lockbox Dad had loaned me.

"Thank you again," I said. "He'll be in great shape next summer."

After Mr. Miller left, I jogged over to Pam's round pen, where we had five of the youngest weanlings. A couple of people stood around the pen, looking into it, and pointing out horses. So far, I'd stayed away from Logan, without being obvious, and he hadn't noticed something was wrong.

"May I answer any questions?" I asked a man and woman who stood arm in arm as they studied a sorrel filly.

The woman smiled at me, tossing her long hair back. "We need another minute to look. We just can't decide on which one to sponsor."

"Take your time," I said with a grin. "I know it's hard! But if it helps, the sorrel filly is quiet and that palomino colt next to her is more high strung. But they're both halter broken and our vet says they're sound."

"Okay, thanks." The man's brows pressed together and he centered his eyes on the filly again.

"Brie!" someone called, and a *Lost Springs Register* writer sidled up next to me as I headed inside the barn. He pushed up his wire-rimmed glasses and turned over a clean piece of paper on his stenographer's notebook.

"How's the turnout?" he asked. "Is it what you expected? Are you happy with the donations?"

"We're very happy," I said. "Look for yourself. We're doing fantastic."

The reporter scribbled on his paper and moved off to take a photo of a woman petting a black filly in the pasture.

Volunteers were scattered everywhere. Logan and I had recruited at least a dozen people who knew enough about horses to help potential sponsors make their choices.

Pam was flitting from person to person and offering advice or any medical knowledge she had on the horses people inquired about. I'd even seen Dad helping an older woman with a cane walk to one of the corrals.

I had just finished giving the training history of a red roan mare to a man when Logan found me.

"It's crazy, isn't it?" he said, shaking his head.

"But it's a good crazy!" I said. "That means horses are getting interest and sponsors. Plus, we're bringing in money to care for them until summer."

My eyes blurred for a second when I said the last line. I wouldn't be here to see the next event. Logan would, but I wouldn't. No more training horses with Logan, spending those long hours in the barn talking, or having a day like today.

"Hey." Logan touched my arm. "You okay? What's wrong?"

I forced a smile. "Nothing. Just sad to think about seeing some of them go next year."

He squeezed my hand. "Me, too. But we'll make sure that they go to good homes."

He smiled at me before hurrying over to Pam, who was waving at him.

I was about to go back outside when Amy signaled at me from her booth.

"Brie, look." She handed me a sealed envelope. "I think there's money in there. I don't know who it came from. I took the lockbox with me when I went to get some apple cider. The envelope was under my clipboard when I got back."

My fingers trembled when I turned over the envelope. Turning away from the crowd, I huddled next to Amy and opened it.

Wrapped in a piece of paper were twenty crisp hundred-dollar bills. A tiny folded note was behind the last bill. *Brie and Logan, thank you.*

"Oh, my God," Amy said.

I nodded, unable to speak. Carefully, I folded the note and stuck it in my pocket and handed Amy the bills. That handwriting. The pen had pressed so hard it almost went through the paper. Half the letters were capitalized and half weren't. It was Dad's handwriting.

Three hours went by and Logan, Amy, and I didn't stop for a second. We had a stack of sponsor papers, and donations had almost filled the lockbox.

On my way to get a filly to show a friend of Pam's, I passed Frogger's stall. Wait a sec. I stepped backward and looked again. There was a red piece of paper taped to the open door. SPONSORED. Frogger was gone—probably being shown to his sponsors right now. Why hadn't Logan told me? He knew I loved Frogger.

My shoulders sagged and I leaned against the door and rubbed my hands across my eyes. Then Logan walked a few yards ahead of me, a blue lead rope in his hand.

"When did Frogger get sponsored?" I asked, hurrying to catch up with him. "You didn't even tell me! I want to meet his sponsor."

"I'm sorry," he said, speeding up and stepping into the round pen. "You were helping someone and it happened so fast. The guy had to rush off—something else to do." Logan looked away from me and haltered a bay mare. "Amy's probably bringing Frogger back now."

"Did you at least like the sponsor?" I choked out, getting angrier by the second.

"He got a *very* good sponsor." Logan turned away and headed for the round pen. I should have been happy, but I loved Frogger. I wasn't going to meet his sponsor until next summer. *If* I even made it back next summer.

Leaning against the wooden fence rail, I stared out at the nearest pasture. Two pregnant mares stuck their heads over the fence and watched the action going on around them. Pam had recommended we keep the mares until they'd given birth and had their foals weaned. Pam had also gelded any stallions capable of breeding with our mares since she didn't want to add to the herd population.

"Excuse me," a woman said. She swiped at her coffee-brown bangs. "I'd like to lead that guy." She pointed to Oscar. He was in a round pen with a couple of colts he'd made friends with after his encounter with Holden. Logan and I had spent hours encouraging Oscar to trust us and every day we spent with him had chipped away some of his sour attitude. He'd lost the wild look in his eyes as he slowly realized we weren't going to hurt him.

"Sure," I said, sniffing and then straightening. "I'm Brie."

"Susan," she said. She gave me a friendly grin and studied Oscar.

I couldn't blow off potential sponsors for the other horses just because I was upset about Frogger. Oscar deserved this chance.

"This is Oscar. We had to work daily with him from the beginning because he was one of our shyest horses. He didn't want to trust us."

"Hmm," Susan said. "How old is he?"

"We can't be completely sure, but our vet estimated he's between six and seven years old."

Susan reached her hand forward and let Oscar sniff her. She moved her hand up his neck and rubbed his shoulder. Oscar didn't flinch under her touch.

"Would you like to lead him now?" I asked Susan.

"Please," she said. I handed her the blue lead line and she clicked to Oscar. "C'mon, big guy."

Oscar followed her without hesitation and she led him twice around the round pen. The colts watched Susan lead Oscar and then halt him. She ran her hands down his legs, checked his hooves, and lifted his lip to check his teeth.

"You put a lot of work into him, didn't you?" Susan said, smiling at me.

"Logan and I did," I said. I patted Oscar's shoulder. "He's a good horse. He just needed time and a little special attention."

Susan eyed Oscar again and then nodded. "I'd love to sponsor him. I'm really impressed with what you've done. Are you going to keep this place open after the adoption event?"

"Yes, we are. We're keeping a couple of pregnant mares and we'll take care of whatever horses aren't adopted." Logan and I had talked with Pam and she'd agreed that we needed to keep the mustangs who weren't adopted instead of moving them somewhere else after all our hard work. Whether the horses got homes or not, they'd all have a safe place to live.

Susan handed me Oscar's lead rope and reached into her pocket. "I'm going to write you a check." She scribbled, and then ripped out the check. "I wish I could give more," she said, handing it to me.

"No, thank you," I said, not looking at it. "Whatever it is, we—" I glanced down at the check. *Ten thousand dollars.* Oh, my God. "This is too much!" I held the check out to her. "You don't have to do that."

Susan shook her head. "I want to. I know what it costs to keep a ranch running and it's not cheap to care for horses. I've got a place on the other side of town. Take the check and use it to have more events like this."

"Wow." I was quiet for a minute. "Thank you so much. It'll be put to good use, I promise."

Susan rubbed Oscar's muzzle. "I have no doubt."

"Let's go fill out the paperwork," I said, and we headed off to see Amy. *Ten thousand dollars.* I owed Holden a trip to his favorite place, the Waffle House, after this. He'd helped Oscar more than Logan and I had.

Half an hour later, I was latching the pen shut when Mom and Dad headed my way.

"Hi," I said. It was still weird to see Dad walking around a pasture in tennis shoes. It was probably only the second time in his life he'd worn shoes that weren't leather.

"It's going so well, hon!" Mom said with a grin. "You're going to be out of horses soon."

"I doubt that," I said. "The older ones will stay until they've had more training. But Logan's okay with that. They just need more time."

"You did a great job, Brie," Dad said.

I wrapped my arms around him for a second. "Thanks. For everything."

"We don't want to interrupt your work," Mom said. She and Dad headed to the barn.

Pam, holding four lead ropes, walked over and gave my shoulders a squeeze.

"What do you think?" Pam asked as we watched Logan lead a newly weaned gray colt for two young guys.

"I think we're doing well. Amy says we've raised lots of money and many people are putting their names on horses as potential adopters." I paused and looked at Pam. "You think we're doing okay, right?"

Pam nodded. "You're doing great. I'm very proud of you and Logan."

"Thanks." I hugged her and she adjusted her blue baseball hat. "Logan's never been this happy. He had me, Jack, and Holden, but he loves being with you. I'm glad you were able to give that to him."

Before I could say anything, Pam walked off toward a group of new people who were getting out of a van. I felt like a fraud. It wasn't easy to walk around like nothing was wrong and not tell Pam or Logan the truth. But it would ruin the day. I clamped my mouth shut and kept working.

The fundraiser came to a close a few hours later, just before Logan and I dropped in exhaustion. We'd sent Amy home, Pam was back in her house, and the last sponsor had filled out the final paperwork.

Wordlessly, Logan took my hand and we headed into the barn. He shut the doors, took me into the tack room, and turned on a small fan. I collapsed on a pile of blankets and he crumpled beside me.

"Too tired to even move," I said, closing my eyes.

"No kidding," he said. "But look." He pulled the lockbox between us and showed me the hundreds of bills inside. "We did it. This is going to take care of all the horses, surprise Pam with a thank-you for all she's given us, and help us at the next event."

I swallowed and looked away. Logan had no idea he'd be doing the next event alone. I'd told him when we were first together that I usually moved every year. But I had *also* told him that sometimes we stayed longer. The worst part was that I now had a date and he didn't know.

"How many horses were sponsored?"

Logan pulled a ledger from the lockbox and scanned it quickly. "Looks like *all* eleven! Plus, a couple of people want to come back when it's less crazy to look at the older guys that we didn't show. We've got five or six left."

"That's great," I said softly. My mind wandered to Frogger. "Tell me about Frogger's sponsor."

Logan sighed and stretched his legs before looking at me. "Well, she got him as a gift from her boyfriend."

"Oh. Good boyfriend."

Logan nodded. "Very good boyfriend. The best boyfriend. She doesn't know it yet, since he got Frogger for her as a surprise. He knew she really wanted him and he thought she'd like to keep him." He elbowed me and grinned.

I swatted at him for elbowing me. Then I froze.

"No," I said. "You didn't. No way."

Logan got up from the blankets and tugged me off the ground. "C'mon! Look!" He pulled me out of the tack room and down the aisle to a stall we'd never used. In a box stall at the far end of the aisle, Frogger stuck his head over the stall door when he heard footsteps.

BY BRIE had been added to the SPONSORED sign taped to the stall door.

"Oh, Logan." I opened Frogger's stall and hugged the colt. Frogger let me wrap my arms around his neck and I couldn't stop my tears.

"Don't cry," Logan said. "I thought you'd be happy."

"I am. It's just . . ." I sank along Frogger's stall wall and sat in the clean sawdust. Logan sat beside me.

"What? Just tell me. I know you're eventually going to move—if that's what you're thinking about. I'm not going to give him away when you move." Logan's eyes locked on my face. My hands clenched and I shut my eyes so I didn't have to see his face.

"That's what's wrong. I'm moving soon." The words almost sounded foreign. I forced down a sob.

"Sooner like when?" Logan's voice was quiet and he rubbed my forearm. "Where?"

"C-California." I ignored his other questions.

"Okay, we'll figure it out." Logan took my hand. "We've got plenty of time to at least—"

"No," I interrupted with a whisper. "No. Logan . . ."

The words weren't coming out. It felt as if I was pulling them out from my gut and my insides were wrenching and twisting until I couldn't breathe. Logan didn't say anything. He rubbed my back while I drew my knees to my chest.

"Two weeks," I finally uttered in a shaky breath. Logan must have assumed Dad had told me at the event, because he didn't ask me how long I'd known. Frogger stepped beside me and leaned down to sniff my arm. I broke down into sobs until I fell asleep in Logan's arms with Frogger watching us.

I don't know how long we were in Frogger's stall or what time it was when Logan carried me out of the barn and put me in his truck. He buckled me into the passenger seat.

"Take me to your house," I said, my voice raw. "I don't want to go home."

He shook his head. "No. You've got to go home." I rested my forehead against the truck window and stared out. I had to tell him the whole truth. He deserved that much.

"I've known for three days."

He took his eyes off the road, slowed the truck, and looked at me for a second. He eased the truck off the road and into the grass. He forced it into park and stared at the steering wheel. Slowly, he turned in his seat until his seat belt was strained. He pushed on the dim overhead light and closed his eyes before looking at me.

"You knew? Why didn't you tell me when you found out?"

I lowered my head. "Because I told myself not to get close to anyone. I never thought it would happen, Logan, I didn't! But then I liked you and everything happened so fast. I didn't want to hurt you."

Logan sat still without saying a word. "I wouldn't have pulled away, Brie. You know that." He turned forward and slammed his back into the seat.

"I wanted to, I swear." I touched his arm and he faced me again. "But if I did, that would have been hanging over us today, and we've been working so hard to have this great event. At least this way, you didn't have that burden today."

"But *you* did."

He leaned over and hugged me. We sat in his truck, in the silence of the deserted road, until my cell rang and jarred us apart. It was Mom.

"We're almost there," I said before she had even asked a question. How fast a place changes from "home" to "there."

I said good-bye and ended the call, throwing my phone into my bag.

"Stop," Logan said.

"Stop what?" I asked. "What's wrong?"

"We can't spend our time together like this," Logan said.

"Like what?" I couldn't keep the twinge of annoyance out of my voice.

Logan reached out and ran his pointer finger up and down my cheekbone. "I feel as angry and sad as you do, believe me," he said. "But if I go there, I won't come back. Time will pass and once we're separated, we'll both wonder where the hell we were those last few days that we had together."

"We would already be living in the future. What we're going to probably experience when I leave."

"I'm sorry to tell you this, but I know that I'll definitely not be feeling great. But I'm already lining up jobs in my head so that I will be busy around the clock from Pam's, to home, Holden, and soon school."

"I should do that, too," I said. "I can still help with the horses on the technical side with the website, and I—"

Logan leaned forward, hands on both sides of my face, and kissed me. I undid my seat belt and slid closer to him. I'd just gotten lost in kissing him when my dad's ringtone went off. I planted a quick kiss on Logan's cheek and reached into my bag. I held up the phone so he could see as I powered it off.

Logan opened his mouth and I covered it with my hand. "I don't care. What are they going to do? There's nothing left to lose."

Logan pulled me gently toward him and I started crying all over again.

CHAPTER FORTY-ONE

Thunder does all the barking, but it's lightning that bites.

Logan and I had been inseparable over the past week and a half. At first, it was hard to do anything but mope, but I'd realized he was right. We spent hours at Amy's house watching movies and playing foosball. We rode Mazy and LG everywhere. Logan even put Holden on an old quarter horse and we took him riding with us.

Logan had worked out a deal with his dad to reduce his shifts in the field and make them up later. For now, he wanted to spend every free second with me.

Mom and Dad were away—gone to Cali to scout out the best neighborhoods—and they were due back tomorrow morning. It was a Friday night, so most of the town was at the movies or bars. But Logan and I were at my empty house. A U-Haul sat mostly packed in the driveway. Dad hadn't hitched it to the SUV yet.

We were leaving on Sunday morning.

Logan was in the kitchen, making us turkey Stroganoff for dinner. We'd rented the latest DVD volume in an action series that we both liked.

"It's ready," he called from the kitchen. It felt like a date. A normal date. Not at all what it really was—our last night together.

"Smells great," I said.

"You'd better say that," he mocked. "It took me five whole minutes to stir this and twenty minutes of waiting."

We ate at the kitchen table and, after we had finished, Logan put the plates in the dishwasher. I flicked on the TV and put in the movie. Logan covered me with one of our throw blankets. We cozied up together on the couch and put our socked feet on the ottoman. We watched the movie and I hid behind Logan during the bloodiest parts. Violence and gore—not my thing. But watching the lead actor was *so* worth it. We didn't talk. We just enjoyed the movie.

"Want popcorn?" Logan asked, getting off the couch and stretching.

"Ugh," I groaned. "Too full."

"You, too full?" Logan teased. He plopped back down on the couch. "Since when, Miss-I-Can-Eat-Three-Hot-Dogs for lunch?"

"Logan!" I shoved him and tried not to laugh. "So what." I sniffed, pretending to be offended. "I like hot dogs."

I stretched out onto the couch and put a pillow behind my head. Logan shifted so my legs were in his lap. "I like you," he said softly.

"Come here," he said, pulling me into a sitting position and getting up and standing behind me, rubbing my neck.

"Thank you," I said. "Want to go upstairs and just—?"

"Let's go," Logan interrupted.

He scooped me into his arms, carrying me through the living room. Giggling, I wrapped an arm around his neck.

"Is this really necessary? My legs *do* work."

"Shh," he said, laughing. "I'm trying to be chivalrous. Just let me carry you up the stairs."

I buried my nose into his neck and let myself sink into his arms. He smelled like sweet hay, soap, and cinnamon. He carried me through my bedroom doorway and I flicked on the light. My room was mostly empty, with only a few boxes against the wall and some clothes hanging in the closet. Logan put me down by my bed.

"Can you lock the balcony door and close the blinds?" I asked. "I'm being way, way over-cautious but if my parents showed up and saw us lying on my bed together—even with all our clothes on—they would *freak*."

While he did that, I rummaged through one of the last boxes in my room and found my container of candles. Vanilla and peach seemed like safe choices—nothing too girly—so I put those on the bare table beside my bed and lit them.

Logan turned off the lights and together we eased down onto my bed. Logan's arms wrapped around me and I snuggled into him. A memory of the first time that we had spoken flashed before my eyes. My body trembled as I held back a sob.

"What's wrong?" Logan asked, squeezing me tighter.

"Nothing," I said, blinking and glad I was facing away from him. "It's just . . . this is the last time we'll get to be together."

"Don't think about it like that," Logan said. He brushed my hair off my face. "It's not going to be the last time we ever see each other. Or the last time we'll ever get time to ourselves like this. I promise."

I sat up and scooted around to face him. He sat up, too, looking into my eyes. "What are we going to do? Do we break up?" I paused. "Or try long-distance?"

If he said he wanted to break up, it would kill me. But most of all, I cared about his happiness. So I had to ask that question.

"Break up?" Logan shook his head. "No, we have to try, Brie. We can do long-distance."

That made me smile. "True. You sure you want to? I mean, you might want to date another girl. One you can actually—" I stopped.

Logan rubbed his hand up and down my arm. "I want to be with you. No one else. We'll do whatever it takes to make this work."

It wasn't long before Logan had coaxed me back into his arms. Shadows from the candles danced on my walls, and soon I drifted off to sleep.

CHAPTER FORTY-TWO

Where the road ends, the trail begins.

In a weird way, I was relieved Sunday morning finally came. Yesterday, Logan had helped me pack the last of my boxes and then I'd spent the rest of the day with Amy. We said good-bye last night, since she knew I only had a few minutes to see Logan this morning.

"I'm going to miss you so much," Amy had said, hugging me.

"Me, too! But we've got webcams and we'll text all the time," I said.

We let go and I looked around her room. Posters of Nashville, Atlanta, and Houston covered her walls.

Amy grinned. "Definitely. And here." She reached for her Watson's uniform and took off two buttons. She pinned them on my shirt. "The horse to remind you of Frogger and the horseshoe for good luck."

"Amy!" I hugged her again. "Thanks."

Turning, I rummaged in my purse and pulled out a large bubble-wrapped rectangle. "Here. For you. You did so much for me—helping Logan with the horses and designing our website. It's a little thank-you."

Amy squinted and carefully unwrapped the package. She pulled out a black picture frame and gasped.

"Oh, my God." She ran her fingers over the glass. Inside was a "window to the South" painting I'd bought in Pensacola. The painting had different squares, or windows, for the southern states. Each state had its name hidden somewhere in the window and there was a recognizable icon for each. Florida's square had a white sand beach and clear waves, Texas had the Alamo, Mississippi had a river barge, and Tennessee had a guitar.

"You like it?"

Amy sat on the end of her bed, holding the painting. "It's perfect," she whispered. "It's the most amazing thing I've ever seen. Thank you so much. I don't want you to leave!"

Amy and I both started to cry, and soon we were sitting beside each other on her bed, trying to stop our mascara from running.

"Will you help Logan with the horses?" I said, sniffing and wiping a pink tissue under my eyes.

"I promise," Amy said, nodding at me. "I'll help him every day when I'm not working. I'll be there when school starts, too." We'd hugged and chatted for a few more minutes before I'd left.

Now I carried the final armful of boxes from my room and set them outside by the U-Haul.

"This it, hon?" Dad asked as he took the boxes and expertly fit them into the trailer. It was barely nine and Dad and Mom had been up for hours loading the rest of our things. They'd double-checked that the electricity was shut off and the post office was forwarding our mail.

"Yeah, that's it." I stepped back from the truck and folded my arms across my chest as I looked around the lawn and driveway. Logan still wasn't here yet. He was supposed to come any minute and say good-bye. I probably looked like a mess. My hair was in a tangled ponytail and I'd barely slept last night. I'd spent most of the night wrapped on my balcony, lights off in my room and just thinking in the dark.

Mom came up behind me and settled an arm on my shoulder. "It's going to be okay. You know that."

I kept staring ahead. She'd be right eventually, but in this moment, I could barely believe her. "Yeah."

She sighed and left me, jogging over to help Dad fold up the trailer ramp.

Yesterday, Dad had taken Mom and me to see the finished site. The steel-and-concrete hotel had been erected, a parking lot was getting lines painted on it, and crews were finishing their installation of the windows. The bumpy road to the job site had been repaved and, according to Dad, it was one of his best jobs—well under budget and in good time.

In the distance, two horses and a rider came into view. Logan trotted LG up the driveway and led Frogger on a lead line beside him. The colt trotted placidly beside the older horse and Logan pulled them to a stop beside me. He dismounted and handed me Frogger's lead line.

"Hey," he said softly. "You want me to go so you can say good-bye to him?"

That was the last thing I wanted. "No. Stay." I put an arm around the colt and he huffed into my hand and sniffed my hair. "Frogger, you flirt," I teased.

"He's a great colt," Logan said. "He's going to be fine." Logan ran his hand over Frogger's shoulder. The colt turned, bumping Logan with his muzzle, and snorted. "I'm going to start his training today and when you come back, he'll be ready for you to ride, and finish training him yourself."

"I'm glad you're keeping him. But I don't know when I'm coming back. It's far and there's no way Mom or Dad will let me come here by myself."

I hugged Frogger and his chin whiskers tickled my neck. He was tall and muscular. His oversize ears made me love him more.

Logan frowned. "Really?" He turned and rummaged in his horse's saddle pack. "Then why did they get you this?" He pushed an envelope into my hand.

I tore it open. *Delta Airlines. Carter, Brie. 26 December.* It was a ticket from San Diego to Casper, Wyoming—a nearby city with an airport. "How did you—" I was so stunned I couldn't finish the question. My fingers shook and for a second, I thought I'd rip the ticket!

"I talked to your dad a couple of days ago," Logan said, grinning. "I reminded him we were having our first adoption event in the summer and we needed you to help with early planning.

"Oh, wait," Logan said, frowning. "Sorry, I mixed these things up." He winked at me.

He pulled out two more envelopes and dangled them in front of me.

I grabbed one. *Continental Airlines. Carter, Brie. 15 April.*

"That's when you're coming back to help plan the event," Logan said. "Hope you don't mind working over spring break."

"Oh, my God," I said. "I can't even believe this. Christmas break with you and spring break? If this is a joke, I'm going to lose it!"

"It's no joke," Logan said. "I promise. And don't forget about this one."

I tore it from his hands. *Continental Airlines. Carter, Brie. 2 June.*

"I'll be here for the adoption event?" I asked, my hands shaking. Frogger nosed my ticket and I hugged his neck.

"Not just for the event, but for a couple of months this summer."

I froze. "What? How? You're kidding."

Logan grinned. "Thank Pam for this one. She called your dad, said you could stay with her, and she promised to keep an eye on you."

"Oh, my God!" I threw my arms around his neck and hugged him. I let him go. "Be right back."

I darted off to find Mom and Dad. They were in the kitchen, both sipping steaming coffee in paper cups.

"Thankyouthankyou!" I said. I tried to grab both of them for a giant hug.

"You deserve it, sweetie," Mom said, squeezing me. She let go and I looked at Dad.

"Your mom is right," Dad said. "You went through a lot this summer. Brie, you matured so much. We know we can trust you to be responsible while you're here."

"Thank you, Dad." Dad pulled me in for a hug and I held on to him for a few seconds.

I left Mom and Dad in the kitchen, promising that I was almost done talking to Logan.

"So," I said, walking toward him, LG, and Frogger. "I *guess* I could come. But only if you promise me something."

"Anything." He held my hand that wasn't still holding the tickets.

"Be careful while I'm gone. And tell Holden I'll see him soon."

Saying good-bye to Holden had been a little tricky. I hadn't wanted Holden to think I was abandoning him. Logan, Jack, and I had told him together about my move and we made it clear I *would* be coming back.

Logan nodded. "Promise." The tickets in my hand didn't make this any easier, but it gave me something to hope for and look forward to. This wasn't a good-bye—it was a see you later. And for once, those weren't just words.

"Brie." Dad's voice interrupted my thoughts. "We'll be heading out in five. Okay?"

I wasn't going to argue. Not with the golden tickets in my hand. Mom and Dad weren't going to get one reason not to let me come back. They were asking me to trust them and take another Carter-Brooks family adventure.

With these plane tickets, I'd actually get to come back. And that made moving forward a lot less painful.

I nodded and Dad moved away to get into the SUV. "You'd better have Frogger waiting for me after Christmas," I said to Logan.

Logan grinned and showed the dimples I'd first seen at WyGas all those months ago. "Oh, I will. I'll send you videos of his training so you can see for yourself."

"Okay." I kissed him hard and he put his warm hands on the sides of my face. When we pulled apart, I pressed my body to his and hugged him, trying to take in everything. The way his hair curled around his ears, how strong his chest felt against mine, and the way his shirt smelled like cinnamon.

"I love you," I said softly.

"I love you." He looked me in the eyes and kissed me again.

"Wait a sec," I said, letting go of his hand and running up to the porch. I grabbed a blue box with white ribbon and handed it to him. "Here. For you."

Logan took the lid off the box and peered inside. A photo that Amy had snapped of us talking by the hot tub was the first thing he saw. I was in a bikini and sitting next to Logan as he sipped lemonade. He flipped through the photos and found some of us on our camping trip. In one, he was fishing in the creek and another was of me holding my phone in front of us while we sat by the campfire.

He'd taken one of me cooking in the kitchen—just before I burned the dinner rolls. My favorite one was of us sitting on the balcony with the sun setting behind us. Logan had an arm around me and our backs were to the camera. Mom had taken it without even telling me. She'd given me the photo last week when she'd realized I was making this gift for Logan. There were pictures of Frogger and the other horses and a photo of Pam with her arm around Logan at the fundraiser.

"It's amazing, Brie," Logan said finally. He carefully put the lid on the box and shook his head.

"There's one more," I said, running back to the porch to pick up the second large box I had stashed there.

"Brie," Logan said. He shook his head as I presented him with the box. "You didn't need to—"

"Stop arguing and open it," I said. "I know my wrapping skills suck. But there *is* a bow."

Logan laughed. He opened the lid and pushed aside some white tissue paper.

I watched his head jerk back a fraction. His eyes flickered from me to the box.

"You probably thought," I said, tears now forming and dripping onto my cheeks, "that I wasn't listening to you that very first time you took me to Pam's shop." I smiled and let the tears flow. "I remember every second of that day we spent together. I didn't forget what you told me about tan hats and black hats."

I reached up and took off his tan hat. I put it down beside me and stuck my hands into the box. I lifted a shaped black hat out and placed it on Logan's head.

My eyes met his and he swallowed.

"You *are* important, Logan. You're in charge of a rescued herd of mustangs. You deserve a black hat."

I picked his tan hat up and held it to my chest. "This goes with me."

Logan looked at me. He opened and closed his mouth. I watched him fight back tears.

"I love you," he said. "I feel like somebody because of you."

"I love you," I said. "And you were already somebody, Logan. You just needed someone to tell you."

The Explorer, with the small U-Haul attached, roared to a start and I handed Frogger's lead line to Logan.

"You'll be back so soon," he said. He smiled. "We'll make it."

"I know." I hugged him again and kissed him quickly before turning away and forcing myself to get into the car. I looked back after I'd settled into the seat, but Logan and Frogger were gone.

Dad put the Explorer into gear and eased it slowly down the driveway. I rolled down the window and stuck my head out to look at the cabin one last time. Mom's flowers bloomed bright and happy. At least we'd leave something behind for the new renters to enjoy. The house was dark and it looked like it did when we got here—wiped clean and ready for new adventures and new people.

We didn't talk as we rode over the bridge and pulled onto the road. Our drive was going to be long and Dad figured we'd at least get halfway tonight.

"Is that . . . ?" Mom's sentence trailed off and she pointed out the windshield.

In grass along the road, two horses' tails streamed out behind them and a guy in a black cowboy hat urged his horse into a faster gallop. We pulled even with Logan and beside him, Frogger galloped easily, his short legs eating up the ground.

I leaned across Dad and waved. Logan snapped his head in my direction for a second, trying not to throw his horse off balance, and raised three fingers, just as someone had done to me on my first day here.

Laughing, I raised three fingers back. We pulled ahead of Logan and the horses and I leaned back in my seat and forced my eyes forward. Tears blurred my vision and I let them fall off my cheeks and splash onto my jeans. Now until December was both short and long at the same time. I had no regrets about letting myself fall for Logan. I'd truly lived every moment—good and bad—in Lost Springs. I had an amazing best friend in Amy, and I had Logan. Best friend and boyfriend rolled into one. Usually, on moving day, I would ask Mom to take a few photos of me outside of the house or somewhere special in town. I'd wanted the pictures so that I could look at them years from now, and they would help me remember where I had lived. But I didn't need photos to remind me of Logan, Holden, or the rest of the town. I had my memories for that.

AUTHOR'S NOTE

Mustangs are a dying breed. They are being subjected to inhumane and inconceivably cruel treatment at the hands of humans. An example? Being driven off cliffs to their deaths by people in helicopters. ON. PURPOSE. Please read more and learn how to help at www.protectmustangs.org and www. wildhorsepreservation.org.

ACKNOWLEDGMENTS

Giant hugs to editor-extraordinaire Caroline Abbey, who said "YES!" to *Wild Hearts*. CA, you started this journey for me and let me venture into YA. I owe you a million milkshakes! ☺

Laura Whitaker and Sarah Shumway, thank you both for taking on this project with enthusiasm! I'm very lucky to not have been orphaned. You've made me feel like a true member of the Bloomsbury family.

Endless thank-yous to Bloomsbury for publishing *Wild Hearts*. The thanks extends to the art department, sales team, and everyone who touched this project. Thank you, all!

Lesley Ward, I can't thank you enough for your support over the years. You're so kind.

Terri Farley, I learned so much from your website and Twitter (@terri_farley) about the plight of mustangs. I hope I did them the tiniest bit of justice in this book.

Lauren Barnholdt, your nonstop #1k1hr shames me into writing! :D <33 Becca Leach, you helped me so much during #BlackHole.

Thank you to my writing friends Aprilynne Pike and Becca Fitzpatrick.

Love to Team Elite: Lexi Carson, Grace Carson, Hannah, Karlee, and Juliett. <3

Special thank-you to Lex and Gracie for being the best little sisters on the planet. I'm grateful every single day that you're in my life. I love you both so, so much and you mean everything to me! <33

Agent Jenn, I'm so glad you're part of my team! You're a dream agent and I'm so lucky!

Finally, thank you to all of the teachers, booksellers, and librarians who put books into the hands of young readers.

Jessica Burkhart is a full-time writer in Kentucky horse country. She is the author of the twenty-book Canterwood Crest series, which has over one million copies in print. Jess is passionate about mustang conservation and hopes to visit the horses in their natural habitat one day.

www.jessicaburkhart.com
Twitter: @jessicaburkhart
Instagram: @jessashley87

As Mimi Blake introduces us to the viewers at home, for the first time, I begin to feel nervous.

After the introductions, she continues with, "Katie, George spoke with you at length last week, so I think we'll begin today with Drew." She turns to me. "Drew. Katie has spent most of her life on the campaign trail with her father. But this is all new to you, isn't it?"

Now I officially cross over into full nervous territory as I realize that some sort of response is required from me. I stare directly into the camera. "Yes, Mimi," I say woodenly. "That is correct."

That is correct? What kind of moron talks that way?

"You're not really like any other candidate's child that we've seen in recent years."

Is there a question in there somewhere?

"Rather than dressing to impress, you dress…" With the back of her hand, she indicates my clothing from head to toe. Again, where's the question? And how am I supposed to respond? Too late, I remember the tie in my pocket. I can't put it on now...can I?

Looking directly into the camera, I say once more, "Yes, Mimi that is correct."

I feel a sharp stabbing sensation around my ankle and realize that Katie just kicked me with the pointy toe of her green high-heeled shoe. Hey! And, ouch! Still, it does remind me of what Katie advised earlier, that I should talk directly to Mimi, not the camera, like we're just two people having a conversation.

This immediately reduces my level of nervousness. And you know what else reduces it? Anger at Katie for getting me into this mess in the first place.

As anger fuels me from the inside, on the outside I suddenly feel distinctly calmer. And, as Mimi proceeds to ask me questions, I realize that this is easy. I know these questions! And how do I know them? Because the TV network forwarded them to Ann in advance to show to me. And *that* happened, according to Ann, because Katie's people set a precedent last time by insisting that that was the only way Katie would do the interview with them—if she could see the questions first. This struck me as cheating at the time. What kind of *wimp* needs to know the questions in advance? What could she possibly be scared of? Coward. But her fear is serving me well now as Mimi continues, "We're told that, despite your family's relatively recent elevation in fortune—unlike the Willfields, the Reillys weren't born with silver spoons in their mouths—you still ride the public school bus and even go to your old public school. Is that correct?"

"Yeah, Mimi." Look at me! No more robotic "Yes, Mimi that is correct" for me. I'm nailing this thing! "I'm a big believer in public transportation," I add. "I even took the train here today."

"Well, don't think you'll be able to do that once you're in the White House," Katie blurts out, adding a muttered, "not that that'll ever happen."

What is it with that girl? And why does she get under my skin so much?

Oh, right. She's annoying.

Plus, could she be right? If my mom wins, will my life really be that different? Excuse me while I retreat back into denial.

I decide to ignore Katie. Mimi does too, practically cooing at me, "Ooh, a real man of the people!"

She swivels her head sharply from me to Katie. I take this to mean that the camera will be swiveling to Katie now too, so I take this opportunity to whip my tie from my pocket and rapidly knot it around my neck. The ends wind up wildly uneven, but whatever.

After a dramatic pause and with a fake smile, Mimi says in a falsely cheerful tone that couldn't be more menacing: "*Katie*."

Just her name, full stop.

I have no idea exactly what's coming next. What I do know is that for Katie, it can't be good.

But for me? This is going to be very good. Because there's nothing I can imagine enjoying more than seeing my enemy fall on her face.

After Mimi's menacing *"Katie,"* she turns to the camera and says, "We'll hear from Katie Willfield after the break," and we pause briefly for commercials.

I can't say for certain what Mimi has in store for me once the break's over. All I know is, it'll be harder than those puffball questions she's been lobbing at Drew. Why, she's all but asking him, with moony eyes, to tell us all the reasons he's so wonderful.

Ugh.

She'll undoubtedly ask me some of the harder questions that George left on the table. Like if I ever felt shortchanged, growing up in a single-parent household in which the only parent spent most of his time focusing on his political career? Or if I have political ambitions of my own?

Both of those would be harder than the questions asked on the previous visit because they're more personal. But that's okay. I'm a professional. And I know how to use the personal professionally. The first question, I'll answer by saying, I don't feel shortchanged at all. When a candidate is as fit to lead the country as my father is, I can only feel privileged, *blessed* to be a part of his manifest destiny. And if it's the second? I'll say, It's a little premature to throw my hat into the ring, don't you think? and I'll accompany it with a smile and a wink to let everyone know that, of *course* that's in my future!

Oh, no. But what if, worst of all, she asks about the china patterns? There was nothing on the list of original questions about that but since George put it on the table with his comments, maybe it is considered fair game now? Still not a problem, I think as I stiffen my back. I'll just fall on my sword. I'll say, My father had no knowledge of what I was doing. Voters should not penalize themselves over childish high jinks that are my sole responsibility. And if she follows it up by questioning, Shouldn't a parent know what his child is up to? Well, she won't do that, because she'll know that I could then counter with a question about her own lax parenting style, and believe me, she *won't* want to go there. Everyone knows the Blake kids are nothing but tabloid trouble.

As we're counted back down from commercial break and Mimi opens again with that eerie smile, followed by "*Katie*," I'm feeling *pret*-ty good about my various strategies.

Then Mimi says, "Is it true what we've heard, that even though you're sixteen, you've *never* had a romantic relationship in your life?"

What? She can't ask that!

"Is it true you've never even been on a single date?"

I'm being blindsided here! How is it possible that she can do this? We had an agreement! These questions weren't on the list! But then, with horror, it hits me: That agreement was for my *last* appearance on the show. We never had them sign one for *this* appearance.

Mimi leans forward in her chair and I can practically *feel* the camera moving in for a close-up of my humiliation.

"Is it true, Katie, that you've never been kissed?"

An hour later, I'm huffing and puffing as I lean in, my hands gripping the carved wooden armrest as I shove, hard, on the couch. It moves only an inch.

An inch.

Stupid freakin' behemoth couch. I feel like I'm trying to move a Mack truck. Trees must have weighed more in the seventeenth century.

Yeah, that makes sense.

I groan and push again, straining with all my might. The leg screeches against the marble floors and then gives way, sliding abruptly. My hands slip off the armrest, and I slam to the ground.

"Oomph," I say, my forehead resting on the cool floor that had, moments ago, been covered by a French provincial sofa.

The ground is musty. Dusty. Like, oh, I don't know, it's been covered by a couch for a few decades. I've gotten so used to the polished-until-I-can-see-my-reflection cleanliness in this place that it's almost foreign to smell actual dirt.

Footsteps shuffle closer, and I suddenly realize I'm not alone. Crap, I hope my mom isn't going to bust me....

I roll over and look up into the amused, warm brown eyes of a boy close to my age. He's leaning over, resting his hands on his knees as he peers down. I blink as if he's a mirage and he'll disappear. Spotting a guy like him in a place like this is harder than finding a lifeboat on the *Titanic*.

But he doesn't.

Disappear, that is.

Awesome. The first boy under seventy I've seen in this place, and he finds me lying facedown on the floor of the billiards room.

"It was the candlestick," I say abruptly, because it's the only thing I can think of and I'm fighting the urge to check him out.

He's cute. Really, really cute. He looks...Costa Rican. Maybe part Native American or part African American...or some combination uniquely his, because I've never seen a guy so totally drool worthy.

In a place like this, a place filled with rich, elderly white people, he stands out, dazzling in a way that has nothing to do with race, and everything to do with...

I blink, realizing that while I've been staring, his lips have been moving.

"... was the sofa?" he asks, furrowing his brow as he walks around so that he can face me as I sit up.

"Oh, uh, no, the sofa's a little too heavy to use as a weapon. It was definitely the candlestick," I say, and then jut my thumb in the direction of an antique brass candelabrum. "And Professor Plum. Because he's weird-looking and I don't trust him."

One side of his mouth curls up as he reaches out to me.

I study him for a second before finally reaching out to accept his hand. It's warm and soft and strong, and he easily pulls me to my feet. And then I'm standing close to him. So close I can smell him.

Cinnamon. I breathe deeper, enjoying the warm spiciness of it. Yes, he smells like cinnamon. As I rake in another breath, I catch him staring.

Abruptly I step away, realizing I'm standing within inches of him, just breathing him in over and over like an idiot.

"Ahhh," he says, once he has room to talk without speaking directly into my ear. "Because we're in the billiards room, of course."

"Yeah," I say, suddenly realizing how lame and outdated my joke is. Maybe if I didn't play board games with old people all the time...

To avoid looking at him, I dust off the seat of my pants and focus *really hard* on my apron.

Oh god. I'm wearing a doily apron in front of a hot boy. "I always pegged it on Mrs. Peacock," he says.

"Oh?" I ask, wondering if there's a way to ditch the apron without looking like it's because of him. I glance around, but it's not like there's a phone booth where I can go from the bumbling Clark Kent to the ultra-suave Superman. I don't even have a pair of glasses to take off. "Why's that?"

"She's the only one not named after a color."

I furrow my brow. "That's not true. Peacock is a color."

"Are you sure?" he asks, crossing his arms. I'm suddenly, acutely aware of how built this boy is. He has serious muscles. Glorious, beautiful muscles, evident even through his stark white button-down and perfectly tailored black vest. He looks like he just left a wedding reception and lost his jacket somewhere.

"Yeah, it's a shade of blue. All the characters in Clue are colors," I say, realizing in some corner of my mind that's still functioning that I should probably shut up about Clue.

"I'll have to take your word for it," he says, flashing a cocky grin. He reaches out toward my face, and I freeze, half-expecting him to caress my cheek like something from a romance novel. But he doesn't. Instead he touches my hair, then pulls his hand away.

The way he looks at me, amusement glimmering in his eyes as he turns his hand and reveals a dust bunny, it's like he *knew* what he was doing. Like he knew I'd think he was reaching out for ... some other reason. And I fell for it.

Sheesh, I am so totally deprived of flirting-with-a-cute-guy opportunities, living in a retirement home with my mom. I need to get out more. I need to get a hobby or something before I swoon at his feet and ask if he wants to play bridge.

He smirks. "Sorry, it was kind of clinging to your ponytail. It was distracting."

"Well, I find your hair distracting too," I say, and then immediately wish I had just kept my trap shut.

I find your hair distracting? That was the best I could do?

"Really," he says, his eyebrow quirking. I'm suddenly, acutely aware that his eyebrows are better groomed than mine.

One of them, the right one, has two slashes through it, like he had it trimmed that way. Like he had them … sculpted to match the lines where his hair is buzzed shorter and little lines swoop and twirl on the sides of his head.

And I'm wearing an apron made of doilies.

"Yeah," I say, my face warming. "Your haircut is, um, crooked."

He smiles, that same amusement as earlier glittering in his eyes. "It's *supposed* to be crooked."

My laughter sounds like a barking seal having seizures, and I can't believe he doesn't back away. Instead, his eyes light up, like my reaction surprises him.

"So you walked into the salon and said, 'Hi, I'd like a crooked haircut?'" I cross my arms, realize I look confrontational, and drop them again. Why do my arms feel so big all of a sudden? It's like I forgot how to function. Like my limbs have become giant noodles attached to my body and I have no control of them.

He laughs, a surprisingly deep, smooth-as-honey laugh that makes my stomach do a flip. "I go to a barber," he says, twisting his big silver watch in circles on his wrist. "And I let him do whatever he wants."

"Brave," I say, motioning with my hands in ridiculous wavy and jerky movements and *oh god what am I doing?*

"He's been cutting my hair for eighteen years," he replies, following my movement with his eyes, his lips twitching.

Oh great, he's picked up the fact that I live in Awkward City, USA. I've become entertainment.

And then his reply finally registers. Eighteen years. So he is at least eighteen years old. Probably nineteen. Although who knows, guys like him probably were born with sculpted hair and Armani suits, so he could still be just eighteen.

I swallow, breathing deeply and trying to calm my racing heart. "And did you like it?"

"Like what?"

"The crooked haircut," I reply, twisting my fingers into the edges of my lace apron. Are my palms damp? Were they damp when he pulled me to my feet or is this a new development? What if I have the dampest palms in the entire world and he's just really good at hiding his disgust?

"I did until now," he says, one side of his lips curling up as he meets my gaze, like an open challenge.

"Oh," I say, embarrassment creeping in. "I mean, it's a good haircut. It, uh, looks good on you."

"Right," he says. "Clearly, you adore it."

I blush harder now, my face so hot I'm sure he could feel it if he reached out and touched it. If he let his beautiful, long fingers slide across my cheek...

I clear my throat. "Um, I mean it. Crookedness and all."

"Mm-hmm," he says, still peering into my eyes as he smirks.

I'm suddenly, completely sure that no one has ever insulted his hair before. Or his looks. Or... him at all. So I basically freeze, staring right back at him, thinking that I've ruined any chance I had with him.

"I was voted best hair, you know," he says after I don't speak.

"I can see why," I say, then wish I hadn't. I want to know who voted him best hair. Other than me.

He laughs and it feels the tiniest bit like it's at me, before he turns away for the first time and studies the couch. With his side to me, I can see the way his button-down strains across his shoulders, the full bulk of his arms under the shiny fabric. Silk. Is it silk? I'm not as good at fashion as I am at art and furniture. Not *high* fashion, anyway. My expertise is limited to cotton and doilies.

"What are you trying to do with this?"

"Move it over there," I say, pointing across the room, relieved to finally have something else to talk about.

"Why?"

"Because every time I walk by this room, it bugs me that it's set up entirely wrong. So I'm fixing it."

"But if you stick it in the middle of the room, won't it kind of…I don't know, block things off? I mean this is one *giant* couch."

"No," I say. "I mean, look at this thing. It's pretty much a piece of art. If I position it correctly, it will provide flow, *and* people will actually notice it and appreciate the design. And over here," I say, pointing to where I'd face-planted, "it blocks the window."

"Provides flow, huh?"

I might have been self-conscious about my Clue references, but my interior-decorating skills—no matter how dorky they are—never actually embarrass me. I mean, if you ask Alex, she'll say it's totally mortifying, but whatever.

"There's an actual science to interior decorating. Just like there's a science to how restaurants lay out their menu to highlight the big-ticket items, and grocery stores position impulse buys."

"I don't think I've ever met a teenage interior-decorating scientist," he says, crossing his arms. "And I know some pretty impressive people."

"Yeah? Like who?"

He shrugs. "Pop stars. Actresses. Inventors. The president's daughter."

"Try not to brag or anything," I say, rolling my eyes to pretend I'm unimpressed.

But really... who the heck is this boy? How does he know these people? And why would he bother talking to me when obviously he could go hang out with way cooler people? People who have full function of their arms, for instance.

"Hey, you asked," he says, one side of his mouth quirking into a Cheshire grin.

Okay, the boy is smokin' hot and knows it. The part of me all wound up at his attractiveness unravels. I will not be intimidated by insanely good looks and a crappy personality.

I meet his eyes, annoyed. "So, fine, you know impressive people, and I'm not one of them. Maybe you think this is stupid, but it's kind of my thing. So if you're not going to help me, maybe you should just move on?"

"Huh," he says, but not like I've annoyed him. More like... he's intrigued. Like maybe I won him over. "Malik." He extends his hand. "And you are?"

"Lucy," a voice calls out, just as I'm reaching for his hand. I swing around to find one of the residents, Henrietta, standing at the entryway, leaning against the doorjamb for support. My stomach sinks. Interlude With the Hot Boy is officially over. Henrietta is seventy-four and frail, and if she needs my help, it's more important.

"Sweetie, can you help me to my room?"

"Sure," I say, pretending like it's totally no big deal that I'm going to spend the entire summer dateless and pathetic. I step away from Malik as he drops his hand back to his side. "See you around?" I give him an awkward little wave. *Dumb.* I should have shaken his hand instead, if only to feel his skin, hot against mine, one more time. Maybe that would be enough cute-boy contact to last me the two months until I head off to college.

I make it all the way to the door before he answers.

"Yeah, see you later, Lucy."

I open my mouth to correct him just as Henrietta finds the crook of my elbow and leans against me. She always thinks I'm her granddaughter, Lucy, who was around my age when she died in a car wreck.

Once, I corrected her. Once, I told her the truth. But watching her eyes fill with tears as if hearing the news for the first time ensured I'll never do that again.

And I don't have the heart to do so now. To tell her my name isn't Lucy, that she has no family left at all, just a giant bank account and no one to leave it to.

And so I simply glance back at Malik one more time, searing his image in my head as I lead Henrietta back to her apartment.

By the time I return to the billiards room twenty minutes later, he's gone.

But the couch is sitting in the middle of the room, exactly where I wanted it.